EX GRATIA

BOOK TWO OF
TERMS AND CONDITIONS

EX GRATIA

M. W. MCLEOD

Ex Gratia
Terms and Conditions: Book Two

Disclaimer: When summoning the Devil himself from the pits of Hell, it is recommended to call him by any monikers with only the darkest of connotations. The King of Hell, Prince of Darkness, Lucifer, and Satan are all acceptable. Use of the name Samael or Lightbringer will end badly for all involved parties barring the fallen angel whose wrath was incurred.

To firnds and griendfriends –
May autocorrect treat us all better.

Your personal and creative journeys continue to inspire every
day.

CONTENTS

ARTICLE I

Ellyria looked up from her book at all that was left of her study group. The holidays and finals were taking their toll on their usual group of five. Today, it was just two of them. "I'm having trouble concentrating today," she admitted.

"I blame the weather." Tucker replied, leaning back in his chair. He looked out the window at the snowy Harvard campus scenery, and yawned. "Today is just dragging on."

She sighed. "Maybe, we should just call it for the day."

"If you want to." He shrugged, sitting upright, and looking at her. "We already made a decent dent in the study guide." He sounded like he was forcing himself to sound as positive as possible about the situation. They really did have a lot of studying to do with finals breathing down their necks over the next couple of days.

"Yeah. I think I just need a mental health break." She smiled, starting to pack up her things.

He returned the gesture, and stood up, grabbing his things as he did so. "I'm thinking about food. What about you?" He asked her curiously.

"I don't know. I've got plenty at home." She shrugged noncommittally.

"Coffee, then?" He countered. His tone more urgent and simpering than before.

Ellyria thought about his suggestion for a moment. Tucker had always been nice, but she got the feeling he was more interested in her than she was in him. She saw how he looked at her, and couldn't help but think about how handsome he was as well. There was just so much in the way of her ever having any sort of relationship with normal men. They were so breakable, and she had so many secrets. After weighing her options, she decided that coffee wasn't too bad an idea on such a cold day. "Sure." She smiled, picking up her bag.

"Sweet." He smiled widely as he led her to the campus coffee shop. "So, what do you like to do in your spare time? You never seem to talk about yourself." He asked conversationally as they walked.

Ellyria sighed. "Because there's not much to talk about. I don't have much family, and, in my spare time, I like to read." She didn't bother to mention the fact that the things she read most often were magical grimoires and ancient Latin.

"Reading is pretty interesting, you can get lost in your own little world." His voice conversational until his expression soured a bit, and his tone became lower. "That sucks. I'm sorry. So, I take it you live alone, then?".

"No, I have a roommate." She told him. "Rent is way too expensive up here to not have one."

"That's good, yeah. The rent can be bad, I guess. I have a scholarship, so it isn't that big of a deal for me." He replied, looking ahead a bit. "So, what is your roommate like, then? Do you two get along well? I've heard the horror stories." He chuckled lightly.

"I rent off campus, so the scholarships don't pay for it." She shrugged. "He's actually a really good guy. We have some ups and downs, but that's just life."

"That's good." He nodded at her. "You must both work hard to afford the rent, then. That's a good trait."

She shook her head. "I'm a full-time student. I pay other ways. He works his ass off, and still complains when I try to do the dishes."

Tucker turned, and gave her an odd look. "Oh. You two are a thing, then. Got it." He looked upset, and took a step away from her as they walked.

"Okay." She tried not to snarl, starting to get angry. She stopped, and reeled around on him., "not that it's your business, but I'm paying for rent with my Mom's life insurance money. I do *not* pay for rent like that."

He jumped a bit at her outburst. "Sorry!" His expression dismayed. "It just sounded that way. Even if you did, there is nothing wrong with that. And," he let out a long sigh, looking completely deflated, "sorry about your Mom." He told her quietly before he reached into his wallet. He pulled out a five-dollar bill. "You can go get the coffee. I've already messed this up. Sorry." He grumbled, turning, and quickly walking away.

Ellyria took the bill with a little surprise, and couldn't summon the nerve to respond before Tucker was already long gone. "Smooth as a dull butter knife." She muttered to herself, not knowing if she meant herself or him. She swung by the coffee shop before heading back to her house. "Hey, Zane." She greeted.

"Hey." Zane replied from behind a computer screen as she entered the house. "How did today go?" He asked as he typed away.

"Classes were fine, but it was just me and Tucker at our study group. Of course, he finally hit on me." She grumbled.

He made a face at that news. "I don't like him." He told her seriously as he continued working. "Something about him is off."

She moved over to give him a peck on the cheek. "That's because he makes your witch uncomfortable."

He shook his head at her, and chuckled. "No, it is because there is something wrong with him. I just don't know what. Yet." He grumbled. He finished up what he was doing, and closed the laptop. "I am guessing you are hungry?" He asked, standing up.

"Getting there, but I can cook. You're busy making us money, Mister Stockbroker." She laughed.

He chuckled, and made his way to the kitchen. "I'm done with that for the day." He smiled at her. "Might have bankrupted a few companies today, but they had it coming. Never embezzle in South America."

"I'm not sure I even want to know." She shook her head. She pulled off her heavy jacket, revealing a sweater. "I'm never going to get used to this cold."

"Thankfully, I can tolerate it." He chuckled at her as she took off her jacket. "Then, you want to go to New York for a penthouse."

She nodded. "It'll be just as cold." She paused. "Now, there's a question I never thought to ask. Is it actually hot in Hell?"

"Depends on the layer," he replied simply, "or if the Dark Prince is feeling spontaneous."

She looked at him, and made a face. "There's a frozen over one, isn't there? Just to prove a point to us foolish mortals."

"Yup." He responded, popping the 'p'. "The look on their faces is priceless." He laughed.

Ellyria kicked off her shoes, and sipped on her coffee. "I don't think I know what to do with myself without the study session this afternoon, but I couldn't focus any longer. So, I think I need a break."

"There is nothing wrong with that." He told her as he began to make her a snack. "Besides, your tests are almost done, right?" he asked idly.

"I've got three more this week." She sighed. "One of the frat houses on campus is having a big party to celebrate finals being over on Friday."

"Do you plan on going?" He asked her as he handed her the snack of pita chips and hummus.

She nodded. "It's been a while since I've relaxed for a bit."

"Well, I can't stop you." He sighed a bit. "I guess, I will be there too."

"You know, you can ask me to not go. Just say the words." She told him seriously.

"I know I can." He replied seriously. "But, I also can't. There is a code I *have* to follow." He told her.

She sighed. "I can order you to tell me how you actually feel." She offered.

He sighed, now. "I think that the parties are stupid. Anything you can do there, you can do here." He told her honestly. He did not want to get ordered around.

"Thank you." She smiled at him. "And, you're right. They are stupid. I just don't know what else to do with myself. Things are feeling- stale? I don't know. I need better hobbies."

"There is always knitting." He joked.

"I would rather take up becoming a serial killer." She deadpanned.

He shook his head at her. "That is too much work. You wouldn't have enough hours in the day to be able to do that and law." He told her seriously.

"Oh, sure, but I can take up knitting." She giggled. "Maybe, it's time we bought that gaming system."

He thought it over for a moment. "I would recommend a computer for that, honestly." He told her with a serious nod. "It would cost more, but there are far more games you could play, then."

"As long as you can play too." She giggled. "I want to watch you play games where you steal cars and cause chaos."

"Then, we get two of them." He suggested. "They have a game about robbery?" He asked seriously.

She nodded. "Along with just about every other crime."

"I'm in." He smirked evilly. "Oh, so much destruction."

"You want to buy them or should I?" She asked.

"I will take care of it." He told her honestly. "What color would you like the lights?" He chuckled.

She thought for a minute. "Assuming they don't have purple, blue."

"Red it is for me." He commented, walking back over to the laptop, and getting the computers ordered.

"You might enjoy some resource management and strategy games, too." She thought aloud. "World domination and conquest."

"I didn't know that they offered that as a recreational activity." He hummed to himself. "I think I might." He smiled at her, going back to the screen for a moment. "And, ordered." He announced with a dramatic click.

She glanced at the screen. "Ugh. I shouldn't have looked at that price."

"Don't worry. Six grand is nothing." He waved it off. "There is plenty more where that came from."

"I really need to start paying more attention to the finances." She winced.

"I can help with that," he told her honestly. "The hard part is dealing with the money and making sure it all goes into the correct accounts. Otherwise, it is straight forward, all things considered."

"I think I might hold off until I graduate." She frowned. "That sounds like a lot."

He shrugged. "It is more and less complicated than I make it out to be." He responded, looking at her seriously. "By the time the deal is done, I will have you set for life."

She nodded. "Thank you."

"Don't worry about it. It is my job." He returned the gesture.

She started to eat her snack, and turned on the television. "I want to see what happens next with Geralt and Yennefer."

Zangrunath looked at her, and shook his head. He already knew the ending. "Enjoy." He commented a bit sarcastically as he went to get started on dinner.

Ellyria began watching the episode, but had to pause it when her phone started to go off with a bunch of text messages. "Oh, for Lucifer's sake." She complained, looking at her messages, and groaning. "Tucker-"

"What is it?" Zane asked from the kitchen. "Is he apologizing like the worthless peon that he is?"

"He might be drinking." She handed him the phone. "I'm going to expect a X rated photos soon."

Zane glanced over the phone, muttering the texts under his breath. "I love you. I'm sorry. You are my world." He sighed after a moment. "There is something wrong with him." He told her seriously.

"Well, he's not prince charming. That's for sure." She groaned. "I should've taken the chance this afternoon and told him we were together."

"That would have, at least, made this easier to deal with." He grumbled. "You should just tell him that and make it easier on everyone." He suggested, going back to cooking again.

She took her phone back, and texted Tucker. 'Thanks, but no thanks. I'm in a relationship.'

'I thought you said that wasn't the case? What happened?' A text replied quickly.

'What I said is that I don't have sex for free rent. Not that I wasn't with my roommate.' She growled as she hit send.

There was a pause in the text before a reply came back. 'Prove it.'

She looked up at Zane. "Do you show up in photographs?"

"Yes, why?" He asked curiously.

"Can you be Zane for a minute please?" She requested, turning on her camera.

He turned into Zane, and walked over to her. "What do you need a picture for?"

"Proof, apparently." She almost snarled, kissing his cheek, and snapping a picture.

He looked at the picture, and shook his head. "At least, make it worth it." He stole her phone, and kissed her firmly on the lips

11

as he took a picture of them. He handed her phone back to her. "There, that should make him believe you."

She smiled, and sent the picture. "Hopefully, that's good enough." She whispered to Zangrunath.

"Hopefully. Otherwise, proving the point will be much different." He smirked, standing up, and going back to make dinner.

"That can be arranged." She offered.

He looked at her for a moment. "Once the dinner is done." He smiled at her. "I refuse to let food get burned."

"That's fine." She smiled. She noticed her old quartz necklace around his neck, and walked up to touch it. She channeled more magic into it. "I should really read into this."

"Into what?" He asked, looking over at her.

"Why this stone prefers people other than me." She smiled.

"It probably has something to do with emotions." He smiled back at her. "I'm no expert on crystals, but doesn't each one help with different aspects?" He asked her.

She nodded. "Yes, they do." She paused. "I have a book on it, actually." She ran off towards her room to grab it, and came back, frantically flipping through pages.

"I wasn't expecting the enthusiasm." He chuckled at her.

"Well, it's the first idea we've had about it for a while. Here it is. Quartz. Draws away negative energy and neutralizes it." She looked at him. "Do you feel any different in that regard?"

"Maybe a little less bloodthirsty." He replied, shrugging a bit.

"Balances and revitalizes. Cleanses and enhances. Aids in concentration. Unlocks memory. Stimulates the immune system." She sighed. "Well, that's not helpful."

"Does it say who it helps?" He asked her as he plated food for her.

"It usually implies the wearer." She shrugged.

"Then, it could imply what your concentration is on right?" He asked, placing a healthy Greek chicken wrap in front of her.

She thought about it. "Are you saying that this stone likes to jump around to the people I concentrate my energy on?"

"No, what I'm saying is, what if the energy you put into it makes you concentrate on it more? Like focusing on a part of yourself." He replied.

She thought about that as she took her first bite of the meal. "Can you turn invisible and move around?"

He did as she asked, and walked around the living room and kitchen while he was unable to be seen. "Is it working?" He asked from behind her.

"Yeah." She smiled. "I can sense it. You can stop now."

"Maybe I like being sneaky." He whispered into her ear.

She shivered as his breath tickled her ear. "Oh." She whispered.

"Finish your food first." He told her as he appeared, moving around the island to get the dishes done. "Then, fun." He smirked.

She continued to eat, and her phone buzzed. "Oh, son of the dark prince." She swore.

"What is it now?" He asked annoyed. He didn't even bother asking who it was sending the text messages. They both already knew.

She unlocked her phone, and looked at the message. "Just more drunk texts." She shut her phone off. "Screw this."

"Just tell him to fuck off tomorrow." He told her as he finished the dishes in record time.

She finished eating in short order, and sighed. "Thank you. It was delicious as always."

"You're welcome." He told her, looking her over.

"You don't have to be Zane, you know." She offered.

Zangrunath kissed her, and turned into his true self. "If you want." He smirked before he kissed her and began to show her the many perks of being with a demon.

During their magical evening together, Ellyria growled at Zane saying, "mine," on repeat, knowing 'love' was a word seldomly, if

13

not ever, used amongst demons. She was okay with this for the time being. She liked their closeness, and, for her, that was good enough. She wasn't ready for marriage and kids and all of that anyway. For right now, she was more than happy with what she had with Zangrunath. As they rested towards the end of the night, Ellyria held onto him. "I like this."

Zangrunath smiled at her, and gave her a kiss. "Good. I'm glad you enjoyed the new things that we tried." He told her as his finger trailed her skin.

"Dangerous question." She whispered as she laid back, enjoying his tenderness.

"What is the question?" He asked curiously.

"Do you want this witch after this is all over?" She asked boldly.

Zangrunath grew quiet for a few moments, thinking her words over. He thought about their relationship so far, and he did enjoy it. But, he also remembered their contract and how it worked. "If I could stay with you, I would." He told her honestly. "I want to see what you will become after you have that dream of yours come true."

"And, after I join you in Hell?" She asked curiously, not expecting that answer.

"It would be nice to have you at my side." He smiled, stealing a kiss. "It would make it far more bearable."

She kissed him. "Good. I've become overly attached to you." She was still careful not to use words like love around him, but attachment and possession. Those were safe. "Mine."

He smirked back, tracing the seal on her back lightly. "Mine."

She shivered, seeing goosebumps come up on her arms. "I didn't know that was sensitive."

He smirked, and traced a slightly different pattern on her back. "It has its uses." He started getting some ideas about how he could show her all the nuances of the seal and its benefits, but, before they continued their fun, he asked. "I assume that you're missing your finals tomorrow?" A smile on his face, and a dark chuckle rumbling deep in his throat.

"Will you go in my place? I just want to be close with my Zangrunath tonight. I already know all of the material." She looked up at him with a tired smile. "For now, it's late. I'd like to rest, if you don't mind."

Zane nodded, and laid Ellyria down to rest in his arms, cuddling into her closer than they had before. He gently rubbed her back, and gave her soft kisses as she grew closer to sleep.

Ellyria breathed deep and slow. She floated in consciousness for quite some time. Her tiredness didn't make her cranky tonight when it might do so on others. Tonight, she decided that simply enjoying the comfort of Zangrunath's arms was enough. She would fall asleep when her body was ready. Eventually, exhaustion washed through her, and she spoke without thought. Her words rang true even though she normally held them back. "I love you." She whispered.

Zangrunath heard her words, and shook his head. He understood the concept of love, but his demonic mind and nature made it so that he could never fully grasp it. He wasn't sure why she would love him. He was, after all, just doing his job.

He watched over her as she fell asleep next to him, and gently placed a hand on her. He did like her. She was better than the other witches he had been bound to over the centuries by a considerable margin. Ellyria was smart and powerful, and those things appealed to him. She was the strongest witch he had ever met. He wasn't sure if he could love her in the way she seemed to love him, but he knew that he could and would protect her in every manner possible. He was sworn to do as much, and he would die and reform as many times as it took to keep her safe. He wanted to see her succeed in every aspect of her life.

He looked over her form under the covers for a long moment before he leaned in to give her a kiss on the cheek. "Sleep well,

Ellyria." He whispered to her, knowing that she was already deeply asleep.

Thursday, December 8, 2022

Ellyria awoke to an empty house late in the morning. She was still exhausted, but she smiled. Last night was fun. She hoped Zangrunath gave Tucker Hell today as she made herself breakfast.

After Zangrunath finished Ellyria's test, he started walking towards the car before Tucker approached him. "Hey, sorry about last night. I was drunk and stupid and-" he started to ramble before Zangrunath cut him off.

"Don't talk to me again." He growled in Ellyria's scariest tone. "No one should have to deal with what you did last night." He tried not to smile and laugh after he delivered the rejection. This part of his job was always fun. His serious tone must've come across given how quickly the young man stepped away looking completely crushed.

Tucker deflated. His shoulders slumping as he looked down at his toes. "Sorry, I-" He began, trying to explain himself before being cut off again.

"Sorry nothing." Zangrunath told him firmly. "You are just a sad, pathetic man who doesn't have the backbone to do anything about it." He sneered, giving Tucker a serious look. "Stay away from me, and don't ever come near me again." He flipped Ellyria's hair, and marched to the car to make his way back home to the real Ellyria.

A few minutes later, he walked into the house, and turned into his demonic self, looking over to see Ellyria resting on the couch. "So, how are you handling today?" He asked, leaning over the back to look at her.

She hummed as she lounged in her pajamas with a book in hand. "Probably the most relaxed I've been in months to be honest. Maybe since Samhain."

"Good." He smiled at her, looking her over. "Are you hungry? It is getting close to noon." He asked, heading towards the kitchen.

She rolled over to watch him. "Maybe for a snack. Somebody let me sleep in."

"You needed it." He smirked back at her. "You were exhausted." He chuckled, starting to make her a light snack.

She nodded. "I was. Actually, I still am. Good thing I can heal myself if need be."

"You say that like I might be offended." He commented.

She shook her head. "No. I'm just enjoying the afterglow of a fun evening."

"The fact you liked what we did makes me savor that time together even more." He smiled, walking over, and handing her the snack. "Dig in."

"Thanks." She smiled, picking up a piece of pear from the fruit cocktail, and crunching into it. She hummed in appreciation. "Yum. Anything to report for the day or was it pretty boring?"

He sat down beside her, and wrapped his tail around her midsection. "Tucker tried to talk to me, and I promptly told him to eff off and not speak with you again." He told her honestly, "other than that, it was pretty boring."

She turned to look at him better. "Well, so much for my study group." She sighed, feeling a little bit lonely. Zangrunath was really all she had for company. "It's okay, though. They were starting to ask questions that I don't want to answer."

"Like us and family?" He asked curiously, looking down at her.

"And, what I do in my spare time." She shrugged. "Can't exactly say occult rituals."

He chuckled at her. "Well, you can, but, then, you will have to come up with a different answer when they think you are joking."

"I don't think I have the charisma in me to pull it off." She smiled, eating a cherry.

"You can be very charismatic." He smiled in return.

She wiggled with his tail around her waist still. "You're right. I did convince a demon to be in a relationship with me."

"Convince and asking are two different things entirely." He rumbled in reply, squeezing her lightly with his tail. "Seriously, though, with the ritual, you could ask me to fulfill your deepest desires."

"I like to think that there was convincing involved; I know the rules about you taking care of me. I've read the code, but I never asked or ordered anything." She took a bit of peach and ate that next. Her mind somewhat wandered to the mystery of how she'd gotten a copy of the demon code into her grimoire, but, once again, decided that it was a problem for another day.

"You still could have." He told her honestly. "I don't mind being ordered by you." He added, looking her over with interest.

"Still, I don't like to. You know that. I could've gone and done that test today. Probably should have. I don't like the servitude thing." She finished her snack.

He watched her for a moment, and took the bowl from her. "I just want to help you get what you want," he told her as he took the dish to the sink, "in every aspect of life."

"I know." She followed him to the kitchen and wrapped her arms around his middle. "I know." She closed her eyes as she held him from behind, trying not to cry as she was once again reminded that what they had between them was on a timeline.

He turned around, and held her for a moment. "It's not that I have to help you." He murmured, looking down at her. "It's that I *want* to help you." He finished, giving her a small squeeze. "You're better than the other witches."

"Thank you." She whispered to him. "I know you don't have to do some of the things you do for me, like investing money."

"You're welcome." He whispered back. "I am making sure you have the funds to fulfill your wants and desires in whatever way you see fit." He told her truthfully.

She smiled up at him, giving him a kiss. "I already have enough for the penthouse. Don't I? I know how aggressive you've been with trading."

"Pretty close." He smirked arrogantly back at her, kissing her in kind. "Give me another few years, and you can more easily afford it."

She shook her head. "That's insane. We started with, like, what? Four hundred thousand, I think, from the house and the life insurance."

"Yup." He nodded. "And, now, you have close to two million dollars." He told her seriously. "It wasn't that hard. Mostly just pattern recognition."

"I- excuse me?" She shook her head. "What?"

"You have close to two million dollars. Yes, you heard me correctly." He deadpanned.

She kissed him firmly. "You're amazing. Shoot. I don't qualify for scholarships anymore. Do I?"

"On paper, you do." He smiled at her. "I have it in a separate account under my name that I will give you access to when you graduate. I wasn't going to ruin free money."

"You thought of everything." She smiled.

"I try." He replied, kissing her lightly. "Now, we just need to wait for the computers to get here."

She nodded. "Can't wait." After holding him a moment more, she let go. "I'm going to meditate. I feel like I'm so close to something." She sighed. "Like my eighteenth birthday, but different."

"Don't tear the house apart." He teased.

"Oh, very funny." She giggled. "I know how to control that, now. I can unmake things just as quickly as I remake them."

He chuckled. "I know. I have seen what you can do."

"I know." She grinned. "I promise not to saturate the gold market."

He made a face. "Please don't. We have too much riding on that." He warned her with a serious expression.

"I can always break into Fort Knox and turn the gold to lead." She chuckled.

"Please don't." He grumbled, looking like he might preemptively wince in pain. "They do tank training there."

"At least, I'm not the Grant that actually suggested taking their seventeen-year-old daughter to a nuclear testing location." She laughed.

"Thankfully, that didn't happen." He chuckled. "You're the Grant that is going to be a terrifying lawyer."

Ellyria smirked, kissing him before walking off to meditate in the warded spare bedroom. "For Hell."

"It will be fun to have you by my side." He grinned, watching her saunter off to go meditate.

She swayed her hips a bit as she turned the corner. "Eternal damnation never sounded better."

Ellyria sat down in the spare room all alone. She sensed Zane moving around the house thanks to the quartz stone around his neck, but, instead of focusing on that, she turned her focus inward. She breathed in and out. She could hear her heartbeat for the longest time until that too became background noise. When that happened, she erupted with power. Her body began to float, not that there was anybody to see or sense it. She'd warded the room especially well for this. She was missing something, but she wasn't sure what. She guessed that it had something to do with Zangrunath interrupting her meditation on the day of her eighteenth birthday, and she had sought out that elusive power ever since.

Zangrunath completed a few chores, and decided to go watch Ellyria meditate. He wasn't sure what it was, but just seeing her with that much power made him want her more. He stepped into the spare bedroom, feeling a blast of natural energy. He closed the door quickly behind him before sitting off to the side where he could enjoy the show.

Like years prior, she delved to the point where she'd discovered the manipulation of matter. She'd been here many times since then, but what came next, she still didn't know. It almost made her afraid, except this was her magic. Ages ago, her father taught her that she never needed to fear her own magic. She pressed forward into her own consciousness, magic, and body. To her, it might have been minutes. Outwardly, hours passed. She was close. Almost there.

He watched as her hair became pointed, and the air around her pulsed with energy. He knew he was safe from her, and she wouldn't hurt him. A good bit of time passed since she'd started this. She seemed to search for something that he couldn't see tangibly there. He watched as her eyes stared at some point off in the distance. Even he couldn't tell what it was.

At the furthest depths of her consciousness, she found it, grasping it desperately. It had defied her for too long, but no more. It tried to move from her grasp, so she used her other power to reign it in, taking it for her own. Her eyes opened, still pulsing with the power inside of her.

He looked into her eyes, which were alternating between different colors. "Did you find what you were looking for?" He asked with a smile.

She floated slowly down to the ground. "Yes."

"Good." He replied, leaning back against the wall. "What was it?" He asked curiously.

She thought for a minute. How could she demonstrate? "You can make fireballs, right?"

"Of course." He chuckled.

"Throw one at me." She told him seriously.

"You know I can't do that." He reminded her. "I can't harm you."

She looked back at him just as seriously. "I'm telling you that it won't."

He a curious look crossed his face. He sighed, conjuring a small mote of fire before throwing it at her like she asked.

When Zangrunath threw the ball of fire, she focused for a second, not even moving as the magic fizzled out of existence before it could hit her. "See?"

He looked at her, and, then, his hand curiously. "What was that?" He asked, shocked by the newfound ability.

"Apparently, I can unmake magic." She pursed her lips. "What are my parents?"

He blinked several times before he shook his head. "I have no clue." He grumbled, looking over at her. "Apparently, they were the two most powerful casters to ever exist."

"And, then, they had me." She replied soberly. She looked at him seriously. "Sometimes, my magic even scares me."

"It shouldn't." He reminded her, moving over, and leaning down next to her. "It's your power. You use it as you see fit."

"Not that." She sighed. "I trust my magic. It wouldn't hurt me, but I could hurt a lot of people."

He looked at her seriously. "Do you want to hurt people?" He asked, lifting her chin up to look into her eyes.

She looked back into the abyss of his black orbs. "No, but the temptation is there. It's so, so easy, Zangrunath. I could see myself at the pinnacle in months if I ever decided to take it, and, with you," she barked one laugh, and snapped.

"You focus on what you want to do, and I will focus on the hurting." He told her seriously. "You just dissipated a fireball without moving a muscle. You should have no worries about hurting people. You will get to the top. I know you will." He told her firmly. "But, I also know you are going to do it your way. Not my way."

She smirked at his words, and kissed him. "You should talk me down from genocide more often."

He smirked at her as she kissed him. "If it means more of this, any day of the week." He growled, pulling her chest against his so that their faces were inches from each other.

She grinned, looking down at him. "Should I be prepared for you to take the rest of my finals this week?"

"Do you actually want to take any of the finals?" He countered seriously.

"Not a single one." She grinned.

Zangrunath lifted her up, and moved them into the living room where they began a fun winter break together. He helped her discover some new things to do with each other, forgetting the outside world altogether as well as the open blinds to the living room. They wrote off any lights coming from outside as headlights from the cars passing by or a rude neighbor.

ARTICLE II

Tuesday, February 14, 2023

Zangrunath roused Ellyria, and, moments later, one of his duplicates offered her breakfast in bed. She yawned, taking the coffee first. "What service this place has." She commented sarcastically.

"Consider it a prize after last night." He smirked.

"You flatter me." She blushed. "We really need to cool it with the late-night fun."

He chuckled at her. "I simply deliver what you want."

"You kept me up past midnight." She half-heartedly complained.

"It's my fault that you enjoy it?" He asked rhetorically with a smirk. "I am just making sure you get what you want however you want it."

She snorted, and held her nose. "Coffee up the nose is not fun! Look, not that I'm complaining, but I didn't mean it quite that way when I initiated things last night." She looked at him with a level gaze.

He sighed deeply. "Fine. We will be less physical with each other. Happy?"

"No." She told him. She moved the tray of food out of the way, gave him a hug, and cuddled into his chest. "We're still going to have fun, but we need to respect my sleep schedule for school." She kissed him before getting up. "I have class soon."

He looked up, and watched her as she walked away. "Fine. Curfew will be ten." He smirked.

She moved into the walk-in closet as he said that. "Thank you for helping me keep a respectable schedule for school even though you're half the problem."

He gave her a look of annoyance and intrigue. "If I remember correctly, which I do, you smirked, bit your lip, and said, 'I will be your dessert'." He quoted.

She came out of the closet fully dressed, deciding to drop the subject for now. "How do I look?" She asked.

"Wonderful." He told her honestly. "Like someone who wants to own the world."

She giggled, preparing to deliver to him the corniest line in her repertoire. She sauntered over, and took his head down to her level before whispering in his ear. "But, I already own the whole world. I have you."

He smirked, and gave her a kiss. "Just say the word, and it's yours."

"The word." She offered with a grin. She waved a hand. "With both of us, the world is too easy. Let's aim for something much more challenging- politics."

"That's why you take the classes." He chuckled, looking at the clock. "You get to school. I have businesses to ruin and money to earn." He reminded her, moving to go to the computer.

She gave him a quick kiss. "Thankfully, today is just the one class this semester. I'll see you by lunch." She grabbed the car keys. "Come on Shelby, baby. Time to go make the men weep."

He laughed as she said that. "Trust me, you don't need the car to do that." He called out as she left the house.

Ellyria made it to campus before she realized exactly what day it was. She groaned as she parked, and rested her head on the steering wheel. "Why does every school have to celebrate this day?" She mumbled to herself as she locked the car, and made her way into a now snow covered and glittery red and pink campus. Thankfully, she'd tested out of most of her math courses, but this one wasn't quite math. It was business and accounting. She hated

25

it on principle, but she needed the credits. She walked into the lecture hall, seeing the room covered in pink rhinestones and sequins. She glared at the decorations, taking a seat seconds before an envelope was all but shoved in her face. She grabbed it, if only to remove the nuisance from her sight. "What's this?" She grumbled.

"It's a letter." Tucker told her quickly, retreating to a different part of the classroom.

She ignored the letter, shoving it into her bag as class started. She could see Tucker trying to steal glances at her all period, but she ignored him. When class ended, she made her way to Shelby before opening the envelope as she sat behind the steering wheel. She started to read, and began to hyperventilate as anger took over.

My sweet Ellyria,

After our blow up back in December, I decided that I had to see you. I needed to explain what happened and why I did what I did. You were difficult to track down, but I was persistent. At least, your car is easily recognized.

I parked in front of your house, and I was going to go knock on the door. The only problem was that it was past dark. I didn't want to bother you if you were eating or something, so I waited. I was glad that I did.

Please see enclosed a photograph of you and your roommate in a compromising position. If you'd like the negatives, meet me in the library at noon.

Tucker

Ellyria looked at the photo of Zane and her on the couch together that had to be taken months earlier since the house was decorated for the holidays. "Fuck." She muttered aloud before switching to her mental voice. "Zane?"

"Yes?" He responded quickly, hearing anger in her tone.

She looked at the picture, and sent him the image she was seeing. "Help."

Ellyria heard a mental wail, which made her wince before Zangrunath appeared in the car a few seconds later in his human disguise. He looked at her for a moment. "Who do I have to kill?" He snarled.

"Tucker." She told him.

He released a growl, and nodded. "I will be back." He grumbled, getting out of the car, and making his way towards the library.

Ellyria sat in the car, locking the door behind him. She couldn't believe the nerve of this jerk. She jumped when a knock came at her window a moment later. She'd been so distracted by emotion that she hadn't thought to pay attention to what was around her. She growled both verbally and mentally, "Tucker."

"Hello, Ellyria." He greeted with a crooked smile. "Did you like the picture?"

She pushed her car door open, forcing him to step back out of her way. "What happens between me and my boyfriend on our property is our business." She told him firmly.

"I know. I wasn't on your property when I took the picture, so it wasn't trespassing." He smirked, looking her over lustfully. "Though, I wasn't expecting you to be into some of those things." He commented, blushing a bit.

"We were experimenting." She gave him more information in hopes that he would keep talking.

"Well, I'm glad you two like to be so active." He sneered, turning, and starting to walk away.

Ellyria didn't think; she reacted. She swiftly made the soles of his shoes so dense that he couldn't lift them. When he fell to the ground with a crack, she knelt beside him, "I'm going to make you pay for every last thing you think you saw."

He looked up at her, shocked by his sudden inability to move. "You can't do anything to me." He threatened in return.

"Why do you think that?" She snarled, using a simple non-detection spell as she used her abilities to throw him into the car and immobilize him.

Tucker looked around, and fear started to overtake him. However, he didn't scream or cry out. He was too interested in whatever Ellyria was trying to do. "Because the internet is a Hell of a place for a video to get uploaded, isn't it?" He retorted.

Ellyria remembered that weekend, and knew what he'd seen. "And, where did you upload it?" She asked calmly as she mentally screamed.

"I haven't. Yet." He told her with a wide smirk. "I just want you to myself."

She leaned into the back seat, and started the car. "Oh, buddy, you just got it." She commented sarcastically as she started driving towards the nearest ley line.

"Where are we going?" Tucker asked, seeing them start to drive away from the campus.

"A place where we can park for a while." She answered. She whispered to Zane, "I'm going to kill him. You get his stuff."

"Already on it." He mentally replied.

She looked back at the pervert pinned to her back seat. "What do you want me to do to you?"

"I want to do what he did." He told her honestly. "It would be beautiful to see you that way in person."

She shivered with disgust as the surrounding area became more forested and she turned down a small outlet road. "What do you want exactly?" She sneered.

"I want to do it all." He told her honestly. "But we can start off slow, if you want."

"You have a phone on you?" She asked.

"Of course. Who doesn't?" He replied.

She waved a hand, and magically took the phone from him, floating it out of his pocket. It shut off with another wave. She made sure she didn't touch it, throwing it on the dash with a little more mental force than she intended. "There are some things you should know about me if we're going to do this."

"What's that?" He asked, eyeing her from the back seat in his helpless predicament.

She could feel Zangrunath's rage, and she borrowed it for a moment, making her eyes glow with fire. She turned to look at him. "I'm a demon." She told him. "And, to have sex with me, there's a contract that sends you straight to Hell."

He tried to recoil in terror, but was unable to do so. He shivered in his place as he gazed at her longingly. "Sell my soul for a night with you?" He reiterated nervously.

"Yep." She told him as she parked the car. She yanked him out of the back seat, feeling the ley magics enter her. She appreciated the calming sensation of the magic for a brief second. Her body pulsed with magic as she looked at Tucker with disdain. "What'll it be?" She asked in a mocking tone. "My body or your soul?"

He looked up at her, and saw the power within her. His expression settling on awe. "Take it." He responded honestly. "I want you."

She kissed him spontaneously for only a second before she used her magic to instantly create spikes from the earth below her that ran through his body. She heard a squelching sound, and watched as the light left his eyes in an instant. Blood splattered on the snow, and she looked away. A lump of emotion settled like a rock in her throat. It was almost painful. She stood up, and wiped her mouth, heaving with frustration and anger. She killed a man, but she'd nearly done something incredibly stupid. "I think I almost actually made a deal there." She muttered to herself.

Zangrunath appeared next to her, and dropped the electronic and otherwise digital contents of Tucker's dorm room onto the ground next to her. He looked at the blood covered area, the corpse, and towards Ellyria. "Do not make a deal with anyone." He warned with a possessive growl.

"I don't understand." She told him honestly, shaking a little bit as the adrenaline from the entire debacle started to wear thin.

"You are mine," he told her firmly. "I will not allow anyone to have you but me." He replied, pulling her close.

"Yours." She muttered as he held her. "His cell is on the front console."

He nodded, and grabbed the phone. He tossed it into the pile with the rest of his things. "Do you want to do it?" He asked, looking her over, and wiping a bit of blood from her face.

She nodded once, waving a hand, and starting an inferno where the gore and technology rested on the ground. She looked at him, trying to ignore anything else. "Order window coverings next day delivery when we get home."

"Of course." He nodded, looking back at her. "No one but me is seeing you like that again." He told her possessively, putting an arm around her, and holding her close.

"I feel like an idiot." She sniffled. "I should've stopped it before it got this bad."

He looked into her eyes, and placed a hand on her cheek. "No, you are not. We were caught off guard." He told her, watching the incinerating remains, which were starting to smell like fried bologna. "He was a twisted individual."

"That's just my luck." She chuckled bitterly. "Take me home, Zane."

He nodded, and led her to the car. "Of course, I will." He responded, helping her get into the car, and shutting the door. He walked around the vehicle, and got into the driver's seat.

Ellyria looked at him. "I finally used my powers for evil."

He reached over, and held her hand. "It wasn't so bad, was it?" He asked in a surprisingly quiet, gentle voice.

"He made it so damn easy." She replied as her voice cracked.

"Of course, he did." He responded as he started Shelby. "He was a bad person. It made it easier to bear."

She held his hand and squeezed it. "I'm glad you were here."

"I am always with you." He replied, squeezing her hand in kind.

She laid down on the bench seat, and rested her head in his lap. "Happy Valentine's." She told him sarcastically.

He chuckled at that, and gently stroked her hair as he drove. "Happy Valentine's Day."

Thursday, May 16, 2024

"I cannot believe that you convinced me to walk for graduation. You're the only person that cares." She complained as she meticulously did her hair for the event.

"You would be upset in the future if you didn't." Zane told her honestly as he helped her get ready.

She lifted her robe, and handed it to him. "I should've put this on before doing the hair."

He chuckled, and helped carefully pull the robe over her head, making sure to not mess with her hair. "There, now, you are all dressed up for the part." He told her, taking a step back, and looking her over.

She smiled, picking up the cap to go with her gown, and gently pinning it into her hair. "I'm assuming that I need to order you into the audience. Or can you be a football field away from me now?" She laughed at her own terrible joke.

"Just tell me to be in the audience." He chuckled. "I'm not that powerful."

She smirked, kissing him lightly. "When we get there, go sit in the audience." After a pause, she added. "What distance are we up to now? I never remember to ask."

"Only one hundred feet." He shrugged. "It just takes time, is all."

"It's been, like, four years." She thought about that. "It would probably take my lifetime for it to be a football field."

"No. It just takes a while." He smirked at her.

She leaned over to the bathroom counter, picking up a medal and a tassel. She placed them around her neck. "Summa cum laude." She commented. "Eat your heart out, Harvard Law."

He gave her a kiss. "You are going to be terrifying."

"I already am." She reminded him. She grabbed the keys to the Shelby, tossing them to him. "Let's blow this pop stand."

He snatched the keys from the air, and moved to the side. "Lead the way."

She sauntered out the door with Zangrunath in tow. "Our reservations are set for tonight?" She asked.

"Of course." He nodded, getting the door for her. "It is set for six."

"Should be enough time, I think. How are we getting there so quickly?" She asked. "New York is a long way away."

He laughed at that, and sat in the driver's seat. "I am one Hell of a driver." He started the car, looking like the epitome of demonic mischievousness.

"Doesn't the ceremony start at three?" She pressed.

"And, doesn't this car have a turbo?" He countered, revving the engine a bit.

She frowned. "I better not have to repair it." She threatened with squinted eyes.

"You won't." He told her honestly. "This car will be fine."

She rubbed the dash with a hand. "Good. I promised to take care of her." She looked over at him. "Let's go get me a diploma!"

"Let's." He backed out of the driveway, hitting the gas, and launching the car forward to the ceremony.

She closed her eyes, and enjoyed the feeling of the speed and power of the vehicle. Her head rested back on the seat. "Miss Ellyria Grant. Bachelor's in English Literature with a minor in Latin Language and Literature." She murmured.

"Truly the most powerful person I know." He smirked at her, shifting the car into a higher gear.

She smirked over at him. As they got closer, the roads started to get congested with such a big group of people all going to one location. She bounced her knee impatiently. "This is why I was fine with them mailing it." She sighed.

He sighed, and slowed the car down, glancing over at her. "Calm down. We will make it there on time." He told her.

"I know. Just impatient. Sorry." She muttered.

"I've noticed." He replied. "You need to relax more."

"I don't know how to relax." She told him seriously. "Not before all of this. There's so many eyes."

"Are you giving a speech?" He asked seriously.

She shook her head. "No."

"Then, don't worry about it. All the people there are looking for their offspring. You just worry about yourself and relax. It will be over before you know it." He reminded her calmly.

"I'll just think about having a nice moonlit dinner with you." She smiled. "You did agree to eat an unreasonably priced meal with me, after all."

He grinned in return. "Of course, you are graduating college. The least I could do is have dinner with you. You deserve a reward."

She thought about that. "I'll have to think of something really good for graduating from law school."

"We can move into the penthouse." He offered with a wink.

"Or go overseas." She chuckled. "Rent a private jet, and see what a certain club is about."

"If that's what you want." He agreed, not looking upset at the idea in the least.

She smirked. "Not going to lie, seeing you nerd out visiting old battle grounds sounds like an oddly good time."

"I wouldn't mind giving you a private tour. I would be the best guide to give them over some jackwagon who simply 'read some words'." He scoffed at the thought, starting to look proud of his accomplishments on the battlefield for a moment. "I think I like that idea."

"It would be nice to take a month off to go see the sights and relax after all of my schooling is over." She glanced over at him. "You just tell me where you want to see some battle grounds, and I'll tell you which museums we're visiting."

He chuckled. "I did most of my business in Europe, so any battles there should be enough." He offered, turning off the highway and onto the main roads.

"As long as we get to vacation, I'm happy." She told him. "I already can't wait."

"You just want to lounge around on a beach." He teased.

"Given that I've never been to the beach, that would be accurate." She told him.

He thought it over in his head for a moment. "Then, I would recommend the Bahamas for that. The water is nice just about all year round."

She hummed. "So, to Europe for a couple weeks and to the Bahamas after that."

"That sounds good." He smiled at her, and, a few moments later, the stadium came into view. "As long as you are happy, that is all that matters to me."

"Well, I want you to enjoy yourself, too." She told him seriously.

"Oh, don't worry about me. I will always find a way to entertain myself." A devilish grin appeared on his face.

She laughed. "Chaos. I know."

He nodded, and pulled the car into the packed parking lot. He got out first, and moved around to get the door for her. "Here you are, Miss Ellyria." His voice was formal, yet lighthearted, as he offered her his hand.

She took his hand, and feigned innocence. "I do declare, Mister Zangrunath, I didn't know that chivalry was alive and well."

"It never died. It was just hiding amongst the plebians." He deadpanned as he helped her out of the car, and shut the door behind her.

"I like that word." She giggled. As they started walking to the building, she saw all the graduates entering at a different door. Pausing, she gave him a kiss. "I'll look for you in the audience."

He gave her a kiss in kind. "I will wave." He replied. Zangrunath watched her go off to join the other students before he made his way to the seating area. He sat down in the numbered seat from his ticket. Annoyance struck him a few moments later when a couple sat beside him. They wouldn't stop talking, and the woman's voice was grating, but he did his best to tune it out. He just watched and waited to see his Ellyria make her way up onto the stage.

Ellyria saw a lot of familiar faces, which she suddenly realized she didn't know. The last four years had been a whirlwind of emotions, studying, and Zane. She smiled, thinking about him. He was her rock, and it killed her that she wouldn't always have him there to rely on. She got in line by last name, and waited for her name to be called. As she walked across the stage, she shook hands with the dean of her college and a couple others she wasn't familiar with, moving her tassel before going to sit and listen to the speeches, and, of course, Zangrunath broke the 'polite clapping' rule. That was just his way.

Zangrunath didn't care about the looks he got from the claps. He was more focused on the person on the stage. His Ellyria. Once she moved off the stage, he waited as best he could for the rest of the whelps to be finished. He did get bored however, so he spoke to her mentally. "Good job. You looked beautiful."

"Thank you, and don't think I didn't see the flash from the crowd." She chuckled mentally. "I want a pretty frame to go with it."

"Of course." He mentally chuckled. "I will make sure it looks good enough to show the world."

She tried to pay attention to the proceedings, even listening to the obligatory Latin speech that she guessed only a handful of people in the crowd cared about or understood, but her attention turned to Zangrunath again. "Let's sneak out."

"If that is what you want. Let's." He replied, happy to get out of the crowded auditorium.

She cast the non-detection spell on herself, and carefully maneuvered around the many bodies unnoticed or otherwise ignored. When she pushed through the outside crash bar door, she found Zane there. She paused for a moment, admiring her love before holding up the package with her degree enclosed. "Let's lollygagging out of here." She quoted an old movie.

He smiled, and gave her a kiss. "Let's. We do have a dinner reservation to get to." He wrapped an arm around her, leading her to the car.

She smirked. "I don't even want to know how much tonight costs."

"Not as much as you think, but more than what a person should spend on a dinner." He chuckled.

"On a rooftop in New York?" She pressed.

"Of course," he replied, "you ask for it, I make it happen."

She shook her head as he helped her into the car, starting to carefully remove the graduation gown. "My guess is several thousand, but seriously don't answer that."

He shook his head at her. "Not nearly that much." He laughed. "The bill will be a few hundred dollars, but not that disgusting."

"Okay." She nodded. "Not that it currently matters. Still haven't bought the penthouse."

"I am working hard on that." He told her as he began to drive towards the restaurant. "Penthouses are not cheap, but it will be worth it."

She smiled at him. "I know that you will make sure it's perfect. Just like our current, 'rental'." She gave him a pointed look, and made air quotes.

"Of course. I will always get you what you want," he smiled, "even if, on paper, you own the house."

"I own a house in Cambridge." She shook her head. "How I didn't notice, I'll never know."

He smiled at her. "I am going to make sure that you are set for the rest of your life when our deal is done." He assured her in a soothing tone. "Not that you would really need it."

She held his hand, and looked away as she tried to control her emotions. She knew he loved her in his own way; she knew love wasn't a feeling demons really had, but the fact that he wanted her to be okay after he was gone proved it to her. She didn't say the words. Instead, she whispered with a thick voice, "mine."

He held her hand in kind, and squeezed it lightly. "I am yours, and you are mine." He replied quietly. He knew she was feeling a mix of emotions right now. His arm moved around her and pulled her close to him as he drove. "Don't worry. Everything will be fine." He reminded her calmly.

"It's just another step forward until you're gone, and I-" She turned into his shoulder, and let the tears fall.

Zangrunath felt wetness come through his shirt, and he pulled to the side of the road. He turned to her, and held her as she cried. "You are the strongest witch I have ever met." He told her as he rubbed her back. "You will be fine without me. You are strong. I know you will be able to keep going." He spoke softly, comforting her as best he could.

She looked up at him with teary eyes. "Thank you for always taking care of me."

"Of course." He replied, resting his forehead against hers. "I will always do the best I can to help you."

She kissed him desperately, and, when she pulled away, she looked into his eyes. "You don't have to say it back, but I love you."

He looked at her, and kissed her like she'd done him. "You are mine, and I will do anything to help you feel better." He told her, trying to be comforting in his own way.

She leaned into him, and closed her eyes. "Let's start by going to dinner." She whispered as she sniffled a bit. Her hand rested on his thigh as she cuddled against his form.

He looked down at her, and kissed her head. "Let's get you fed." He whispered, putting an arm around her, and driving the car towards their destination.

"I think I'd like you to show me how my finances work this summer." She told him. "It's time I understand all of that."

"I will." He promised as he rubbed her shoulder. A smile pulled at his lips. "It is not as complicated as you think it is, I assure you."

Ellyria nodded, wiping her eyes a bit. "I can't summon you again, can I?"

Zane released a sigh before shaking his head. "No." He told her in a simple, straightforward tone. "The deal doesn't work that way."

"Can I summon you on Samhain?" She asked hopefully.

He made a face, and replied in a somber tone. "Demons are not applicable to that."

She nodded. "I guess, I'll just have to be ready when it happens. I have no other choice."

"I'm sorry." He told her, softly rubbing her shoulder. "I would stay longer if I could."

"It's okay." She sighed. "I'm not sure I really wanted you to watch me grow old." She shivered. "All while you're still," she waved a hand over his form. "I'd look like your grandmother."

"I can look like anyone. I can even make myself look older." He corrected reassuringly.

"You'd be my silver fox, then." She giggled.

"I would be okay with that." He responded with a small smile. "I could be there to take you to Hell."

She held his hand and squeezed it. "I thought that was death's job. You can't take me if you're already there?"

"I just want to cut out the middleman." He kept his words open and honest. "If anyone is going to take you to Hell, I want it to be me."

"I can be yours there?" She asked. "Do you have enough sway as a general for that? I don't really understand the pecking order. You still need to teach me about that."

"I'm not the highest ranked general, but I don't think there should be a problem." He smiled at her. "You could be mine forever."

"Yours." She promised.

His smile grew wider, and he squeezed her hand. "Forever."

"You would definitely make damnation worth it. Only problem would be if you get summoned." She mumbled.

He rubbed her hand with his thumb. "It takes a lot to summon me. The only real way that would happen is if World War three started, but we missed that bullet years ago." He chuckled.

"And, could I be summoned?" She asked.

"If you get made into a demon, yes," he replied, thinking that idea over. "Given your strength, it would take a world ending power to do that." He suggested with a laugh.

"Do I keep my powers at all?" She hummed.

"Some of them, but that depends on what they decide you would be best used for." He responded with a thoughtful frown.

She looked up at him, and made a face. "What are the options? Where do you think they'll choose?"

"Honestly, I'm not sure." He sighed. "Given your power, though, probably a general like myself."

She thought about that. "I would have been fine being in your legions."

"I would like that." He smiled.

"Having to obey your orders." She added with a smirk.

"Of course, you would enjoy that." He moved his hand to gently rub and squeeze her thigh.

Ellyria let out a little surprised yipping sound when his touches tickled her. "So would you." She argued.

"Yes, I would." Zane smirked at her as they began to enter the outskirts of New York City.

She looked up at the skyscrapers and lights. "I love this city."

"It is nice." He smiled, watching her for a moment as he drove them to their destination.

"And, so much sin for you to create chaos with." She offered with a little chuckle.

"It would be too easy." He chuckled. "I would just need to walk down a street and say a few words."

She smiled. "Living here will be interesting."

"It will." He told her with a nod. "You won't be able to open up Shelby as easily on the streets."

"We'll just have to take trips for that." She offered.

He smirked at her, and, when he turned to watch the road again, he saw their destination close by. "Oh, we will." He pulled the car into the parking garage, shutting the car off after pulling into a spot. Then, he walked around to help Ellyria out. "Shall we go eat?"

"Yes, we shall." She took his hand, strolling beside him.

He gave her a kiss, and led her towards their destination, past a sign that he was sure to walk by quickly. Once they reached the elevator well, he hit the button for the sixty-fifth floor. "I hope you enjoy the view. There are very few buildings you can't see while up here." He told her.

She leaned into him. "I can't imagine not enjoying this."

"I am hoping. I rented the whole restaurant." He informed her as the doors opened, revealing the beautifully decorated Manhattan restaurant. The room was large and open with windows looking out over the New York skyline. The smell of bread coming from the kitchen was delightful. As they stepped into the main foyer, a well-dressed waiter appeared.

"Welcome, and good evening. You must be the reservation for Grant?" He asked with a smile, giving a slight bow.

"Yes." Zane smiled at the man before looking towards Ellyria. "Ready?" He asked.

"Ready." She smiled widely as they followed the waiter.

The waiter led them to the rooftop section, and helped seat them. "Are there any drinks I can get you?" He asked the two of them.

"I'll take a vodka soda with squeezed lemon and a splash of sour mix." Ellyria responded decisively.

"Of course, miss." The waiter responded, writing her drink order down. He turned to Zane. "And, for you, sir?"

Zane looked over the menu briefly. "Let's go with the gin and tonic." He replied.

"Of course, sir, we will have those out for you in just a few moments." The waiter smiled, leaving them alone out on the magnificent, starry rooftop.

"I didn't expect you to rent the whole place!" She quietly complained.

"I thought you would like the quietness." He admitted. "This place is normally pretty busy."

She blushed. "I do. You just spoil me. That's all."

"Alright, then. Next time, we will choose something with a drive through." He joked.

"Not for my graduation from law school!" She raised her voice, and covered her mouth.

He laughed at her. A goofy smile gracing his features. "Never stop being you."

Ellyria nodded, waving over herself. "Ta-da."

As she did that, the waiter came back, and placed their drinks on the table. "Here we are. Are you two ready to order or do you need a few more minutes?" He smiled.

"I think I need another minute." Ellyria replied, looking at her menu, now.

"Alright, I will return shortly." The man nodded before leaving them to ponder the menu.

"It all sounds great. Well, the stuff that I recognize." She told him.

"I have heard good things" He smiled at her, placing his menu down. "I know what I am having."

She looked up. "Oh?"

"I'm going with the dry aged New York strip." He told her with a nod. "Seems simple enough."

"I was looking at that." She chuckled.

"Two of them, then?" He asked her seriously. "Make it easy?"

She nodded. "Sounds like a plan." She paused for a minute. "And, the strawberries and cream for dessert."

"Sounds good to me." He smiled, waving over the waiter.

The man came over, taking their orders, and giving another bow as he left them be again. As he strode with purpose, it was almost like he was dancing throughout the restaurant.

She gave Zane a look. "Is he normal? He gives me- a feeling-" she hummed. "I didn't make sense, did I?"

The demon chuckled at her. "No, it made sense. He simply made a deal."

She looked from Zane to the waiter. "I honestly can't tell what for. Maybe theatre given the area."

"I have no clue." He shrugged, looking at the man before looking back at her. "Doesn't concern us either way."

"Do people with deals know that they made a deal?" She asked.

"I certainly hope so. Otherwise, there would be problems." He reminded her.

She shook her head. "I'm an idiot. Forgot about the code."

"It's fine. There is a lot to it." He smirked, taking a sip of his drink.

"I should know it, though. I might need to live by it." Ellyria whispered.

He reached out a hand to hold hers. "You have plenty of time." He told her honestly. "For now, enjoy tonight. We can worry about that later."

She nodded. "I know." She looked around and up to the sky. "This is beautiful."

"Yes, it is." He smiled, gazing at her.

She looked at him, and saw him watching her instead of the scenery. "Oh, you." She blushed.

"What can I say? I literally cannot lie to you." He smiled at her.

She took his hand from across the table, and held it. "Sometimes, I wonder how I got so lucky."

He rubbed her hand with his thumb. "Sometimes, I wonder the same thing." He told her honestly. "I have done this countless times, and this one has been different in every single aspect. No wars. No real bloodshed. No backstabbing or deceit. Just helping someone become successful."

She didn't realize that she'd leaned in to hear his words. She sat up a bit. "I can't even begin to fathom where that scared, sad seventeen-year-old would be now had you not shown up. By far, you are my biggest and best mistake, and I would never change it."

"Same." He replied with a sincere smile. He was going to speak before the food came to the table.

"Here you are, folks. Enjoy." The waiter told them, placing the food in front of them.

"Thank you. It looks delicious." Ellyria commented.

"Thank you." Zane added, looking at the food, and smiling.

Ellyria took her napkin and put it in her lap before picking up her utensils. "Not going to lie, it's kind of odd to see you actually eat after all this time."

He smiled, and began to cut into his steak. "I can eat," he told her, taking a bite. "I just don't need to."

She cut into her perfectly cooked steak, and took a bite. "Oh, this is delicious."

He nodded, enjoying the taste for a moment. "The cook might have made a deal."

She laughed. "I'm fine with never knowing." Her eyes closed as she chewed the melt-in-your-mouth meat.

He smiled, and watched her eat for a moment before he cut into his own entrée again. He took a sip of his drink. "This is nice, not having to cook." He commented conversationally.

She took another bite. After a minute, she replied, "thank you for always doing that. I know you know that I can cook."

"It's fine," he replied, waving her off. "You are busy becoming the world's best lawyer."

Ellyria gave him a soft look. "I can't wait to start learning legal writing and business law. Hearing about it from you is great, but I want to be able to hold a conversation. No offense."

"None taken." He responded. "It mostly deals with clear language, expectations, and making sure that both ends of the deal are achievable. That and taking care not to give too much power for too little in return." He explained, taking another bite of his meal.

"I wonder who I'll eventually work for." She hummed.

"I'm not overly sure, but, knowing you, anywhere you really want to work." A mischievous and knowing smirk forming on his lips.

She thought for a while as she chewed. "I think I'd want to start off at a firm."

"Smart move. It helps get your foot in the door as well as experience." He responded with a nod of approval.

"Then, I think I'd like to work for a company, maybe a talent agency or a book publisher. Something that would be a bit more specific and detailed." She explained.

"That can easily be arranged." He told her with a nod. "As long as you know what you want to do, we can make whatever vision you have a reality."

She looked down at her plate, trying to ignore the sour thoughts that Zane might not be there for all of it. "I do." She smiled, but it didn't reach her eyes.

He set his fork down for a moment, and held her hand. "No matter what, you will always be mine." He whispered for her ears only.

"Yours." She told him.

"Now and forever." He added reassuringly.

She finished her plate a moment later. "This has been the best night of my life."

He finished his plate at about the same time as Ellyria. "But, we haven't even had dessert yet."

"Oh, trust me, I didn't forget." She smirked.

The waiter walked over, and took the empty plates. "Are we interested in dessert?" He asked the pair.

"Yes, please." She looked to Zane. "Do you want towards share?" She asked.

"Yes, please." He playfully parroted her words.

"What would you like?" The waiter inquired, silently enjoying the cute couple's flirting.

Ellyria looked over at him. "The strawberries and cream, please."

The waiter nodded. "Coming right up. I will have that out for you in just a few moments."

Ellyria held Zane's hand. "Are we going home tonight or did you have plans?" She asked.

"My only plan was to come here and have dinner with you." He told her honestly. "Where we go next is entirely up to you."

"I don't know." She thought aloud. "Hotels are nice, but the beds aren't as nice as ours."

"Then, we should head straight home." He chuckled.

She looked him up and down. "I am more than fine with that."

"I figured you would be." He teased, looking back at her in kind.

As they were eyeing one another, the waiter came back with their dessert. "Here you are. Enjoy." He smiled, leaving them be.

Ellyria grabbed her dessert fork, and took a small piece of the decadent looking fruity dish before offering it to Zangrunath. "A sweet for my sweet." She teased.

He looked at her offering, and took a bite. He chewed the bite of food, and replied mentally, "you will regret that later."

"I'm counting on it." She winked.

He winked back at her, and took a piece of fruit, offering it to her in kind.

She took the bite, and hummed. "Oh, yes."

He chuckled. "You are too easy to figure out." He smirked, stealing a small piece of the strawberry.

She took another forkful for herself. "Zane?"

"Yes, Elly?" He asked in turn, hearing the little telltale pitch in her tone.

She glanced over at the waiter who was watching them intently. "You're not going to propose to me, are you? The waiter is watching like you are."

He chuckled at that. "No. We are fine the way we are. Besides, marriage doesn't work the same with demons." He explained as best he could, offering her another piece of fruit.

She nodded. "Oh, thank goodness." She whispered. "I don't think I'm a marriage and kids sort of person, and, if I am, I don't think I'm ready for that yet. Not by a long shot."

"Also, marriage involves churches." He reminded her. "No go for me."

"Even if I wanted to get married, it would be in court." She smiled, taking one last forkful.

"Are you ready to get out of here?" He asked, already knowing the answer.

She took his hand. "You bet your ass."

"Can I bet on yours?" He countered, waving the waiter over to get the check.

Ellyria nodded. "Sure."

Zangrunath paid before leading Ellyria back down to Shelby. "Let's get you home." He smiled, pulling her close to him.

She leaned against his side. "I think I'll take a nap so we can have fun times later."

"By all means." He agreed with a wink, leading her to the car.

She smiled. "I want to get in the hot tub together, too."

"Will do." He helped her into the car. "I will make sure you are nice and relaxed."

ARTICLE III

Ellyria sat at the dining room table, looking over a document. She looked away from her assignment to see Zangrunath. "Can I talk this over with you?"

Zangrunath nodded, and pushed the vegetables he was cutting to the side. "What is it?" He asked, walking over.

"I'm supposed to write a document using Bluebook citation," she showed him the assignment. "Basically, I need to make the best deal for the company that I theoretically work for." After a second, she paused. "Originally, I thought that I'd outline the money changing hands, but that is already pretty clear. It would take me a paragraph at most. Would it be wrong to make the bulk of the content about control of assets that are changing ownership instead?"

He looked over the assignment carefully. "That would work as long as you clearly define what the 'assets' are. One person might think it is the money while another might think it is the stock in the company or equipment." He explained, giving an example.

She nodded several times. "Okay, that's about what I was thinking. Thank you."

"No problem." He replied, smiling, and going back to working on the dinner he was making.

She started to frantically write, mind going a mile a minute while her hand struggled to keep up. "I'm going to be a bit."

He waved her off. "Take your time. I just barely started making dinner. It will be a while." He told her honestly.

She took out a red pen, and started properly marking the document, registering when Zangrunath brought her dinner. Then, she started to eat and write. While multitasking, she worked deeply into the night. She looked up at the clock when she finally finished, yawning widely. "I sleep too early. Apparently, eleven thirty-four is late for me."

He walked over to her, and wrapped an arm around her. "That's because you work like a maniac." He told her honestly as he guided her to bed.

"I just," she yawned, "don't want to revise on the weekend."

"If you do, it won't be much after all of that." He reassured her as he lifted her up and brought her to bed. "You work hard. I know you will be fine."

She curled up into him. "Goodnight, Zane."

"Sleep well, Elly." He smiled at her, giving her a kiss as he tucked her in for the night.

Wednesday, April 22, 2026

Ellyria came back home around six at night with a wide grin. "Zane!" She jumped up and down excitedly as she offloaded her belongings, and pulled a document out of her backpack.

Zangrunath blinked a few times as she ran into the house. "Yes?" He asked, watching her enthusiasm with infectious joy. "What makes you so happy?" He asked curiously.

"I got the legal writing essay from Friday back!" She held up the documents to reveal a red '100%' circled.

He smiled. "Good job." He told her, pulling her in for a hug. "You are doing great."

Ellyria hugged him back. "Thank you, thank you, thank you."

"For what?" He chuckled. "Giving a small bit of advice?"

"Everything. Ever." She mumbled.

He held her close for a moment longer. "Well, thank you, but you did most of the work." He reminded her in a simple, matter of fact tone. "You're already pretty smart. You just need to be nudged in the right direction, is all."

"It's starting to come together." She smiled, kicking her shoes off near the door.

Zane waved a hand, and moved to put her shoes in line with the rest of them before looking at her. "It was always there. You just needed guidance."

"With a lot of things." She added.

"You would have figured it out. It would have just taken longer." He commented, moving into the kitchen. "I bet you are hungry."

"Yes, I am." She murmured. After a minute of waffling between going to get changed and just staying in the living room to chat, she sat down at the kitchen bar. "Things are starting to get competitive."

"No wonder you are back home so late." He commented, glancing at the clock as he made her dinner. "You do like to win; you are competitive like that."

She nodded. "There's this internship over the summer, and there's a lot of politics kicking in."

He let out a sigh. "Ugh. I hate politics. So much they said, we said nonsense. That's why I prefer deals. It's an even divide where everything is laid out." He smiled, "easy."

"I'm not even sure I want it, but the temptation to get ahead is there and it's strong." She sighed, rubbing her temples.

"Then, go for it." He told her seriously. "It will get you closer to what you want."

"So much for our summer vacation." She frowned. "I like distracting you while you try to concentrate on video games."

"As do I." He smirked at her playfully before he let out a sigh. "We will manage." He told her seriously. "It will just be one summer."

She sighed. "I guess. It's time that I become the lawyer and not just Ellyria."

"You will still be my Ellyria." He assured her as he placed her dinner in front of her.

She picked up her utensils, and looked up at him. "I can't believe I'm saying this. This is not who or what I thought I'd be one day, but I need a wardrobe upgrade and a stylist."

He smiled, and released a self-assured chuckle. "And, why do you think I am here?"

"You what, now?" She asked, baffled.

"Wardrobe upgrade? Easy." He responded without pause, waving his hand at all of her. "As for a stylist, I have been bound to enough women to know what trends will never go out of style." He smirked at her. "This is nothing."

"Well, make me a lawyer." She shrugged, starting to eat.

He looked her over with a critical eye, but not because he needed to. "It won't be difficult."

"I didn't think so, but, honestly, I still dress and carry myself like I did in high school and college. I need to be ready sooner than I thought." She commented.

"Don't worry. I will whip you into shape in no time." He promised.

She eyed him. "In the least sexual way I can summon, make me a woman."

He chuckled, and gave a little shrug. "Walking and talking will take time and practice. As for clothes, the internet."

"I don't even know where to start." She giggled, starting to get a little excited about shopping. "Any suggestions on clothes you wouldn't rip off?"

"I would rip them off of you all the same." He commented idly as he thought. "Well, I think several department stores will have what you're looking for. There must be a website for this. Either way, I think a black-on-black look will suit you well. It is slimming and formidable as well as easy to clean."

"I know for a fact that I want a pencil skirt. They look so powerful in TV and movies." Ellyria commented before she groaned. "I'm going to have to start dry cleaning things."

"You can have people do that for you." He responded quickly, waving the concern off. "Seriously, the number of things you can have done for you in this day and age is astounding."

She nodded. "I guess it's not so bad if I'm paying them." She thought aloud. "This whole I play and you work thing has never sat right with me."

"I have plenty of play time." He chuckled darkly. "It is fun getting gaming profiles banned."

"Yeah, I never expected the love for first person shooters, but you do get to torment kids." She shrugged, though she still looked like she was thinking about the previous conversation of major wardrobe purchases.

"If you are worried about the money, don't be. You are going to be fine. Besides, lawyers make a pretty penny. I know you will become miss money bags before too long."

Ellyria finished her meal, and looked at him. "Thanks to you, I haven't been worried about money since high school."

"It was my job to help you." He reminded her in a serious tone. "You having no worries is a good thing."

She stole a kiss from him, and cleaned her dish. "I have an essay to write for Friday." She groaned.

"You can do this." He encouraged, his voice almost chipper by comparison to his usual timbre. "It will be a cake walk."

"It's for the internship. Yay." She waved her hands with her lack of enthusiasm.

"Then, make it fun." He suggested. "Just because it's work doesn't mean you can't enjoy it."

She nodded. "Dear Parker, McDonough, and Hannon, please choose me because I'm witchy. Thanks."

He shook his head at her, and released a scoffing snort. "Not like that." He sighed. "Dear Parker, McDonough, and Hannon, I am a strong and independent woman who is more than capable of working at your company. I have language and social skills which make me well suited to helping your clients. Knowing this, please consider me to work for you."

"Well, it's not a full letter, but it's a start." She smiled.

"It's all about the word play." He smiled at her. "It's the difference between eating with grandma and eating grandma. Word choice and punctuation matter. If you get it, I'll make it worth your while."

She giggled at his example. "Oh, you. How am I supposed to concentrate while thinking about that?"

"You have to get accepted, so you better work hard." He teased.

"Eff me." She whined, averting her eyes from the literal demon who was enjoying taunting her far too much. She grabbed some paper and a pen from her backpack, sitting at the kitchen table, and thinking for a moment before starting to write.

"If all goes well, I plan on it." He chuckled, watching her get to work.

Dear Parker, McDonough, and Hannon,
Please accept this letter as my formal request for entry into your summer internship program.

She looked at him reading over her shoulder. "No pressure or anything."

He chuckled, and walked away. "Just wanted a brief idea of what was ahead."

"Sure." She sighed. His distraction made her lose track of where she was going with the letter.

He whistled too casually as he left the room so she could work. She just needed a goal, and he knew what she wanted.

She looked back at the paperwork, and started again.

As a female embarking in a male dominated industry, I feel that it's of the utmost importance that I take every opportunity to put myself in a position to be ready for the future. It takes a certain amount of strength and dedication to be in this industry. It also requires subtlety, attention to detail, and that certain electric something that you can't quite express with words.

Energy. Energy is something I have in spades, and one thing I've learned about energy is that energy is power.

Ellyria looked at the document, grumbling her frustrations under her breath. "This is way too much information. I'm basically telling them about my life story in the most bass-ackwards roundabout manner there is."

"Then, tease them with what is to come!" Zane called out from the other room in a playful singsong manner.

She tossed the draft in the bin.

Dear Partners,

Did I get your attention? I hope it did. My name is Ellyria Grant, and we'll be working as partners in a firm together one day, but the first step requires that you take the chance to hire the strongest, most independent future lawyer that you've ever met.

She hummed. "Okay, this one, I like."

The most important thing you should know about me is that I have a certain magic about me. Sometimes, I can just make things happen out of nowhere when things are stuck.

She smiled. "Thank you!"
"You're welcome." He replied.

Thursday, April 30, 2026

Ellyria wore her freshly purchased black blouse with a rounded neckline and a black pencil skirt with a pair of heels. She paced back and forth in the living room as she wrung her hands together. She saw Zane out of the corner of her eye, but ignored him in favor of her worry. "Everybody else has interviews tomorrow." She mumbled. "Why was I invited to dinner tonight?"

Zane looked at her for a moment, and chuckled. "Oh, I think I have an idea." He smirked knowingly." Who are you meeting tonight?" He asked seriously as he watched her pace.

She looked at her shoes. "Mister McDonough's assistant, I think."

"Then, why do you think he invited you to dinner?" He asked her rhetorically. "To show you his baseball card collection?"

"To politely tell me that my letter had balls, but not just 'no' but 'Hell no'." She worried aloud.

He chuckled at her. "Calm down. Everything will be fine." He walked up to her, and rubbed her shoulder reassuringly. "I will be right there next to you the whole time."

"Invisible." She added with a sigh. "I can do this. I can do this."

"Yes, you can." He agreed. "If not, I know you will give them Hell."

She nodded. "I would kiss you if it wouldn't smear my lipstick."

"You can save that for later." He smiled. "Just go get the job first. I can wait."

She smiled, and grabbed her purse and the keys to Shelby. "Let's do this."

Zangrunath smiled, and disappeared. "Break a leg." He told her mentally as they left.

She hopped into the car after locking the door. "Thanks. Time to go eat an overly expensive dinner." She sighed as she punched the gas, accelerating towards the restaurant. When she arrived, she parked, putting her keys in her purse before walking with purpose towards the building. Her heels clicked on the pavement, and she held her head high despite her worries. She smiled at the hostess. "Hello. I'm here for the McDonough reservation."

"Hello, Miss. Mister McDonough is waiting for you. Right this way." The hostess smiled before leading her to a private table.

Ellyria mentally spoke to Zangrunath, "did she just say Mister McDonough? I thought it was supposed to be his assistant."

"She did." He replied. "That is odd. Why would one of the partners want to see you?"

"I guess we'll find out." She replied mentally, offering her hand to Mister McDonough as she approached the table. "Good to meet you, sir."

He stood up as she approached, and gently, yet firmly, took her hand. "Hello, Miss Grant, it is good to finally make your acquaintance." The gentleman with a stylish crew cut smiled. His brown hair looked somewhat red against the navy blues of his suit.

She returned the smile as she took her seat across from him. "I'll admit. I'm surprised. I expected your assistant."

"That was the original plan, yes." He chuckled, taking his own seat. "But, I figured he wouldn't be able to do a proper interview."

She nodded, but lied when she responded. "I understand completely. Thank you for taking the time out of your busy schedule to see me. I understand that most of these meetings are taking place tomorrow at the University." She still didn't get what was happening here, and wanted more information.

"That is one of the reasons my assistant couldn't make it, yes." He chuckled. "But, for you in particular, he wouldn't be able to understand your- innate ability." He smiled, waving the waiter over.

The waiter came over, and took their drink orders, and, when he left, Ellyria looked towards Mister McDonough, feeling a bit baffled. "How so?" She asked, trying not to audibly gulp.

"Well, I look over all prospective new interns. I like to make sure I know who I am hiring." He told her seriously. "I was a little curious after seeing your background check. It seemed quite mysterious. Unnatural, even."

She hummed a little. "Oh, I'm sure it's all easily explainable. What was it that was in question?"

"Mostly, your senior year of high school." He told her simply.

She frowned in false upset. "That was a rough year for me, but my grades remained high despite everything."

"You did well, considering you had issues with the Vatican." He replied quickly, looking directly at her as the drinks arrived.

She froze as she took her drink from the waiter. She looked up at the man, and saw the dazed look on his face. Magic. She leveled a gaze at McDonough. "I handled it." She hedged. Internally, she was screaming to Zane. "What the Hell?!"

Zane didn't respond.

"Zane?" She asked quietly.

"You look like you are having some trouble there. Is everything alright?" Mister McDonough asked with a straight face.

She nodded, and lied through her teeth. "Oh, yes, of course. Thinking about the Vatican just makes me think about my parents. I'm sure you can understand." She didn't bother to mention that her constant companion was being maddeningly silent.

"I can understand. Really, I can. Losing those close to you can be tough. Not being able to hear them talk back can be nerve wracking." He not so subtly taunted, taking a sip of his drink.

She raised an eyebrow at him. "Mister McDonough, sir. May I ask the real reason you wanted to meet me?"

"Of course, but I will answer that when we have food and the room to ourselves." He told her, waving the waiter over. "You will thank me for the discretion later."

She ordered her meal, and waited for him to order his before looking towards him again. "Do you speak Latin?" She asked curiously.

"Fluently." He smiled back.

She switched over to the language. "So do I."

"I had a feeling you would." He chuckled.

"Why is that?" She replied curiously, smirking over at him. She was starting to enjoy this, which only further proved that there were things wrong with her.

"Well, at first, I wasn't sure." He told her honestly. "But, after seeing the timing of certain events and how well you 'took care' of things, I figured you might also have friends in low places."

She nodded. "That would be accurate. Care to explain why he's being uncharacteristically silent?"

"Because mine talks way too much." He sighed. "I needed to be able to think."

"So, you turned off the volume or are they having their own little tête-à-tête?" She asked, taking a drink.

"Turned off the volume. They can still hear us, but, unless they show themselves, we won't be able to hear them." He explained, taking another drink as well.

She eyed him carefully. "So, you wanted to meet me because of him and not because of my internship letter."

He shook his head. "Not quite. My real intent was to learn more detail about your deal. I wanted to make sure that you and I aren't going to be butting heads with one another. That would be problematic for the both of us." He told her as he sloshed his wine around in his glass a little, and took a whiff of it in the glass.

"Without going into details, I'd like to be a respected business and contract lawyer." She smiled.

He looked her over with a guarded and curious expression. "Really? You sold your soul to become a lawyer." He asked seriously.

"That is an embarrassing and complicated story." She responded.

He nodded. "I understand that." He sighed before he regarded her seriously. "So, you just want to be a well-respected lawyer, that's it? No plans on world domination or money?" He asked, half-joking.

"If I wanted to take over the world, I could've done that years ago. It would've been easy, and money isn't going to be a problem." She told him honestly.

He raised an eyebrow, and chuckled at her. "I saw the car pull in. I am impressed," Mister McDonough replied honestly. "But, that was a curious choice of words. You must have an impressive friend if you think you could have done that."

"Indeed." She smirked at him. "But, I wouldn't need him to do it. I just don't want that. Conquest is easy. Politics are harder."

He nodded still eyeing her curiously like she was a puzzle he was trying to piece together rather than a young woman and a supposedly terrifying witch. "Indeed, it is." He replied, giving pause as their food arrived. When the waiter left, Mister McDonough looked back at Ellyria. "It appears you like challenges, then." He surmised, taking a bite of his parmesan crusted chicken. "I admire that."

She cut into her fish, and started to eat as well. "So, you've learned an awful lot about me. Tell me, why do you think we might butt heads? What's your endgame?"

"The same as yours." He told her honestly. "However, we have different specialties. I am a defense lawyer."

She nodded. "It shouldn't be a problem, then."

"Correct. In fact, I think it could be beneficial for both of us." He smiled. "I can help you gain that reputation you want, and you can help me with some of the more- troubling clients."

"Troubling clients?" She quirked her head to the side.

"To put it simply, other demons and the like." He explained, taking a bite of his meal. "We have a few people on our business team, but they are not the best. If you can become our lead for that, I would be extremely thankful."

She smirked. "That shouldn't be a problem. I have a wonderful teacher."

"Good. We need the help." He told her seriously, but the smile on his face lightened the mood. "To be honest, I am trying to see if I can get out of mine, but time is kind of running out." He sighed. "The sooner you are able to get up to snuff, the better."

"Good luck getting out of that deal. You would be the first." She told him honestly.

"That is what I am hoping for." He replied. "I have a feeling my demon tricked me, but I still can't figure out how. Legal writing isn't my specialty, so help would be appreciated."

"I'm assuming you used the ritual and didn't just make a deal?" She asked.

He shook his head. "Not quite. I did make a deal, but I needed help to do it. Just wasn't expecting the consequences to be so dramatic." He sighed.

She nodded. "Well, if you didn't use the ritual, you stand a chance." She told him honestly. "Did you see the contract? How was it worded?"

"I can do you one better. I have a copy." He told her. "Not with me, obviously, but I have one. The wording is convoluted to say the least, and I know that there is some form of loophole. I'm just not sure what I am looking for."

"Well, if there is one, I can find it." She told him confidently. "I might have magic, but my words are my weapons." She realized that she'd been so interested in the conversation that she'd hardly eaten, and took another bite of food.

"Good." His tone rang out clear and decisive between them. "You're hired," He extended a hand.

Before she took his hand, she asked, "are we shaking on the internship or an actual job offer contingent on passing the bar exam next year?"

"Both." He replied without missing a beat. "If you are even half as good as what I have seen your scores are, you will pass it with no issue."

"I have every confidence in that." She grinned, taking his hand. "Does your firm write employment contracts? Because I'll need to review it before I sign."

"We do, and that is perfectly fine." He smiled as she shook his hand. "I only want to be a lawyer, not take souls."

Ellyria joked. "What's the point in going to Hell of you don't have the power to trap souls there with you for eternity?"

"To save the ones you love." Mister McDonough sighed. "Sometimes knowing you will be damned, makes life a little better knowing someone else won't be."

She smiled, and her eyes got a little distant as she took another bite to eat. "I know exactly what you mean."

"Was it worth it?" He asked. "Making the deal, I mean?"

She looked at him seriously. "I cast the ritual. I didn't make a deal."

"Then, you still have time to figure it out." He decided with a small nod. "Just don't regret your decisions." He told her in an encouraging manner as he finished his meal.

"I don't regret anything. I don't want to get out of it, and, furthermore, I can't get out of it." She told him. "Nobody's ever gotten out of a deal after using that ritual, and I know that I won't try to be the first. I'm going to Hell." She shrugged once as if to punctuate her statement.

He saw her resolution, and gave a simple nod. "Good. At least, you know what you're in for."

"Yes, I do." She nodded. She finished her last bite, and looked up. "If you don't mind, I'm going to turn the volume back up, now."

"I can do it. After all, I cast the spell to begin with." He replied, waving a hand, and Ellyria heard Zane's voice again.

Ellyria smiled. "Aww, you ruined my fun. Learned a new trick a while back, and haven't run into people like me to try it out with."

"A new trick?" Mister McDonough asked curiously.

"Oh, my family magic goes as far back as the crusades, as far as I know. There's some interesting abilities that I have because of it." She told him mysteriously.

He chuckled. "I have heard of your father, but never knew what he was capable of. So, it wouldn't surprise me to hear that the heir would be just as strong." He chuckled, waving to the waiter for their check.

"Heard of?" She asked. "I didn't know he was well known. We lived in the middle of nowhere."

"Us casters need to stay together, so we try to keep an ear out for one another." He smiled. "Sam was strong from what I heard before he ran off somewhere with someone. My guess is to that town of yours."

"Yeah, that sounds about right." She sighed. "I'll have to ask him more about it in October."

He raised a curious eyebrow at her response. "Apparently, he wanted to make sure whatever he was hiding was a secret, even from his own daughter." He commented, looking a little shocked.

"Let's just say that my coming of age was a bit jarring." She deadpanned.

He made a face. "I'm sorry to hear that." He replied soothingly as he stood up, leaving the money on the table for the check. "I hope you do find the answers. There are a few of us who are curious as to what happened." He told her, placing a hand on her shoulder. "Have a good night, Miss Grant. I look forward to working with you in the future." He smiled, taking his leave.

Ellyria felt a little baffled as she was left behind with nobody but Zane. She grabbed her purse, and started to walk towards the car. "That was interesting." She mentally spoke to the invisible demon.

"Indeed, it was." He responded simply. "He seemed to be telling the truth, too."

"I agree. I didn't catch any falsehood coming from him." She nodded as she unlocked the car, and hopped in.

Zane appeared in the passenger's seat next to her, and looked at her. "I wasn't expecting another witch up here." He chuckled in shocked surprise.

She shook her head, working through a similar feeling. "We should expect more. The Puritans came here for freedom of religion. There's probably a bunch of old Pagan and Wiccan families."

"That, I was not expecting." He told her. "We should be on the lookout, then. It would be nice to have allies besides your future boss."

"I'll have to look at my book. I think I remember seeing a magic sensing spell." Ellyria surmised as she started driving them towards the house.

He nodded, placing a hand on her thigh, and smiling. "Congrats on getting the job."

"Thank you." She grinned. "I almost can't believe it."

"I'd pinch you, but I'd have to pinch me, too." He joked.

Ellyria shook her head. "No, thank you." She looked over at him with a little sadness. "One more step closer to the dream."

"You are going to be great with or without me." He replied. His voice both soft and encouraging.

"I wish I had worded it differently," was her only response.

He massaged the place he was holding lightly. "If ever there was someone to try and change the ritual, you would be the one to do it." He told her with a sigh. "This world is starting to grow on me." His eyes looked towards the window but focused their attention on Ellyria through the reflection.

She thought about his words. "I'll make it happen. Hell is about desires, after all."

He turned to look at her with a serious and mildly impressed expression. It looked both doubtful and hopeful. "You would be the first person to change the terms." He told her. "No one else has ever had the power to change them."

"You can just start calling me Karen because I'm going to need to speak with your manager." She chuckled.

He laughed in kind. "Good luck. You will need it." He smiled, looking a little more hopeful for a brief second before it disappeared again.

"How do I summon the Dark Prince?" She asked.

"Honestly, I have no clue." He grumbled, and sighed.

She thought about that and how she could speak to her father. How she could summon Zangrunath in the first place. "I'll make a way."

He smirked. "If anyone can. It's you." The hand on her thigh gently squeezed. His thumb softly rubbing in little reassuring circles. "The most powerful witch I know."

She smiled. "If I have to, the seven seals won't stand a chance against me."

He looked at her, and blinked. "If nothing else, we would see each other, then, but I would refrain from doing that. The requirements are more like prophecies, and you would anger both sides if you did that." He explained. "Please don't do that."

She took his hand, and squeezed. "Mine." She growled.

He growled in kind, squeezing her hand. "Yours, and you are mine."

She parked in the driveway, and stopped the car. Her body angled to look at him better in the cramped space. "I will do whatever it takes to keep you here with me. You are mine, and I am yours."

He leaned in, and kissed her. "I will do whatever it takes to help you make that come true." He assured her.

She got out of the car, and strolled up to the house. "For now, let's celebrate."

He grinned a wide, toothy smile, and followed her into the house. "Yes, I owe you." He shut the door behind him, and turned into his demonic form.

Ellyria looked up at Zangrunath with trust in her eyes. "Please either go to my classes tomorrow or send an email to my teachers about my absence." She asked him as they began a long weekend of fun.

Friday, May 1, 2026

Zangrunath lovingly helped feed Ellyria the next morning. After she was taken care of, he sat behind her on the couch while a duplicate Zangrunath hugged her gently from in front of her. The original behind her was tracing the seal on her back, and, when he finished running his hands over it, she shook in his duplicate's arms. "What was that?" She whispered to him nervously. "It feels- different."

"I just unlocked the seal more." He explained to her. "I wanted to feel closer to you." He whispered to her.

She looked up at the copy in front of her, so she could look into his eyes. "It feels so," she shook her head. "Exposed. Intimate."

"It is." He whispered to her as he gently caressed her arms. "I want to give you something that can only be shared between people like us." He explained to her as he looked into her eyes. "There is more to it if you are comfortable with that."

"Something between a witch and her demon?" She asked curiously, leaning on the couch, and finding the material scratchier than normal. "I don't understand. What does it do?"

"It makes you experience things as if you were in Hell. It is very intense." He explained. "It can only be done by a caster and demon who are in love." He added while looking into her eyes.

Ellyria's eyes watered, and she nodded. "Oh." She murmured as surprised, happy tears fell. Her lips pulled into a smile. "That seal is connected to- you want to touch my soul?"

Zangrunath nodded, and turned her head to the side so he could kiss her. "I love you, Ellyria, and I want to be as close as possible with you." He smiled, wiping away her tears.

"I love you, too, Zangrunath." She murmured, nodding, and looking into his eyes. "Please do it."

"Are you sure?" He asked before he started tracing the seal.

She nodded. "I trust you with everything that I am."

He kissed, enjoying the rest of the weekend with his love.

ARTICLE IV

Monday, June 29, 2026

After nearly a full month of dropping off mail and delivering coffee, Ellyria was finally pulled into Mister McDonough's office. It was around lunch time, so she guessed and brought her food in with her, knocking on his door politely. "Hello."

"Come in." Mister McDonough called from behind the door as he worked on a document.

"You asked for me, sir?" She smiled, closing the door behind her.

"Yes." He replied, gesturing for her to take a seat. "I need you to look into something for me." He began seriously.

She nodded. "Of course, I'd be happy to help. What is it?"

"It has to do with one of our clients." He told her as he laced his fingers together on the table. "I think they are a caster like us, but I am having trouble trying to track them down." His expression started to turn from conversational to one of annoyance.

"Do you have an address? I can go check for wards or spells on the place. Worst case, I douse them out." She offered.

He thought it over for a minute, and nodded. "It would be great if you could do that, but, be warned, they are known to be aggressive." He made a slightly apologetic face.

"I am not concerned in the least." She told him honestly.

"You must be pretty confident in that demon of yours, then." He responded, once again impressed.

She leveled him with a gaze. "Frankly, I'm disappointed that you think I need him to protect myself, but, yes, Zangrunath is a high-ranking demon. I have trusted him with my life for six years. Nothing will change that."

"I'm jealous. I don't have that kind of trust in mine." He sighed. "But, you did the ritual, so it would make sense that it's different for you."

"Yes, there are things that the ritual does where a simple deal does not." She whispered. "And, you never showed me that contract."

"If you can find the client and make sure he is still alive and well, I will show it to you." He offered. "Nothing against you or anything. I'm just nervous about letting people see it."

She nodded. "I understand. Just know that whatever I see is between me, you, and the Dark Prince. Oh, and the other two people in the room." She dispelled the volume control spell McDonough favored with a thought. "I wonder what they think of it?"

McDonough sighed as a female demon appeared next to him, leaning on his shoulder alluringly. "I think she is a lying little shit." The demon smirked.

A second later, Zangrunath appeared in front of Ellyria. "Be quiet, whelp." He demanded, looking down at the lesser demon.

"Why would I lie?" Ellyria asked. "If I were going to lie, why not go straight to the top?"

"Because you are a manipulative little bitch." She sneered almost instantly with disdain in her voice.

Ellyria used her magic for a moment to keep the demoness's lips closed. "Okay. I see why you like that spell. Zangrunath is much calmer."

"Oh, I will make her quiet permanently." Zangrunath told the room, glaring at the female demon with a look in his eyes that told them clearly that he was imagining stabbing the other demon and tearing her apart limb from limb.

"Yes, Astratoth is a bit difficult to deal with at the best of times." McDonough sighed, glaring at the female demon before he looked at Zangrunath. "You, however, have much more self-control. That's good."

Ellyria gazed at Zangrunath. She was enjoying this moment more than she cared to admit, and caught herself staring. "Do as you please, but no messes."

Zangrunath smiled, and released a small growl. He walked up to the female demon, and grabbed her by the back of the neck. "You and I are going to have a talk." He snarled before disappearing with Astratoth into a cloud of mist.

Ellyria looked to her boss, holding out a hand. "Address?"

He sighed, and pulled out a sticky note, jotting down the address. "Here you go." He replied, handing it to her. "Just stay safe, and, please, don't let your demon kill mine. That hurts."

"Don't I know it." She rubbed her head where she remembered feeling being shot years before. "Trust me. If they're casters, I'll be fine."

He looked her over skeptically, and gave her a nod. "Okay. Just go make sure he is alive, and don't hurt him. We need him for the case we are working on."

"They'll be fine." She told him. "I'll go check on your witness. Real subtle there."

"The case is already causing enough problems. I didn't want to somehow make it worse." He explained simply.

She turned, and left the office. "Time to go open Shelby up."

As Ellyria hopped into the car, she noticed her discarded planner in the passenger's seat. The little symbol next to the date reminded her that tonight was a full moon. She'd need to do cleansings tonight. After typing the address in the GPS and starting to drive off, she could sense Zane's glee. She wasn't entirely sure why. It was a first. Could he do this all along or was this new? Or, maybe, he was just projecting the emotion like he would thoughts. Either way, she'd need to check sometime. She and Zane had an interesting relationship that had probably never happened before, or, at the very least, happened so infrequently that she wasn't sure any of those other couples were currently alive. She turned her attention to the road, following directions, and getting there in record time thanks to turbo drive.

When she parked along the street in front of the house in question, Zane appeared in the passenger's seat, grinning like he had won the most sublime of battles. "So, this is the place?" He asked, looking it over. "It seems normal enough but so does our house."

"Yeah. I'm not sensing strong magic, but that might be the point." She thought for a minute. "Can't douse it. Too obvious. I do have the magic sensing spell, but that could be obvious, too, depending on the type of magic folk."

He looked at the house and, then, to her. "So, we walk in?" He asked seriously.

"Either that or I use my Mom's power to forcibly rip apart any magic there is in the place." She shrugged.

"I am fine with either option." He smiled at her. "I could always try to go scout the house out as well." He offered.

She thought for a minute. "Steve called them aggressive, so I vote for the option that keeps us off their property."

"Fine. We can do it the boring way." He sighed, making a face.

She rolled her eyes at him, and started to concentrate in the back of her mind on taking magic away from the property. Outwardly, she asked, "what did you do to Narzgaloth or whatever her name was?"

"I simply gave Astratoth an ultimatum." He explained, pronouncing the name carefully for her. "Stay quiet around you or I rip her tongue out through her pancreas." His tone was lighthearted despite the threat coming from his lips.

She shivered. "That's wonderfully barbaric." She sensed something in the house, mentally grasping onto it. "Prepare for a rather violent reaction in a minute." She warned as she started to dismantle the magic from the domicile.

Zane watched as the glyphs and wards that were once invisible started to glow and pop like magic confetti all throughout the yard. He smiled over at Ellyria, and saw a man with shaggy blond hair angrily marching out of the house. "I think he noticed us."

"I would hope so." She murmured, eyes closed in deep concentration. "I think I just tore apart a summoning circle or something similar inside the house."

"What in the world were they summoning?" He asked oddly as the man came up and banged on the window of the car.

"I don't know who you people are, but get the fuck off of my property!" He yelled at them.

Ellyria turned to look at the man, rolling down the window. "Actually, we're parked on the street. This is public property." She looked at him innocently. "Is there some sort of problem?" She asked as another sigil exploded like a firework.

The man looked back at the decimated wards, looking upset and scared. He knew they could probably see what was happening, running a hand through his hair. A nasty look overtook his face. "I know what you're doing! You're trying to get me to hurt more people," he trailed off. "I won't do it!" He growled, trying to grab Ellyria through the window.

Ellyria felt Zane take hold of her and move her out of the way. She lost concentration, and found herself on the passenger's seat, looking at the back of his head. "What are you talking about?"

Zane grabbed the man by the neck. "Answer her question." He demanded.

The man sputtered and coughed as Zane's hands gripped his throat. "Th- the wards p- protect me from the moon," he gasped, struggling for air.

"Son of a bitch." Ellyria muttered, getting out of the car, and storming into the unsuspecting man's house. "I was a mythical creature before it was cool." She muttered under her breath like an occult hipster.

Zane watched her get out of the car, and followed her. His fist still holding, and now dragging, the man. "Show us." He grumbled, letting go of him, and pushing him towards the door.

Ellyria growled as she entered the living room to see an actual cage in the center with chains attached to the ceiling and walls. Beneath and around the cage, she saw a sigil carved into the ground- the one she'd torn all the magic from a moment before. "Lucifer be damned werewolves."

Zane followed them inside, and released his grip on the man, lightly pushing him inside. He slammed the door closed behind them. His lips opened to let out a biting snarl of anger, but he was cut off.

"Now, I have nothing to keep me safe for tonight." The man ran his hands through his hair as his throat rasped from the rough handling Zangrunath had given him moments before. His eyes looking from the now magicless circle to the young woman who had intruded in his home and destroyed his safety net. His eyes flashed angrily, and his nostrils flared. "Thanks for that." He sounded like he was about to let out a string of curses and oaths before Ellyria cut him off violently.

"No, you're not." She growled at him in impressive fashion. It almost seemed demon like in nature. "Magic should come with warning stickers." She turned around, assessing the room and the area for the best course of action for a moment.

He gave the back of her head a dirty look. "I knew what I was doing. I was just trying to make it easier on everyone else!" He yelled.

"No, you didn't." She reeled around, and seethed at him, poking him in the chest as her eyes flashed with lightning. "Had you warded this place right, it would reek of danger so nobody with half of a sixth sense would come near it. Instead, you made it as unassuming as possible. *I* couldn't even tell there was magic here until it started going off like moist rock candy, and I'm one of the most magically gifted witches on the continent, if not the world!"

"I did what I had to do to live a normal life." He growled at her. "You try explaining to your coworkers and loved ones why you have to call off every full moon."

She took a breath, and shook her head. "You are so lucky that I'm a good witch." She conjured her wand, and started casting proper wards this time. She wiped the old sigil away with a single swipe of her wand, and meticulously started to redo the sigil in the center of the room. As she did so, recreating the correct symbol from memory after many years of studying her grimoire. Midway through, she muttered, "who all knows? Just us?"

"A lawyer, you two, and one other person." He sighed. "Not even my girlfriend knows."

"Which lawyer?" She grumbled as she started to infuse the seal with her magic. She glanced over at Zane, looking emotional and dangerous.

"Steven McDonough." He told her with a frown. "He has been helping me with a mess I made.

Zane chuckled darkly, and asked curiously. "How bad was it?"

"I killed seven people. Woke up covered in their blood." He explained in a broken sounding voice.

Ellyria looked to Zane as she was casting. She looked livid. "He sent me to you, knowing full well that it's a full moon tonight, and knowing a good deal about what you were." The strokes that she was moving her wand in looked violent, like she was considering how she was going to slit the lawyer's throat with it after she got done with this.

"Sorry." The man replied as a pained groan. "It's hard for me to deal with people because of all of this." He gestured to himself and around the house.

"Had he had an iota of respect, he would have warned me." She raged. "He sent me here to test me." She finished with the sigil, and moved out into the yard. "This will take a while."

Zane called out to Ellyria. "We are going to be home late." He sighed, deciding to help clean a bit in the meantime.

"We're staying the night. We're not going home." She replied from just outside the door. "I need to make sure the magic worked."

"Really?" The man asked, glancing between the two strangers. "Why are you going through all of this trouble to help me?"

"Because I made a mistake, and I'm a decent person. Or, at least, I try to be most of the time." She looked over at him from where she was marking the front door with new runes. "You're not dangerous to me. Not in the same ways as a normal person."

Zane regarded the man, and shrugged. "If you were an actual threat, we would have much bigger problems to worry about." He told him seriously.

The man looked at the pair, and nodded. "Thank you." He murmured. His expression was clearly overwhelmed and grateful. Zane noticed him wipe away a tear.

"Don't thank us yet." She told him seriously, walking clockwise around the house as she made more runes. "Thank us tomorrow morning."

He nodded, moving to a closet to grab supplies to help Zane clean. "Okay."

Hours passed and the sun was close to setting. "When's moonrise?" Ellyria eventually asked as she finished infusing the wards with magic.

"Moonrise is 8:43, but the moon is full at 7:56. It is the moon being full that you need to worry about." He explained, getting into the cage, and starting to lock the chains on his wrists and ankles.

Ellyria sat back on the old, beat-up couch, relaxing for a minute. "You won't require that." She told him seriously. "Had this place been warded properly in the first place, those seven people would've never been a problem."

Zane took a seat next to her, but pulled her close to his side protectively. "She fixed your failure of epic proportions." He chuckled darkly. "Just calm down, now."

Ellyria looked at the clock, "nearly time." She assessed the man in the cage with a little annoyed eye roll. "What's your name, anyhow, werewolf?"

"Tom." He replied simply just before the transformation started, and a pained howl ripped from his lips.

She watched as he started to double over, turning to look at Zane. "Are they wolves or are they more, like, half-people with hair?" She asked curiously. "I only know they exist because of the spells in my book."

He shook his head. "It's neither. It is more like a spirit possessing him." He told her as Tom's body began to change.

"Aww, I thought he was going to turn into a cute puppy." She complained playfully. "That's no fun."

"If he worked on it, he could." He told her.

She watched with morbid interest as Tom gripped his head in pain. "So, he's just him, but feral?"

"More like trying to drive a car blindfolded while high as a kite." He explained.

She made a face. "So, like, when you're possessing someone, but on steroids?"

"Well, kind of. He still has some control, but the other half is trying to take full control." He told her as best he could.

She nodded. "Okay, so the Strange Case of Doctor Jekyll and Mister Hyde."

"That is accurate." He smiled, glad he was able to help her understand.

"Well, can he talk like that or are we in for a lot of screaming and howling?" She asked.

"That depends on him and what his relationship with the spirit is." He responded, watching Tom like a hawk. The other man was looking far more wolf-like. His frame becoming muscled and bulky.

Her head tilted as she watched. "So, he could theoretically turn me into one of them or is that a myth?"

"Myth." He chuckled. "It is genetically inherited."

"That makes sense." She thought for a moment. "I'm willing to bet that his girlfriend has already figured it out. Any idiot who read that series of seven popular fiction novels about wizardry would be able to make an educated guess."

Zane looked around the room, and laughed. "You need to remember that people are idiots. She still might not know."

"She might not." She turned her attention back to the wolf boy as he was starting to stand back up in an almost upright manner. "Better?" She asked.

Tom's body looked around the room and met the two sets of eyes that were watching him. A far more animalistic voice came out. "You two talk a lot." He grumbled, stretching, and flexing his freshly supercharged muscles. "Yes, it is better." He replied honestly, looking at his hands, and flexing them. He looked impressed at himself. It was the first time in his life he'd ever felt this way, and it was incredibly freeing.

"So, you *can* talk like that." She hummed. "I was honestly starting to expect snarling." She crossed her arms, and got a haughty look about her. Pride swelled in her chest. "That's what proper wards are like. They don't just keep you in. They help you regulate and keep control."

Tom nodded, and let out a sigh of relief. "I actually can't hear the other guy." He told them, looking around the room with wonder. "Thank you. This is the first time I have had control."

"Just don't trust what you find on the internet again." She told him. "I did, and I wound up with this big galoof." She gestured to Zane with a playful grin.

"You don't regret a second of it." Zane smiled down at her. His arm pulled her towards him lightly, giving her a little squeeze.

"It clearly worked out for you two." Tom sighed. He shook his head at the strange and very intimate couple. "Just, please, don't talk about whatever you two are into."

Ellyria's lips pulled into a playful smirk. "Uncomfortable, bondage man?"

"I just don't want to hear about what a human and, I'm guessing since you look normal, a demon are doing behind closed doors." He rumbled, shivering a bit as revulsion rolled through him.

Ellyria rolled her eyes. "If we were in Europe, you'd be more concerned about violence. America is all about Puritanical sexual stigma. It even shows in our literature."

Tom sat down on the floor, and removed the cuffs from his wrists and ankles. "Well, of course, that would make sense. The country was founded by Puritans seeking refuge away from a dictatorial king at the time, so it only makes sense that it would bleed into modern day social life." He replied eloquently.

"Huh, a literal animal and well read." She smirked, looking to Zane. "I like him."

"We are not keeping him as a pet." Zane grumbled argumentatively. A serious expression on his face as he met her eyes.

"Like Hell you will." Tom threatened from his place inside the cage.

Ellyria held up her hands. "Yikes. I didn't mean it like that." She held up two fingers. "I've got like two friends including you." She pointed at Zangrunath. "At least, I can be myself around him."

Zane gazed into her eyes for a moment longer before he released a sigh, nodding decisively. "Fine." He told her, looking at Tom. "I know he won't do anything anyway."

She glanced over at Tom and back to Zangrunath. "So, can we come visit once a month? The full moon is a relatively restless night for me being a witch anyhow."

"That's fine." Tom told her with a serious expression and nod. His voice started strong and slowly got quieter as he spoke. "If you guys don't mind, of course. It would be nice to be able to control him fully. He's caused too many problems. I don't want to live in fear of him anymore."

She looked at the runes on the ground and up from there to the cage and chains that uselessly hung limp inside of the miniscule prison. "Well, the first thing you'll want to do is move this mess out of your living room so your girlfriend can come visit."

"That's why I have a rug." He replied, pointing towards the rolled-up area rug that was pushed flush against a wall. "It makes it easier that way."

"Alright, then. Now, tell me. What happens if she decides to move in and sweep?" She countered.

"I will say I like the design?" He suggested with a lackadaisical shrug.

"You're missing the point. You need permanent accommodations if you want to rise above this," she gestured to all of him, letting out a long, weary sigh. "Rather than just living with it."

"It will happen in time. This is the first time I have been able to talk. Up until now, I have usually blacked out only to wake up in a destroyed room the next morning. I'm still trying to process this." He grumbled, looking at them with a mix between ire and gratefulness that was hard to get a beat on. It seemed like his expression was changing from moment to moment based on swiftly fluctuating emotions. Clearly, there was still, at least, a small fight for dominance happening inside of him that they were no longer outwardly seeing.

Ellyria decided that it was best to leave Tom be with his thoughts. She barely knew him. She couldn't even begin to imagine what he was feeling right now. The best parallel she had was how quickly her life began to change for the better after Zangrunath came into her life. "You think the garage thing will work here like it worked at the old place in Oklahoma?"

"It's possible. It really doesn't matter what the room is like as long as the runes are right." He replied.

She nodded, standing up. "I'm going to put my stones out to be cleansed. Then, I'm going to go line the walls of your garage in lead. You're welcome."

Tom blinked with some surprise, but nodded. "That's fine. Thank you again."

Zane watched her walk away, admiring her form before turning back to look at the werewolf. He gestured throughout the room. "So, how long has it been like this?"

Tom gazed about his room, and shrugged again. "About a decade?" He responded as more of a guess than anything. "It's hard to tell when it started. I was in college and liked to drink."

"So, you moved into the house ten years ago?" He asked curiously. Tom didn't look that old.

"No." Tom replied, shaking his head. "I moved here after the accident about a year ago. I've just been scraping my life together, making ends meet. Trying to get by, you know? That is, until she showed up." He sighed right up until the moment that he thought about Ellyria. A small smile gracing his somewhat twisted features.

"If you even attempt to hit on her or give her any type of flirtatious look, I will rip you apart and mail the pieces across the United States." Zangrunath's eyes flared with a possessive fire that hadn't been there a moment before. After a moment, he took a breath, calming down. "But, yes, she is strong."

Tom froze for a moment, realizing that Zane meant every part of his threat. "I wasn't planning on it. My girlfriend is pretty awesome as it is." He replied defensively, averting his gaze from the demon.

"Good." Zane nodded. As he saw Ellyria come back into the room, he smiled.

She yawned as she laid down on the couch with her head in Zane's lap. "Well, I would normally stay up, but that always takes a lot out of me."

Zane nodded, and sighed. "And, you work tomorrow. You need to get some rest."

"I'm sure I will after that. I just feel rude since we're somebody's company." She complained.

"I know, but you still need rest." He told her seriously. "Get it while you can."

She closed her eyes, and tried to relax. Instead of saying the words out loud, she whispered them into his head. "Night. Love you."

"Love you, too. Sleep well." He replied mentally as he gently rubbed her scalp and hair as she fell asleep.

Tom looked at the two of them, and smiled. "You two are adorable."

Zane glared, which made Tom retreat in his cage before turning around, laying down, and falling asleep not long afterward.

Tuesday, June 30, 2026

After speeding home to get changed and picking up take out, which Zangrunath was never happy about because it wasn't healthy, Ellyria stumbled her way into the law offices of Parker, McDonough, and Hannon. There were dark circles under her eyes as she approached Steve McDonough's office, knocked, and heard a female voice through it.

"It's that tramp again." Astratoth crooned. "Don't show her that. She can't help you. Nobody can help you but me. Isn't that right?"

Steve looked over at the demon, and shook his head. "I think she can. Come in!" His features held a victorious grin as he called to Ellyria.

Ellyria opened the door, and walked in. She closed it with a little wave, letting a breeze close the door with a decisive click. She sat down, glaring daggers at the demon. "If you say anything further about me- in mine *or* Zangrunath's presence, I will make you suffer so badly that you will beg for the fires of Hell."

Astratoth glared at Ellyria, and saw the fire in the witch's eyes. She gulped. After that, she didn't speak another word before disappearing in a puff of smoke.

Ellyria looked to Steve. She was somewhere between exhausted, grumpy, and furious. Her expression almost coolly unreadable after such a large amount of magic use and lack of sleep. "Where were we?"

"Well, other than that impressive display, good job with Thomas. He told me that you made him feel normal for the first time in ages." He smiled.

"I actually like him. After I stopped feeling blindsided and completely infuriated at the situation, I decided that it was fun." She smiled, but it didn't reach her eyes. "We have plans to visit next month." She added.

"I heard." He replied, giving her a small nod of approval. "You're going to see if he can get it under control, right?" He asked, leaning back in his chair a bit.

She waved a hand. "He was normal last night, but all that stuff needs to not be in the living room. Normal people don't have cages and chains right in the middle of sigils."

He chuckled at her lightly. "Normal is a very loose term with magic folk. For instance, how any person would think we were normal, until they knew more than what can be seen at the surface." He smirked, turning around, and rummaging through his desk.

"I grew up normal until my sixteenth birthday." She told him honestly. "Then, boom. Magic. Dad barely had a chance to teach me anything before he passed."

"Then, you know better than anyone why we need to work hard to hide what we have." He responded, looking at her, and placing a piece of parchment on the desk. "Now, we can work together to deal with this as well."

She looked at the parchment. "I honestly expected a scroll." She took out a legal pad and red pen. "Bring it on."

He pushed his contract towards her. "As I promised, here it is. It is well written, but I know that there is something there. I just can't figure out where it is at." Steve furrowed his brow while gazing at the paper in front of him. "It's right under my nose."

She picked up the document, and started to carefully read. "So, it's been about three years since this started? And, you asked to be an influential lawyer, yes?"

"Correct." He responded with a nod.

Ellyria read for a bit longer. She hummed. "This is odd."

"What part?" He asked curiously.

"Article two, subsection 'C' states that the deal is sealed when you influence not just your current colleagues, but future generations as well. You hire the interns. By all rights, your deal should be done." She explained.

He raised an eyebrow, and nodded. "True, but the next part states that it must also be by my own hand directly. I don't always hire them. I oversee them, yes, but not directly."

Ellyria glanced up at him with a look of concern. "You hired me."

"Yes, I did. It isn't that part I am worried about. I knew that would be a factor regardless. What I am worried about is article six, subsection 'B'."

"Let me get there." She interrupted, reading on, and taking a few notes as she did. She read over the article in question. "What's your worry in particular?"

"It says that, upon completion, my soul will go to Hell. That, I knew, but what it doesn't state is any of the ways for it to be completed. There was the hiring, yes, but it has no real factor for which I would be able to say, this is finished. And, I just can't figure out a way around it." He sighed.

She read through the rest of the contract. There wasn't much left of it. A sigh escaped her. "This contract should both be done and shouldn't exist." She told him honestly. "Unclear terms are grounds for voiding a contract, which is probably why it hasn't been completed yet either." She told him seriously.

Steve closed his eyes, and sighed. "Of course, demons would have some weird issues, making a contract active and voided at the same time." He looked over at her. "So, what would you suggest in order to make it work out?"

Ellyria flipped the page on her legal pad, and wrote out a clause, which could be added to the bottom of the contract. She ripped the page out, and handed it over to him. "Find yourself an intern who doesn't already have a demon bound to them, write this at the bottom of that document, and have them sign it. Should fix your problem. This defines the terms of contract termination and constraints while also transferring it as you've requested."

He read over the document, and nodded, letting out a long sigh of relief as he did so. "Thank you." He told her seriously. "It won't be hard to get the intern, there are only a handful of demons around here." He waved flippantly. "I will figure it out and have it done soon enough."

"Alright." She yawned, covering her mouth with a hand. "I'll accept my fat bonus check whenever you've got that handled."

Steve sighed. "The check will be directly deposited." He responded. His expression was serious and grateful; the relief palpable. "Now, go home, and get some rest. You look like a mess."

She sighed. "I'll take you up on that. Used a lot of magic yesterday."

"Good job again, by the way." He smiled. "That is the happiest I have heard him in a long time."

"Who knew that ripping apart his wards and replacing them with the correct ones would be the solution?" She quipped sarcastically.

"Go get rest, Ellyria." He chuckled, waving her off. "I will see you tomorrow."

"Thanks." She muttered, giving a little nod. She dragged herself to Shelby, and got into the driver's seat before thinking better of it. She scooted over. "I shouldn't be driving."

Zane appeared in the driver's seat in her place. "I will get you home. You just rest."

She laid down on the bench seat, resting her head on his thigh. "There was another loophole." She whispered. "I could've gotten him out without taking another soul, but," she paused, "I didn't think Hell would like me getting people out of deals."

He shook his head, and gently stroked her hair. "No, they wouldn't. I can do many things down there but saving you from the code is not one of them." He sighed before starting the car.

Her eyes closed. "When he transfers the contract, can we switch Astratoth out with someone tolerable?"

He thought for a moment. "That should be doable." He told her seriously. "There is nothing saying it can't be done."

"Transfer of contract should mean terms can be changed." Elly murmured. "Night."

"Sleep well." He told her softly.

ARTICLE V

Ellyria stretched out on the bed with her eyes still closed. She felt Zane there next to her, and grabbed him, taking his arm. "Mine." She murmured quietly.

"Mine." He replied, pulling her close, and kissing her softly. "Happy birthday."

A smile pulled at her lips, and, finally, she opened her eyes. "Do I have to go to class today?"

"Not if you don't want to." He told her honestly. "Just say the word. I will take care of the rest for you."

"Can your copies go far from you? I want the real Zangrunath here with me." She asked, having never had a copy leave the house before now.

"They can go as far as you order them." He told her.

She nodded. "Send your copy to class in my place for the day, and, from the original, may I please have breakfast?"

Zane nodded, making a copy of himself. It then changed it to look like Ellyria. "Yes, and yes." He chuckled lightly, going to go make her breakfast.

She crawled out of bed, and shuffled out to the kitchen where she sat in a pair of boy shorts and a tank top. "I want to wear nothing but pajamas today."

"I'm perfectly fine with that." He agreed, looking her over as he started to cook. "You know me."

"Yes, I do." She grinned. "I don't really have any plans for the day. Just didn't want to summon the energy to leave the house."

"Nothing out of the ordinary." He shrugged as he cracked some eggs into a pan. "Either way, I will do whatever you want to do."

She nodded. "I just want to hang out with you to be honest. We don't get many days like this."

"Well, we have options. I just need to do a small amount of work, but, once that is done, I vote for games." He told her as he quickly began to plate the food.

She took the plate from him. "That sounds nice. I'll take a bath while you're working."

He nodded, moving to the computer. "If I get done early, I will join you."

She started to eat. "I will let you get to it. Rob them blind."

"Will do." He replied darkly as he began to go through spreadsheets and double check sites.

Ellyria ate her bacon and eggs, savoring the flavors for several minutes before stealing a kiss from Zane's cheek as she retreated into the bathroom. She turned on the faucet, and let the water get warm while she stripped down. Once it was a nice warm temperature, she stopped up the drain, and slipped in. She sighed in content as the salts and bubbles rose in the tub. Once it was full, she used a toe to turn the water off. Laying back, she closed her eyes for a bit. She could wash her hair in a few minutes. This was nice.

Zangrunath worked fast, not because it was Ellyria's birthday, but because he liked to get things done expeditiously. He bought controlling stock in a company, and, then, sold for triple the price when he saw it spike. He smirked as emails came rushing in, but he ignored them. He wanted to be with Ellyria, so he stood up to go join her in the bath.

Ellyria's eyes opened when she heard the door move. How long had it been? Hadn't she just gotten in the tub? She rubbed her eyes tiredly. "Zane?" She murmured, looking over at him.

"Yeah, it's me." He smiled, turning into his demonic form before he joined her. "Relax. I will wash you." He grabbed a bath puff, and gently started to massage and clean her back.

She sighed, leaning into the touch. "Thanks." The sudden irony of the situation hit her. She laughed. "So much for years ago when I said I wouldn't make you bathe me."

"You didn't say anything." He chuckled. "I wanted to do this." He reminded her, scrubbing her lightly. "Mine."

She turned her head around to look up at him. "Mine." She replied.

He held her close, and, once he was done with the soap and bath puff, he helped lower her head towards the water. "Hold your breath for a moment. I need to wash your hair."

She followed his direction, and held her breath as he gently washed her hair and massaged her scalp. When it was all cleaned and rinsed, she turned to him. "Thank you." She told him in earnest, kissing his cheek lovingly. "Let's go play some games."

"Name the game." He smirked back at her.

"Let's play a strategy game. I've got a feeling. Today is the day I finally beat you in world domination." She giggled.

"We shall see." He chuckled in kind. "Bring your 'A' game."

She smiled. "Let me go grab a drink and snacks." She hopped out of the tub, grabbing her towel to dry off. She pulled on a big shirt and pajama pants. After that, she went to the kitchen, choosing a package of cheese crackers and a cola. "I know you love it when I drink soda." She giggled as she booted up her PC.

He followed her lead, and shook his head. "At least, drink alcohol at that point. It will taste better." He sighed, starting up their favorite turn-based strategy game.

"I get it, but I think it tastes good." She opened her game, and joined the online game he started. "My only request is that you don't choose Germany."

"It is too sweet." He commented as he chose Mongolia instead at her request. "It won't matter what I choose." He teased, relaxing in his chair a bit, and opening a card game up as his side game.

She carefully selected the Aztecs before starting the game. She would try her damnedest to win, but, regardless, she was enjoying her time with Zane. When round one started, she grinned at her spawn drop. "Good luck." She singsonged, grabbing her head a bit as a headache started to build.

Zane quickly moved his troops to take out the surrounding barbarians. Then, he started building his actual army. He rubbed his head as he felt her headache hit him. "You need to drink water." He told her seriously.

She nodded, and stood up, letting out a sigh. "You're right." She agreed. She poured out her soda, grabbing water, and a couple pain pills. "Sorry." She took her turn, and started to build up her defenses. There was only ever one way to get close to beating Zane at this game, and this was it. Several rounds passed until one of her scouts found his land on round forty-eight.

"Hello, pretty." He sneered evilly, sending several squads to destroy the scout. "And, goodbye." He chuckled as the unit was obliterated. "Your turn."

She rubbed her temples, drinking more water, and closing her eyes for a moment. "I should've expected that. By the way, you know you get penalties when you declare surprise war, right?"

"Yes, and?" He asked in return, looking at her with concern. "Are you alright?" He asked.

"Yeah. It's just a little headache. Nothing to worry about." She told him even though she closed her eyes against the pain for a minute. "It's probably just the weather."

He looked out the window, and saw that it was a nice sunny day. "Just take it easy." He told her seriously. "If you need to, go lie down."

"I'm fine." She murmured, forgetting that he helped take away most of her pain. "I don't need rest. I'm good."

He gave her a critical look, and nodded. "Fine. Just don't try too hard to beat me." He warned. If she was this insistent, then, the ritual wouldn't let him do much about it. He went back to moving armies around to strategically flank her.

She cursed, seeing his moves, but unable to do much to stop him. She bought another unit. "I don't think I stand much chance," she replied honestly, "whether I hurt myself or not."

He checked his resource output, and smirked as he found what he needed for his long game. "You can always throw in the towel. It won't cost you anything."

"What did you find?" She grumbled with a little chuckle immediately following. A moment later, pain lanced through her forehead.

He turned, gazing at her seriously. "Okay. There is something wrong with you."

She winced, grabbing her head, and massaging her temples. "Yeah."

Zane moved in front of her. He held her close, taking as much pain as he could. "What is wrong?" He asked.

"I don't know. My head just hurts." She shook her head. Tears started to streak down her cheeks. "Something's wrong."

"I can tell." He replied, wincing as he felt the pain. He carried her to the bedroom. "Did anything weird happen in the last few days?"

She tried to think. "Nothing. It was normal. Just my birthday."

"When was the last time you meditated?" He asked, guessing that this was magical in nature.

"Two nights ago on the full moon." She answered, holding him tight, and sobbing into him.

He held her close as the pain wracked through the two of them. Unsure of what else could be done, he gazed at her, taking more pain from her. He was nearing the limits of what he could help with, which made even the ancient demon concerned.

"It's been since Samhain at the leys." She whispered through broken sobs.

"Then, let's get you there." He decided, pulling her close against his chest. "Hopefully, it will help."

She curled into him. "Are you okay to drive? I know you feel this."

"I'm not driving." He assured her, stretching his wings. "We won't get there quick enough." He told her as he made his way to the back door.

She nodded into him. "Is your copy okay?" She worried.

"He will be fine." He murmured quietly, rubbing a thumb in her scalp gently. "Just focus on feeling better." He shrouded them in mist, and they took flight a moment later.

"Be quick." She whimpered, thinking to herself, but saying aloud, "why is this happening?"

"I don't know." His words were honest, but strong and reassuring. He would take care of her and help fix this. She was his. She would be safe and alive. He flew as fast as he could towards the ley line. "Just stay calm. I will protect you."

Elly nodded. "Okay." She took deep breaths, trying to remain calm, but the pain kept her from relaxing or meditating. "I love you." She muttered, starting to fear for the worst.

Zane flew quickly, rubbing her comfortingly as they got closer. "I love you, too." He told her quietly as he landed next to the ley.

She opened her eyes, squinting as she looked around the clearing. It made her head hurt to do even that, so she asked, "put me down in the center."

"Of course." He agreed as he walked her to the center of the clearing, and gently set her down.

She looked up at him as she felt the magic connect with hers. The pain was still there but, somehow, less, if only just a little bit. She reached up to touch him. "Mine."

"Mine." He smiled, seeing the pain in her expression soften slightly. He leaned down to give her a kiss.

"Sorry." She sighed, looking up to him. "I ruined our nice day."

"No, you didn't." He told her. "Now, we just have a day out." He gestured to the field.

She closed her eyes. "I think I need to sleep this off, now, but I'm scared."

"You sleep. I will watch over you." He sat down beside her, and placed her head in his lap.

Her voice broke as some more tears escaped. "I don't want to die like this."

"You won't. I would die countless times before I let you die once." His tone was firm. The earnestness apparent in every urgent syllable.

She curled close to him, and tried to focus on relaxing. Her eyes closed, and she breathed, using her meditation techniques to calm herself over a few minutes before she finally drifted off to sleep.

He held her close to him, wrapping his wings around her to give her some shade to rest in. He stroked her hair, and thought hard. He had never seen anything like this before, and he needed answers. When she woke up, he was going to ask the only person he knew who might be able to help- Steve McDonough.

A little over an hour later, Ellyria started to mutter in her sleep. "Dad, help. Daddy. Something's- something's wrong." The words twisted and reordered but cycled on repeat.

Zane held Ellyria, and nodded. "Yes, any help would be appreciated." He muttered quietly to the open field. He would take any help they could get.

Ellyria opened her eyes. Strangely, she wasn't in an open field. She was at her old house in Oklahoma. "Dad?" She asked, walking around, and searching for him.

She walked around the house for several minutes. It was like she was walking through gelatin. Her limbs were so heavy and slow. When she walked into her room, a voice called out from behind her. "Hey, sweetie. It's been a while since we last spoke."

Her father smiled at her. He looked like he did when he was living with a soft smile and kind, brown eyes identical to hers. His short black hair in the last haircut she remembered him having.

She turned in slow motion before a jarring sensation overtook her, and she suddenly ran up and hugged him. The weights on her somehow magically lifted. It felt like she could move freely, now. "It hurts."

"It will be okay, sweetie." Sam held her tightly. His tone was quiet and reassuring. A hand rubbed her back gently.

"What is this?" She murmured. "Our book doesn't say anything about this birthday."

He pulled back, and looked into her eyes. "I'm not sure what is going on." He told her honestly. "I never went through this."

She shook her head in confusion, and pain lanced through her forehead as strong and powerful as it had when she was awake. Her vision blurred for a second as she rubbed her temples. "What? No-"

"This probably has to do with your mother." He replied apologetically, letting out a quiet sigh.

"I'm already strong enough. I don't need anything else." She cried.

"I don't think it's about strength or power." Sam tried to explain. "It might be about lineage."

"I don't understand. What does that mean?" She asked quietly. She didn't understand any of this. It made no sense.

He held her chin, and looked into her eyes. "Remember when I said your Mom was an angel?"

"Yeah, you she's dead. In Heaven, I guess." She whispered.

"I never said she was dead. I said she was no longer around." He told her seriously.

"Dad?" She asked. Pain was still at the forefront, but confusion and fear started to overtake that now. "What do you mean?"

"I mean that, when you were born, your Mom had to go back home- to Heaven." He kept his words simple, not mincing them in any way.

She looked into her father's eyes as the pain and turmoil started to drag her into consciousness. Her vision went blurry again, and her father blinked from existence for a moment before reappearing a moment later. "No. No. I have more questions!" She screamed in panic.

"I wish there was more time. We will talk again." Sam smiled. "He will keep you safe."

Elly blinked, and the scene changed. She opened her eyes, and saw Zane above her where he was when she'd fallen asleep. "No." She grunted in pain. "No-" Her voice became filled with the panic she'd felt moments before in the dream. Fear started to take hold, settling into her chest.

Zane held her close. "Everything will be alright." He reassured her, trying to think of what the problem could be. He could still feel the agonizing pain she was in, and it wasn't improving.

She took his hand, and muttered brokenly, "Eiael."

He looked at her curiously. The name sounded familiar for some reason, but it didn't click immediately. "What?"

"My Mom." She whispered. "It's my Mom."

He shook his head. Now, he understood even less. "How? What thing is this?"

"I don't know." She whined, grabbing her head, and sobbing. "Woke up too soon. Dad- Dad said," she sniffled, and her lip quivered.

"What did he say?" He asked almost desperately.

She held him tighter. "She's an," Ellyria looked up at him, tears still streaming down her face. Would he still love her if she spoke the words? Was this even real? "Angel." When she said it, it was like the other shoe dropped, making it real. She waited for him to disappear in fire and leave her.

Zane froze as she said the word. It was like a the darkest of curses. He shook his head, and released a growl before he picked her up, flying towards the nearest church that he knew of. He only knew its location because they passed it whenever he went to campus with her.

"Where are we going?" She asked exhaustedly.

"To the experts on those beings." He told her seriously, spitting the last two words. His body shifting from his demonic form into his human one.

She looked at him, and nodded, trying to concentrate despite her pain to give him the power he needed to help her get into the church. "Please, work." She muttered.

He could feel himself growing stronger, and looked down at her. "Focus on feeling better, not on me." He glowered.

"You need it." She whispered.

"No, I don't!" He shouted, flying faster as her magic spurred him on. "You need it more. I am expendable."

She shook her head, and cried. "Not to me."

He let out a snarl of pain and frustration, seeing the consecrated grounds of the church in sight below them. He landed, pausing just before the fence that marked the entrance to the property. Taking a couple of deep breaths, he stormed in and yelled. "Somebody fix her!"

One priest and two other men dressed in seminary garb walked over with an urgency to their steps. The oldest man, wearing priestly vestments, looked down at the young woman in the man's arms. He could see that the man was smoking as if slowly being purified. Parts of his disguise faded to reveal patches of red skin before reforming back to that of his human 'Zane' moniker. "What on Earth is wrong with her? Shouldn't you be bringing her to a hospital?"

Zane growled at the man. "Her mother is an angel." He replied, spitting each word with disdain. He hated them, knowing them to be true. He had missed the signs. "Fix her." He ordered.

The youngest, and strongest looking, clergyman took Ellyria from Zangrunath's arms. The fully ordained priest, who was the oldest of the small group of men, looked towards Zane unflinchingly. "Are you sure?"

Zane's eyes flared red. "Her mother's name is Eiael! Go to your books and fix her already!" He demanded as he felt Ellyria's power quickly beginning to fade from him. He started to feel pain, now. A sigh, that came out as a rumbling growl, escaped him before he made his way towards the doors where the holy aura of the church could no longer hurt him. "I will be waiting." He called out before stepping outside and leaning against the brick fence of the church building as his wounds now healed unimpeded.

Ellyria felt her magic coming back to her, but she also felt Zane getting further away. The pain got worse when he got too far. She desperately reached and groped for him. "Zane! Zane! Zangrunath!" She panicked as impatient hands started to hold her down and unfamiliar voices tried to soothe her. Why were they doing this? She needed him. Her Zangrunath. "Mine." She murmured as she sobbed there on the floor with her eyes closed tightly against the pain.

The three clergymen looked at each other, and, without speaking, the youngest ran to grab a specific book. He returned, frantically flipping pages. "Eiael." He paused. "It says he's male not female. Rules over changes, longevity of life, and material things. Governs occult sciences." He read, looking at the older, more experienced holy men. "Why aren't you doing anything? Don't we become priests to help people?"

The eldest man knelt beside Ellyria, holding her head firm and still as she screamed in pain, writhing, and kicking on the floor. She was shouting incoherent words and phrases in English and Latin. He looked to the youngest man. "She is nephilim." He explained quietly. "And, Hellspawn brought her onto consecrated ground."

"So?" The youngest asked, gesturing to the woman who was clearly in agony. "This is no way to live. If you won't help her, I will."

The third man stood. "I will contact the Vatican."

Ellyria snapped out of pain for long enough to shout, "no!" She dragged the priest back beside the others with her magic. Her eyes were open, but she wasn't seeing between the pain and panic she felt. "No. No. Not the Vatican. Please." She begged without realizing what she was saying. "They killed my father. I don't want to die." She gripped her forehead, and screamed. "Zane!"

The one who was just forcibly moved recoiled, backing away from her. Shock and fear danced in his eyes. "Kill it. It's a danger to-"

The youngest priest pulled Ellyria away from the others. "No! She didn't hurt you. She's in pain, and you're talking about informing the Vatican. What sort of men of God are we if we just let this keep happening?"

Hearing Ellyria's continued screams and feeling her pain growing instead of waning, Zane strode into the church with determination. Even though the pain was intense, he needed to be there for her. Like the priest, he knelt beside her, and held her hand. "I'm here." He told her as calmly as he could before looking at the man across from him with dark fire in his eyes. "Let me make this clear. Help her or I will make sure that you meet your God much sooner than he intended."

The eldest priest looked at the demon, gave himself the sign of the cross, and began to pray. The second ran. The youngest shook his head at the other two. He pursed his lips, and looked at the demon. "I'll try my best." He promised, picking Ellyria up, and bringing her into the back area where baptisms were given to adults. He took a few deep breaths to prepare himself for any disturbing possibilities, and walked straight in, muttering prayers under his breath. Internally, his prayer was much louder and more fervent as he begged silently for this to work.

When Ellyria's body hit the water, it convulsed, and she gasped for breath as her head submerged. Her lungs found air again, coughing before the process repeated until she passed out, falling limp in the small baptismal pool in the stranger's arms.

Zane followed the man, watching carefully. He wanted to make sure that his Ellyria was safe. When she passed out, he looked at the priest that held her. "Is she going to be okay?" He asked seriously.

"I think so, but I've never seen such a violent reaction to holy water." He saw the girl's chest rising and falling. "I can try frankincense as well." He offered, climbing out of the oversized bathtub, and handing her to Zane. "If nothing else, it gave her a break from the pain."

Zane winced as he felt the holy water hit him; it felt like acid. He released a growl. He didn't let go, however. He had to make sure that she would be better. It was the ritual, but he wanted it as well. "Try it. Do whatever it takes to fix this." He told him.

Ellyria didn't know where she was. Nothing looked familiar. There was nobody around. All she knew was pain. She walked until she couldn't take anymore; she fell, crumpling onto the ground, and sobbed. "Zane. Zane. Help." She muttered as she cried.

Several minutes passed before a hand touched the back of Ellyria's head and stroked her hair. The person didn't speak. It was a simple, gentle comfort. They pulled Ellyria into an embrace, holding her tightly and protectively.

"Zane." She whispered as she cried in this new stranger's arms. She had no more strength or words. She feared to move or open her eyes, but the embrace was nice.

"I'm sorry." A whisper came in a soft, feminine voice. "It will be over soon. I promise."

Ellyria couldn't see straight, but she blinked up at this new person several times. She didn't get a good look. It was a blur. "Who are you?" She whispered back between wracking sobs.

The arms pulled her tight. "You already know."

Tears stained Ellyria's cheeks. "What is this, M- mom?"

A sad smile crossed the other woman's face, not that Ellyria could see it. "*Destiny.*"

The response was clear and silent in her mind, whispered there almost like a thought as her eyes opened to find a censer of smoking incense swinging over her body. Zane held her hand while recoiling from the smoke. The pain in her head was gone. She didn't even get a chance to feel relief before she realized that it was now replaced with Zangrunath's pain. She looked up at him with watery eyes. "Zane." She whispered painfully, worried about how his flesh looked. His disguise fluctuated from intact to sloughing off in large chunks.

"Ellyria." He smiled. "Do you feel better?" He asked in a much more serious tone.

"A little." She mumbled.

"Good." He looked to the priest in training. "Good job." He told the man with a smirk.

The clergyman nodded. "Thanks. Honestly, I'm not sure what I did, if anything."

"You made her feel better." Zane responded, looking down at Elly. "That is all that matters."

Ellyria closed her eyes. "I want to go home."

"Then, let's get you home." He nodded, picking her up, and walking her out of the church.

She curled into Zangrunath's chest. "Zane."

"Elly." He whispered, rubbing her upper arm and shoulder soothingly. When they were outside, he shrouded them in mist, and took flight.

"Thank you." She whispered. "You didn't have to hurt yourself for me."

He leaned in and gave her a gentle kiss. "It's fine. I wanted to make sure you were safe."

She kissed his chest so she didn't have to move too much. "I feel different." She whispered.

"Good different or bad different?" He asked seriously. His tone morbid.

She shook her head. "I don't know."

He sighed, giving her a squeeze. "It is fine. You will be okay. You are strong."

She grew quiet the rest of the way home, and, once they were inside, he laid her down to rest on the bed. "Will you help me get comfortable? My clothes are soaked."

"Of course." He agreed, moving to help her out of the wet clothes. He walked around the corner to the bathroom. Grabbing her towel, he helped dry her off, being sure to be extra gentle given all the pain she'd recently been in. "I am sorry your birthday was a bust." He sighed.

Once she was comfortable, she rolled over, laying down on her stomach. She hugged a pillow. After cuddling into the blankets and pillows, she mumbled. "It's okay. I think I'll take tomorrow off, too. Just to make sure I'm up to snuff." Her words were muddied by sleep. She was too tired to notice Zangrunath's reaction to seeing the new design on her back. The new symbol there was familiar to anybody under the Dark Prince's rule. The symbol of the fallen. "Maybe, you can go see if there's anything to learn back home."

"I think I know what the problem was." He sighed, moving to sit down next to her. His eyes gazing at the new symbol on her back without blinking or breaking away for a long moment. "You are a fallen angel." He told her, tracing the new marking lightly with a finger.

"I was already going to Hell." She whispered. "Didn't need the theatrics, big guy." She spoke to God as if he were listening.

"I think it means that you fell from grace or that you are cut off from your Mom." Zane guessed, trying his best to help.

She shook her head. "I had no grace to begin with." She did a quick mental check. "I think I still have my powers. I don't get it."

"Maybe, your Mom can't help you anymore." He suggested.

"I never met her." She turned over to look at him. "I don't know how she helped me."

He shrugged. "She might have kept you out of His eyes, but I am not sure. He works way differently than we do. We are straightforward."

She opened her arms for him. "Just come over here and hold me. I want to sleep this off."

He nodded, and laid down next to her, holding her in his arms. He wrapped one of his wings over her. "Of course. Get some sleep. You need it." He whispered, giving her a kiss.

She kissed him back, and fell asleep quickly. At the end of the day, while Ellyria slept, the disguised Zangrunath that looked like Ellyria came home, and his memories rejoined the original. 'She' had been followed by a man, starting after they'd left the church. The man himself wasn't familiar, but his disposition was. The clothing and wary glances almost gave him déjà vu from Ellyria's senior year. The van that followed him on the way home only confirmed Zane's suspicions. The Vatican had found them.

Zane sighed at the news. Of course, they would find her after the mess that happened earlier. He thought about what he could do to try getting them out of this again, but he was drawing a blank. They had almost no scapegoats this time around. With Ellyria's schooling and the large amounts of money currently invested, they had even fewer ways to get away, now. He needed to figure something out. She needed things to be as easy and normal as they had been for the past few years. He could tell that she wanted the end of law school to go smoothly. He just didn't have a clue how to fix it.

Thursday, March 25, 2027

Ellyria awoke in the morning sore all over from the debacle the previous day. Zangrunath was still holding her, and she kissed him. "Good morning." She whispered, but her voice sounded a little different. Even to her own ears, it was deep and sultry.

"Good morning," He replied, kissing her back. "Are you feeling better today?"

She sat up, and shook her head. "I feel different." She explained poorly, looking at him with eyes that were closer to black than their usual chestnut brown.

He turned her face to look into her eyes. "Your eyes are different." He told her.

She crawled out of bed, and looked at herself in the bathroom mirror. "What's happening?" She asked, sounding seconds away from tears. "Would anybody know?"

"I don't know." He sighed, powerless to help her with this. "The only ones that might know are the church or your Mom. I am not sure who else."

She rubbed her temples to think, remembering his words from before falling asleep. "What about fallen angels? There have to be some."

He nodded. "Several. The Black Prince was the first. The only problem is finding them. They generally stay hidden." He told her, walking up to her, and wrapping his arms around her middle. "We will figure this out."

She turned to him with fresh tears in her eyes. Panic was clear in her features. "Would he say? Would he tell you if I sent you and ordered it?"

He held her tightly. "I don't know if he would say anything. And, if you did order me, that could take a long time."

Ellyria gulped. "I need to know what's happening to me." After a long moment of thinking, she sighed. "Call Steve. Have him cover at school for me. I need- I need-" she shook her head. "Take me to Stonehenge."

Zane's expression flashed from confusion, to understanding, to shock in an instant. Finally, he settled on a simple nod. "Okay, let me get everything in order." He responded, going to make a few phone calls to get everything sorted out for their spontaneous trip overseas.

She got dressed, noticing that her skin had a slightly different hue to it than before. She was normally pale. She lived in the Northeast and wasn't exactly active outdoors. Why was she more tan than normal, now? After another inspection, her hair was still near-black, so, at least, some things never changed. She walked past Zangrunath in the living room, and grabbed an energy bar from the pantry. She didn't have time for a proper meal right now. She needed results. Mentally, she started planning, and she started scribbling notes down on a paper frantically. "I need the world's biggest ley convergence."

"I figured as much. That is why we are headed to England." He replied, finishing the last call, and dialing Steve. "We need you to cover for Ellyria for the next week." Zangrunath didn't bother greeting the lawyer when he answered. His words the demanding orders of a general on a mission. "Something is wrong with her, and we are trying to figure it out."

"Is she alright?" Steve asked with concern in his voice.

"Yes and no." Zane responded honestly. "She is experiencing strange symptoms. We think it is magic related. We are heading out of town to try to get it fixed. I will keep you updated."

Steve took a moment to respond as he tried to think about any magical ailments he knew of. Coming up short, he sighed. "Let me know if there's anything else I can do. I'll see if I can find any information."

"Will do." The demon replied before hanging up. He looked towards Elly. "You ready? We have a plane to catch."

She took her notebook, pen, purse, and nothing else as she finished her energy bar. "Yeah." She sighed, trying to remain calm as she walked out to the car.

"Good." He replied, turning into his human self before leaving the house. He got into the car, and began to drive them to the airstrip. "I chartered a private plane, in case anything else changes." He told her calmly.

"Thank you." She mumbled in her altered voice. She let out a frustrated growl, and it sounded like one of Zangrunath's. Her eyes closed. "Fuck." She whispered.

He placed a hand on her leg as he drove. "We will figure this out." He quietly assured her.

"I'm scared." She admitted quietly.

"So am I." He gave a stalwart nod. "I want to help you so much more than I can, but this is beyond me."

"Thank you for being here." She gripped his hand tightly. "I love you."

"I will always be by your side. I love you." He replied, squeezing her hand in kind. Zane quickly got them to the airport thanks to turbo drive. He pulled the car up to a security guard, flashed his ID, and wheeled into a parking lot. He parked as close to the hanger as possible, and helped Ellyria out of the car.

She closed her eyes, waiting for them to get to the airport, and following his lead to get to the private plane since she'd never been on one before. She was solely focused on this one task, and the few small things that she could control. One of the first lessons of magical control was to calm your emotions, and she tried her best to do that now.

They walked through the large doors of the hangar to find a private jet with seating for eight waiting for them. Zane got them into the plane, and sat Ellyria down in one of the seats, making sure that she would be okay for a moment. After that, he moved to the cockpit to check on the flight plan with the pilot.

Ellyria looked up at Zane with a sad expression when he returned. She was at a loss for what to do or say. She was feeling so helpless.

He sat down next to her. "Don't worry. We will be in the air in a few minutes and arrive in about six hours." His tone was reassuring as he held her hand.

She leaned into him, and closed her eyes. "What time will it be when we get there? Late would be good, but I don't care about low profiles right now."

"We should be there by midnight London time." He informed her, doing some quick math in his head. "Secrecy won't be a problem."

"Okay." She nodded. "Hopefully, travel will be fast after landing."

"It will be. There will be a car waiting for us." He rubbed her shoulder reassuringly as she leaned on him.

"So much for a fun trip to Europe this summer." She grumbled as she felt the plane start to taxi.

He sighed, and looked out the window for a moment. After takeoff, he looked back at her, and gave her a kiss. "No matter what happens, I will still love you. No physical transformation could change that." He told her seriously.

Ellyria looked up at him. "I know. I just need to know what's happening. Simple as that."

"We will. If anyone can figure it out, I know you can." He smiled.

"Zangrunath?" She whispered.

"Yes, Elly?" He asked.

"I can't believe I'm going to do this." She shook her head in bafflement after a long, serious look.

"Neither can I." He told her honestly, feeling just as shocked as her. "If you can pull this off, there will be nothing that you can't do."

She held him close. "I'm summoning the Prince of Darkness tonight."

He smirked. "That is the strangest and hottest thing I have ever heard you say."

"Am I going to be smote?" She asked.

He made a face. "I am not sure. If he casts spells, you should be fine, but, if he attacks you, I will be able to take the hit. Once." He groaned, trying not to imagine the pain.

Once the seatbelt light turned off, she stood up. "I need to get changed." She announced.

"Into what?" He asked her curiously. "You brought next to nothing, and have all of your clothes on you."

"I can remake them. I just don't do it, like, ever." She shrugged.

"Oh." He trailed off for a moment. "I forget that you can do that sometimes."

She nodded. "It's okay. I'd rather spend money than use magic on clothes most of the time." She moved into the small bathroom, and remade her shirt into one with a bare back. She wanted to be able to show her seal and the freshly added sigil, if necessary. When she returned, she sat beside Zangrunath.

He held her close when she sat down, looking her over. "You look good." He complimented. He glanced down at her back, seeing the sigil now bare for all to see. "Let me guess, to prove to him that you are one?" He asked seriously.

"Whatever helps at this point." She smiled, but it didn't reach her eyes.

"You will be fine." He assured her, rubbing her arm, and kissing her forehead. "I won't let anything happen to you."

"I know." She whispered, resting against him. "I'm going to try to sleep before we get there."

"Get some rest." He told her, moving her head to rest in his lap. "I will let you know when we are landing." He murmured.

Ellyria's eyes closed. Even though she hadn't been awake for long, sleep swiftly took her. While she slept, she dreamt of the summoning she needed to do, ways to improve her plans, and she felt like someone was guiding her, helping her make it right.

They made it over the Atlantic in a few short hours. Zane kept a constant vigil, soothing Ellyria by rubbing her back. He watched her like a hawk in his worry, and noticed that her skin had gotten even more tanned. She almost didn't look like herself. Her figure was the same, but the pallor of her skin made her look different. He saw his hand against hers, and tilted his head to the side as morbid curiosity rolled through him. He let his disguise fall on just his hand, and saw how much closer hers looked to his now. It was jarring. He quickly made the disguise shimmer back into place, and distracted his mind with the details of the next steps after they landed. When the time was right, he gave her a gentle shake. "Elly, we are going to be landing soon."

She hummed sleepily, grumbling a bit, and sat up in her seat as her eyes opened. "Hi."

He looked into her eyes, and saw that they were even darker than before. "Hey." He responded, looking her over critically for any other changes.

"You look worried." She stared down at her hands. "What's wrong?"

"Your eyes are darker. Almost as dark as mine." He told her seriously.

She sighed. "Okay. I'm- It's okay. We'll figure it out."

He held her close for a moment before gazing into her eyes. "I know we will."

"I'm becoming demonic." She murmured more to herself than anything.

"I think it suits you well." He smiled a bit mischievously. "I will still love you no matter what."

She kissed him. "Thanks. It's just confusing and concerning," she paused before adding, "and all sorts of other things. I expected this to happen after I died."

"You still look beautiful to me no matter what; now or after the deal is done." He reassured her.

She buckled up when the seatbelt light illuminated, and held onto his hand as they waited for the plane to land. "I love you,

Zane. Thank you. Even if you are kind of excited that I'm," she waved at all of her.

He gently squeezed her hand. "Anytime." He promised, adding one word at a whisper. "Mine."

Before she could respond, the plane's tires hit the tarmac. She sighed. "Never did like the landing."

He rubbed her thigh reassuringly as the plane taxied around to the hangar. When they came to a stop, Zane stood up, and held out his hand for Ellyria. "Let's go have a meeting."

She stood, and took his hand. "I'm ready. I think." Her voice filled with anxiety.

He squeezed her hand once more. "Relax. He might be the ruler of Hell, but he doesn't *look* terrifying." He gave a soft, reassuring smile before he added mentally to himself, 'in his angelic form.'

"I'm more worried about the power I need to summon to get him here at this point." She murmured as an unfamiliar looking sports car appeared in her vision. She squinted. "I don't know European vehicles."

He smiled, and led her to the passenger seat on the opposite side of the car from what she was used to. He opened the door for her. "This is a supercar manufactured by a local company. They lend out their engines to vehicles that participate in some long-standing international racing championships." He explained simply for her, since he knew she didn't really care much for motorsports. He walked around the vehicle, and got into the driver's seat next to her. "I figured you would want to get there quickly."

"I don't own this beast, do I?" She asked him seriously as she buckled herself up.

"No, I only rented it, but, if you want one, it can be arranged." He replied, stepping on the gas, and rocketing them forward to the biggest ley line in the world.

"No, no." She laughed, gripping the seat a bit as he took off like a bat out of Hell. "I just know you, and wouldn't be surprised anymore."

He chuckled. "I only buy things that you will use on a regular basis. It would be silly to buy you a car that you would never drive."

She nodded. "That makes sense. So, I don't own the private jet either, right? I honestly don't even know all the holdings I have anymore. I try to keep up with what you do, but you do a lot. I just get busy with school and the internship."

"No. Unless you start taking international jobs or work across the states regularly, there is no reason to do that." He told her. "As for holdings, you have the same as you did before. I don't buy anything unless you ask for it or you actually need it." He glanced at her before turning his attention back to the road.

"Well, thank you for being conservative." She grinned. "Still don't own the penthouse. Yet."

Zane laughed at that. "You can afford it now. Just tell me when and where you want. I will take care of it."

"I'm contracted at Steve's firm for three years after graduation, so hold off for now. Just keep growing what I have." She told him.

"Of course." He smiled. "I will make sure that you can get whatever high end penthouse you want." He promised as he pulled the car off the highway, and took a round-about to get onto another road.

She tapped her toes impatiently as she started to sense magic. "We're getting close."

He placed a hand on her leg. "Yes. Just breathe. I know you can do it." He reassured her, fully believing in her ability to make this happen for the first time in history.

Ellyria nodded. "I will need you to make sure nobody gets into the circle while I'm forming it."

He looked out the window, seeing how dark it was as they left the city proper. Then, he looked at her. "You should be fine, but I will make sure that no one stops you."

"Once it's started, it shouldn't be a problem." She informed him. "Then, I want you with me."

He nodded, and a smirk curled his lips upwards. "I will follow you anywhere."

She looked at him seriously. "Should I speak English or Latin?"

"Well, he speaks all of them, but Latin would be the best option." He responded as he saw the old structure appear in the distance. "Just try to keep yourself contained. He is the most beautiful creature you will ever see." He warned with a sigh.

"No, he's not." She told him, looking at Zangrunath.

He smirked. "Remember when I showed you that really beautiful man? He is far more impressive."

Ellyria nodded. "I understand, but he's not the demon I love. And, to be honest, not really. I was drunk."

He pulled the car into a parking spot, and leaned over to kiss her. "Thank you. I love you."

"I love you." She whispered before stealing one last kiss and hopping out of the car. She instantly felt a connection with the earth here, but she took off her shoes and socks, tossing them into the car all the same. She took in as much of the magic as possible, and found herself unconsciously floating towards the wonder.

Zane watched as Ellyria began to spark with lightning as she moved towards the old structure. He was shocked to see the electric current, but figured it was due to the intense magical power here. He started to move around the area, making sure there would be no intrusions to her. He was a little nervous himself, but didn't show it. No mortal had ever made a deal with the *actual* Devil before. Those stories were made up. He was starting to be excited to see history in the making.

Ellyria walked to the north side of the monument, and started activating the near invisible ancient runes. Walls of force appeared, forming into a circle. When she finished, it became a dome as she 'walked' in. In truth, her feet were moving as if walking, but she was still hovering a foot above the ground. Her hair was standing fully on end as it had in years past. She summoned magical lines in the circle, and the power became thick and palpable. "Zane." She whispered before she started to concentrate, closing her eyes.

As he watched the impressive magic, Zangrunath noticed a few guards begin to quickly approach. He growled, knocking them out. He would have killed them, but he didn't want to possibly make the ritual go haywire by adding human sacrifice to the equation. He turned back towards Elly when he thought he heard her call him, but he saw she was busy working on the last few parts of the ritual. So, he hung back, continuing to keep her safe.

Ellyria felt something huge about to happen. She started to push her own magic into the summoning without realizing that she was also partially draining Zane due to their connection. She felt a surge of energy and somebody or something circling her. Her concentration was still needed for a moment before she could stabilize the magic. Only then, could she open her eyes.

Zane continued to guard the area. As he did so, he began to feel weaker. It was subtle at first, but, now that the magic was flowing faster and stronger, he started to feel his movements become more sluggish. He shrugged it off initially, and, then, needed to turn into his demonic self in order to keep moving. He looked back at Ellyria, and saw the spectral form of two wings coming from her back. It was an incredible sight to see. He felt his movements slow down even more, gritting his teeth through it. He knew she was determined to see this through to the end.

Ellyria opened her eyes to find what could only be described as an angel, but with altered features. Before her stood a man in stature, and, like Zangrunath had described, more beautiful than any she had seen before. His hair was the darkest of black. His eyes were two obsidian orbs to match. On his back were six wings; all of them were upside down, looking like they would move the wrong way. Their color was the same shade of black as his hair, but they had an aura of divinity that was almost too much to bear. The fallen seraphim looked around the area before he turned his gaze to Ellyria. "What is this?" He asked with a voice that demanded authority while clearly confused and intrigued by his predicament.

"My name is Ellyria Grant." She stood tall, hovering in the air, and defiantly looking back at him. "I summoned Zangrunath to me seven years ago. My father was a human, and my mother an angel." She started in perfect Latin before turning slightly, showing her bare back with the new symbol upon it. She didn't notice the spectral wings there. "Something happened yesterday, and I need to know what's happening to me. What is this?"

Lucifer gazed at her with a perplexed expression. He raised an eyebrow, noticing the all too familiar seal on her back before he glanced over to see one of his generals moving closer. He smirked at the two of them before landing on the ground. "To put it into the simplest of terms, you are cut off from divinity." His head tilted to the side, and he started to walk a slow arch around her. "Your body isn't used to your powers without their help, yet. It will take some time before you can properly control it." He explained, leaning down, and critically looking at her sigil.

Zangrunath tensed up as he watched his King circle his witch and inspect her. He got as close as he dared. He wouldn't hazard touching the man who ruled all of Hell. "How long will that take?" He asked quietly, not looking at the Dark Prince directly.

Lucifer turned to look at his general, and smirked. "Well, Zangrunath, that could take a few days, a few months, maybe even a few years." He chuckled at the demon before he turned towards Ellyria, leaning down slightly to meet her gaze. He searched deep into her eyes and even her soul. "You, however, Miss Grant, are strong." He told her seriously. "Strong enough to summon me here." He hummed.

Ellyria gulped, but didn't have the mental capacity to feel fear at the moment. She had a lot more questions that she doubted she'd get the chance to ask, so it was time to cut to the chase. Her eyes darted towards Zangrunath, and she licked her lips before she finally spoke again as she pulled a document out of her pocket, which was hastily scribbled in the airplane bathroom in her own writing. "I'd like to make an addendum to my ritual contract while you're here."

A curious look crossed the ruler of Hell's expression. He moved one of his wings over the contract in her hand, and it appeared in his hands. He began to read it over. "And, what addendum would that be?" He asked as his eyes quickly moved across the page.

"I want Zangrunath by my side for the rest of my natural life." She told him seriously. "I'm prepared," she looked at Zangrunath with a little smile and a significant look, "for a soul binding, if necessary." She remembered looking at one part of her grimoire that was next to the demon code that Zangrunath didn't particularly care for. "In return, you can have my copy of the demon code."

"Ellyria!" Zangrunath called out to her before his whole body was stopped by a gesture from Lucifer.

"This is between me and her, general, not you." The Dark Prince smirked at the demon before he gazed at Ellyria. He thought it over for a moment, closing his eyes in thought. When dark eyes opened, he gave her a serious look. "To spend the rest of your natural life with a demon, I find to be a little less than my services." He told her simply, giving a pause. "But, having a copy of the code back in its rightful place is very tempting, and one such as yourself amongst my ranks will be useful in what is to come." He paused, and he extended his hand for her. "You, have a deal." His eyes glowing like smoldering embers, now.

She looked at him seriously. "Let me see that the contract hasn't changed first."

He released a sigh, and waved a hand, summoning her contract to his hand. "Once the deal is struck, the change will be made." He told her, showing her the document.

She nodded, looking at Zangrunath for a moment before she took Lucifer's hand. "Are you okay with this deal?"

Zangrunath felt his body relax a bit, and he looked at her and his King. "I want to be with you." He responded. "I will follow you anywhere." His lips curling into a smile just for her.

Lucifer raised an eyebrow at the display, and began to laugh at the pair. He laughed for several long moments; this was the most hilarious entertainment he'd had in quite some time. A moment later, he quieted himself, wiping away merry tears from his eyes. "A half angel and a demon fall in love and talk with the Devil to stay together. It sounds ludicrous. Yet, here it is." His piercing gaze shifting between the pair.

"If nothing else, we will be an eternity of entertainment for you." Ellyria replied as the corners of her lips tilted upwards. She knew that Zangrunath would be intrigued by the words in years previous. "He is mine. I am his. We are one." She took his hand, and couldn't see the power glowing in her eyes. "Make it happen."

There was a visible pause when she said that. "Fine." He smirked as flames quickly enveloped her and Zangrunath. The seal on Ellyria's back began to burn and shift, becoming more intricate as a sigil burned itself into place on Zangrunath's back as well.

Lucifer smirked at the couple, and the contract in his hand changed, adding the new addendum she requested. He let go of her hand, taking a step back. "There. It is done. You two are now bound together mind, body, and soul." He gazed around, becoming a little bored, now. "Is there anything else that needs to be done?" He asked seriously. "I am a busy man."

Ellyria looked up at Lucifer in pain, confusion, and, maybe, the first bit of fear. Her words, however, didn't show any of that. They were calculated and very much demonic in nature. "Nothing now, but I can already tell that things will be fun when I join you down there."

He waved her off, and made his way back to the center of the circle. "You will be busy while down there, so enjoy your fun while you can." His expression knowingly mischievous. "Enjoy." Lucifer singsonged in a low baritone before he spread his wings, vanishing from sight in a blinding light that seemed to outshine the sun for the briefest of moments. Moments later, the magic settled, and the dark, stillness of night returned to the area.

Ellyria turned to look at Zangrunath before the massive use of magic finally rebounded, hitting her full force. Seconds later, she fell to a heap on the ground, unconscious.

Zangrunath took a knee as the magic subsided. He looked at where his King was moments before. Then, he walked over to carefully pick up Ellyria. She was out cold, and he knew she would be for quite some time. He walked back to the car, and, as he set her into the seat, he saw the seal on her back, making a face. He sighed, seeing that Lucifer had changed her seal. The soul binding worked into the annihilation ritual, now. Anything either of them felt from now on would be on a soul deep level. He shut the door, and changed back into his human form. "We are going to need some time to figure this out." He grumbled, getting into the car, and driving her back to the airport so that they could fly back home.

Friday, March 26, 2027

Ellyria awoke with a pounding magical hangover. She was laying down on a small bed, and looked at the unfamiliar surroundings before she realized that she was back on the private jet. The sheets slid across her skin, and she groaned at how sensitive it was. "Turn it off, turn it off, turn it off." She begged.

Zane stepped into the small room, and leaned down next to her. He looked into her eyes, sighing deeply. "I can't," he explained, a frown taking his features.

"W- what? I didn't ask for this." She closed her eyes tightly as she tried to remember the now somewhat blurry conversation and her request, which was a terrible idea since it also made her focus on how her body was feeling. She was a live wire right now.

He nodded. "That is why I called out. What I feel all the time, you feel all the time." He explained to her. He wanted to soothe her, but knew that it wouldn't help her while she adjusted. "That is soul binding."

Ellyria nodded. "Okay. I guess I didn't fully understand this part." She gripped the bed sheets tightly to distract herself. "So, you have this headache, too."

"Yeah." He replied with a frown. "It sucks." He sighed, going to get her some water.

"Did I mess up too badly?" She asked seriously.

He came back into the room, and handed her the glass. "No, it was just bad timing, I guess." He replied. "Drink this, slowly."

"Is there something in it?" She asked as she followed his instructions, trusting him regardless of his answer.

"It is water with lemon." He told her. "You will just take a while to get used to this."

"I have goosebumps all over right now." She admitted.

He smirked. "I figured as much." He replied, seeing the telltale bumps on her arms. "It will take some getting used to. I'm sorry in advance.

"Yeah. The car ride will not be fun." She frowned. "I'm sorry I screwed this up."

"You did not." His voice firm as he smiled at her. He wanted to be reassuring and give her a kiss, but that would cause more problems than it was worth. "Things will just be different for a while."

She handed him the glass of water, and laid down. "Mine." She whispered.

"And you are mine." He whispered back. "I will let you know before we land. Try to get some rest if you can." He told her, knowing it was going to be difficult at best.

"Body, mind, and soul." She muttered, thinking about the Devil's words. "What else changed?"

"Well, I know that I don't have to follow your orders verbatim now." He explained, already halfway out of the small bedroom door into the cabin. "I realized that when I was driving back to the jet."

Ellyria sat up, realizing the bed sheets weren't doing her any favors. "How so?"

"Well, normally, when I am driving you somewhere, I am focused on just getting you to that place. Nothing else. When we drove back, my mind was wandering, trying to process what you had done." He replied, shaking his head a bit. "You made a deal with Lucifer." He chuckled at the words.

She crawled out of the bed, and pulled him into a hug despite herself. "I'm glad that you've got more freedom."

He slowly wrapped his arms around her. "Thank you." He rubbed her back automatically out of habit. "It will be nice to be able to do more."

She tensed up at the feeling of his hands on her, but grit her teeth through it. This was normal now. She didn't have a choice. "And, in Hell, we can be together. I think."

He pulled away slightly when he felt her tense up. "Sorry." He apologized, gazing into her eyes. "Yes, we will be together. This can't be undone."

"He looked at me strangely." She commented after trying to relax for several moments. She looked up at him, pulling away, and holding his hands. "I don't know what to think of it."

"It was probably because he knew what all of this was going to be like for you now." He offered by way of explanation. "Why do you think he said, 'enjoy'?" He sighed.

She rubbed her temples. "I thought it was more like, enjoy your mortal trifles because I'm going to work you like a dog when you get to Hell."

"That too." He groaned. Out of the corner of his eye, he noticed that he was starting to see land out of the plane's window. "We will be on the ground soon."

She nodded, taking a seat, and buckling up. "I'll prepare for the landing to be a rough one."

He nodded, and sat down next to her, offering his hand. "Don't worry. I will be right here." His tone calm and reassuring.

She took his hand, and sighed when she noticed the odd hue of her skin. "I'm hoping this is only a couple of days. Much more, and I'll look like you."

"A few days. A week or two, at most." He nodded. "You are strong. You will have this under control in no time."

"How am I supposed to go to school like this?" She asked.

"You did well when we opened the seal the first time. You will be able to do this." He encouraged her.

"Any suggestions to help with this?" She groaned, leaning her head back on the headrest and looking at the ceiling.

He nodded. "You will want something to counteract it. Perhaps, a pin in your shoe or something." He offered. "It isn't a perfect fix, but it will help."

"We'll figure it out. At least, you'll be there to help." She sighed.

"Of course." He smiled at her, squeezing her hand. "Always. Now and forever." He whispered as the plane landed. He watched Ellyria with worry. He didn't like seeing her like this. "I will try to get you home as fast as possible."

She nodded several times. "Thank you."

Sunday, March 28, 2027

Ellyria sprawled and stretched out on the bed. Her skin was a normal color, but her eyes were still darkest of obsidian. Content and happiness washed through her. She was simply happy that she was getting control over the changes. She was several decades away from being comfortable with looking like a demon. She gazed over at Zangrunath. "Can we talk?" She asked quietly.

"Are you not doing that right now?" He chuckled.

She swatted at him lazily. "Oh, eff off." She complained. "Can you tell me more about this soul binding thing? I don't think I really understand it all yet."

Zane nodded. "Of course." He moved his fingers to his thigh, and pinched until it stung. "It is similar to the deal in many ways, but much more powerful."

She winced. "Ouch."

"I am sorry." He responded automatically. "Simply proving a point."

"Okay, so it's just that? That's it?" She asked, rolling over a bit to look at him better. "Given the name of it, I thought there was more."

He hummed. "It binds two souls together permanently." He started. "When our deal ends, we will still be able to do the mental talk. My constitution will still aid yours. You will be healthier and live longer."

She tilted her head. "It sounds like the annihilation ritual for people who never cast it."

He nodded. "The ritual is based on soul binding, yes."

"But are there differences?" Ellyria asked seriously. "Other than the fact that, in the annihilation ritual, souls are forfeited to Hell?"

He shrugged. "Not much, really. It's mostly subtle things that aren't necessary. You'll hardly notice them. Better eyesight and senses, but nothing nearing what I can do. The sterilization thing I never really understood the reasoning behind-"

She sat up so fast that her head spun. "The what?!"

Zangrunath blinked, clearly surprised by her quick and violent reaction. "Soul binding sterilizes the two bound together. I thought you knew that when you suggested it. You've never really mentioned that you wanted children, and we've always been careful about that. So, I thought you were fine with that end."

"No, no, no-" she muttered, shaking her head, and placing a hand on her chest as her breathing started to hitch. Tears pooled in her eyes. "Zane, you never thought that, maybe, I was waiting to be done with school before being ready for children? You're a master tactician. How could you be so-" she caught herself before she blurted something stupid that resulted in an argument.

"Despite our connection, I cannot actually hear your thoughts." He responded with a low growl before releasing a sigh. He sat up, and pulled her against his chest. A hand moved up to stroke her hair and upper back. "I'm sorry." He told her in a soft voice. He tried not to sound begrudging, knowing that this was not going to be fun for him.

The tears streaked down Ellyria's face. She sobbed into him. "Fuck!" She wailed. Her fists balled up, and she pounded his chest in frustration, making herself grunt in pain. "How could I be so stupid?"

"You're not stupid." He responded. "You just do things without thinking them through or without knowing all of the details first."

She pulled away, looking up at him. Her face was puffy and red, but not in the demonic way. "I did want to be a Mom." Her voice broke.

Zangrunath sighed. "You can still be. Just not like that."

She gulped audibly, and nodded. Her throat thick with emotion. "I just wanted-" she looked down at herself for a moment. The dream she had of their future together destroyed before it could even happen. She sniffled, and pushed away. "I'm sorry." She muttered as she climbed out of bed. "I need a minute."

He looked at her, and sighed. Sometimes, Ellyria's greed was a pain in the ass. He watched her stalk off, hearing the door to the warded spare bedroom slam shut. He thought he heard a muffled scream. He stood up, and went about cleaning the house, sending a duplicate to make a dessert for her. If there was one thing he knew for certain after seven years, he knew that she liked her sweets after crying herself dry.

ARTICLE VI

When Ellyria got dressed, she ignored her professional clothing and outfits. Instead, she chose a comfortable shirt and a hoodie with jeans and sneakers. The bar exam was long, and she anticipated a cold room. Zangrunath, as usual, had her breakfast ready. "I don't want you to take this for me, but," she mumbled between bites, "I need a favor."

He looked back curiously, leaning on the counter. "What's that?" He replied, tilting his head to the side.

"I want you to watch my answers. If I go below the passing rate, I want you to tell me which questions to try again." She sighed. "This is just for insurance. Otherwise, don't interfere."

He nodded. "Will do." He smiled. "All you ever have to do is ask."

"I know." She smiled in return. "It feels like cheating, but I want this."

"You will get it." He reassured her.

She finished her meal, and kissed him. She groaned, realizing her mistake. Mornings were still rough on her with the seal. Sleeping was a battle for three weeks but became relatively normal after they'd purchased a sixth pair of soft sheets, which she deemed soft enough. Zane didn't mess around, and subsequently purchased ten more sets of the sheets and controlling stock in the company. "Calm down." She muttered to herself with closed eyes.

Zangrunath chuckled at her. He knew she was having some difficulty with this transition still, but it was in his nature to enjoy other people's suffering. "Do you want me to drive you, so you don't have to take longer to get there?" He asked.

"No." She shook her head. "I'm never going to get used to it that way." She took a breath. "This is normal now. I'm still just getting used to it."

"You are doing a great job." He encouraged. "I knew you were going to push yourself to overcome this, and I am impressed by how well you are doing." He smiled. "I'm proud of you."

She pulled him into a hug. "I love you." She whispered before grabbing her keys, purse, and lunch. "Today's going to suck." She announced with a groan, trying to sound positive. "Let's do this thing!" She locked the door, and walked to the car. When she noticed her friendly local Vatican agent at the end of the street, she paused, walking over to him. She knocked on his window. "Hey, Larry." She greeted with an apologetic smile. "I'm taking the bar today. You really don't have to follow me. It's not going to be exciting."

Larry sighed, and shook his head. "Sorry, Elly. It's my job." He told her seriously. "I will stay in the parking lot."

"I would hope so." She laughed. "All of this over casting a couple little spells in high school." She shook her head, straightening back up. "Sorry in advance for the boring day."

"It is what it is." He replied, waving her back towards her car away from his surveillance van. "Good luck today."

"Thanks." She smiled, walking back to her car, and hopping in. The car looked empty, but she spoke to the open air, knowing that Zane was inside and invisible. "He still has no clue, right?"

"Could not have any more of a clue if we spelled it out for him." Zane replied with a dark chuckle.

She smirked, taking a breath to steel herself before starting the car. "I will get used to this." She grumbled to herself.

"You're doing great." He replied, trying not to mock her misfortunes too much. He liked to tease her, but knew not to anger the woman who could theoretically rearrange his atoms.

"Thanks, Lucy, buddy ol' pal." She groused, throwing the car into reverse, and heading towards the school.

"You like it when you get home." Zane countered, whispering the words into her ear.

Goosebumps raised up on her arms at his words, and she shivered. "Oh, it has its benefits, but the drawbacks outnumber them at the beginning." She complained, letting out a sigh. "I'll stop calling him Lucy. Don't look at me in that tone of voice." She joked.

The invisibility covered up his smirk. "I would appreciate it if you would refrain from angering the Prince of Darkness. It will work out better for us in the future."

"I get it." She told him while she parked. She eyed Larry parking a good distance away, and sighed. "At least, it's just the one. Like Corbin. Should've expected it after the fireworks at that church."

"Yeah, I didn't help with that either." He agreed with a sigh of his own.

She grabbed her things. "Alright. Mental talk only. Can't have them think I'm cheating."

"Of course." He responded as she asked. "I will try to stay quiet for the entirety of it. I know how much you like interruptions while working."

She looked at her phone, and saw a couple of text messages. One was from Steve, and the other was from Tom; both wished her luck on her test. She tossed the phone on the seat, and locked the door. "I will bend this test to my will." She grinned as she walked towards the building to take her exams.

"You've got this." Zane mentally encouraged as she walked into the building. As Ellyria went through security to get into the exam room, Zane checked on the exam itself. He quickly scanned the pages, no one being able to see an invisible demon, and smiled to himself. He wouldn't need to tell her anything. She had this in the bag, and he knew it. So, he would still double check her answers like she asked, but he knew he wouldn't have to say a word to her. Everyone else, well, he would enjoy watching the worry and panic on their faces as they struggled.

At the door, Ellyria showed her photo ID, and took off her hoodie for them to check it and her arms before she pulled the garment back on. She knew this was serious business, but she never realized just how much. She saw a few of her fellow classmates in the room with her along with a few unfamiliar faces from other schools. She smiled at those she knew, and ignored the ones she didn't. At nine, she got her exam. She wiggled and adjusted in the uncomfortable seat, looking at the clock. This was going to be a long day, and, after six hours today, she would still have to return for another grueling six hours tomorrow. On the proctor's go, she opened the booklet, and got started.

Several hours later, Ellyria was ravenously eating dinner at home. "How'd I do for day one?"

"You did just fine." He smiled at her. "I didn't think you would need help to begin with."

"Me either, but I still was worried." She sighed, almost inhaling another bite. She forced herself to slow down.

"Calm down." He told her seriously. "There is plenty of food, and you are not going anywhere. You don't have to inhale your meal."

She nodded. "Sorry. Didn't realize how hungry all of that testing made me." She took a sip of water, and looked up at him. "If you don't mind, I'm going to go relax in the tub for a bit and pass out for the night. I'm exhausted."

"Have fun." He smirked at her knowingly as he started to clean the kitchen. "And, sleep well." He added, moving to give her a kiss. "Love you."

"Love you." She muttered before heading off to bed. "I do require cuddles later, though."

"I will hold you close as you drift off to sleep." He promised.

Thursday, May 20, 2027

Ellyria nearly overslept. She'd forgotten to set her alarm the previous night, but, luckily, Zane was there. Her eyes peeked open to see his black ones. "Hey." She murmured as she started to feel their bond for the day. Her skin crawled just feeling his hand on her shoulder, but she leaned into it instead of recoiling. This needed to start feeling normal again.

"Morning." He whispered, giving her a kiss before giving her some space. "Come on. You need to start getting ready for school."

She growled impressively for a human before forcing herself out of bed as she saw the clock. "Ugh. I slept in."

"I know. That's why I woke you up." He told her as he got up to make her a light breakfast. "You just have a little longer before this is all done." He called back to her.

"Waiting on my scores will be the hardest part," she complained, "but we are going to Europe. So, it'll make it tolerable."

"Oh, yes, it will." He smirked while working on her food. "I will get to show you all of the sights."

She came out of the bedroom in an outfit similar to the previous day, seeing his look. "I'm not even dressed nicely right now."

"And, I would still wreck you like Diana." He chuckled. "I don't care what you wear. I always want you." He told her honestly, putting a plate of fruit in front of her.

She gaped. "You can't just say that!"

"Why?" He asked seriously.

"Well, generally, there's respect for the dead." She blushed, covering her face. She grabbed some fruit and started to eat. "Okay. I was hungry."

"I know. I could tell." He told her, leaning on the counter as he looked at her. "Also, you love it." He smirked.

She nodded, and smiled. "Seven years together will do that."

"It has been a fun seven years." He nodded in kind. "I wouldn't change it."

"It has." She smiled, raising an eyebrow as a thought occurred to her for the first time. "Wait a second. What's the soul binding mean regarding marriage and that whole token?"

"Well, we are connected together, so I guess you could say we are married." He answered, thinking it over. "Even if we aren't, I don't care. I am glad to be with you."

"I just wish there was one choice that hadn't been taken away." She sighed wistfully.

He looked back into her eyes sympathetically. He wished he could give her everything she desired, but, this one thing, he couldn't. "Sorry but that is beyond the both of us."

"I know." She mumbled. "I hadn't even thought hard enough on whether I wanted kids to know whether I should feel cheated or not. I was busy focusing on school, thinking about all of that took a backseat."

He reached across the counter, and held her hand. "I would rather just have you."

"I probably would've died trying anyway or so say all horror movies." She laughed.

"Not too far off, but not right either," he shrugged, looking at the clock. "Alright, enough baby talk. You've got to finish your exam. We have a plane to catch later."

She looked over at the clock. "Shoot. Sorry." She shoveled the last bit of food into her mouth, put the dish in the dishwasher, and grabbed everything she needed before rushing to the car. She looked at her watch and over at Larry in his van. "Great." She jogged over to his car. "I'm running late, so I'm going to be speeding." She told him through the window. "See you after my vacation."

He gave her a nod. "Drive safe. Have fun!" He smirked as he started the surveillance vehicle, so that he could vainly attempt keeping up with the muscle car.

Ellyria took off down the street, peeling out. "I can't believe I screwed up my schedule today."

"Calm down." Zane soothed, using their mental speech. "You will be fine. Just get there and the rest will take care of itself."

"I swear, I'm going to teach myself to ley walk one of these days." She murmured as she weaved between vehicles.

"When you do that, I might not be able to keep up with you." He told her honestly, thinking about his ability to move between sigils and minor teleportation over short distances. "Stupid limits."

She shook her head as she pulled into the parking lot, finding only the furthest spots available. "I can take you with me according to my grimoire."

"I have just never done that." He explained as she walked towards the school. "I don't really know the specifics."

"My understanding is that it's watered-down teleportation for normal witches, but, since my family can tap the leys anywhere," she trailed off, arriving at the door to the testing room with about two minutes to spare. She went through the same process as the previous day's screening before she was allowed into the testing area, sitting down as the clock struck nine.

"You could teleport anywhere." He replied, sounding impressed. "That would save a fortune."

She gave a mental nod. "Only problem is, I'm not entirely sure how discreet it is."

He hummed in agreement. "It might raise some concerns. It's okay. We will worry about that later. For now, ace this thing so we can go to Europe." He mentally smirked as she got her testing booklet for the day. "We have a club to join."

Ellyria adjusted uncomfortably in her seat, but her focus shifted for the next several hours. When she turned in her documents at the end of the day, the proctor reminded the group about the results being mailed to them in about ten business days. A few groans filled the room, but celebration was the general feeling all around as the group shuffled out of the testing area.

Ellyria hopped into the Shelby a few minutes later, waving at Larry before heading towards the airport. "Well, three years of school didn't go to waste. You didn't stop me at all."

"You didn't need it." Zane smiled, appearing next to her in the passenger's seat. "You had it in the bag."

"You already know my score, don't you?" She giggled, knowing Zangrunath very well by now.

"Of course." He teased. A dark chuckle emanating from his chest.

She looked at him impatiently, and grumbled. "For the love of Lucifer, Zangrunath."

"You can wait like everyone else." He smirked. "Besides, you are going to be very distracted in Europe. You won't have time to worry about the score."

Ellyria sighed, but nodded. "And, when we get back, I'm a lawyer."

"With a job already lined up." He added lightly. "No need to worry."

"Yeah, Parker wasn't happy about my contract, but McDonough and Hannon overruled him." She reminded him again.

He nodded, having heard it several times before, but proud of her nonetheless. "And, I didn't help with any of that. It was all you."

She started to get irritated at the thought of Mister Parker. "That standard contract was a joke, and he knows it. Besides, after three years, New York calls."

He sighed a bit, knowing she was getting herself worked up for no reason. "I was saying that most of it didn't need my help. That was you having your own connections." He reached over, placing a hand lightly on her thigh. Looking at her seriously, he added, "and, when New York does call, the penthouse will be ready for you."

"I've actually got my eyes on a new development I noticed from our last visit." She smirked.

"Really? Which one is that?" He asked curiously.

She shook her head. "Can't remember the name, but I have the website saved on my phone." She pulled it out of her hoodie pocket. "It's going to be open for buyers next year. All the companies seem kosher, and the prices are going to start at twenty million, so I'm assuming the penthouse will be somewhere in the thirties or forties given the current market."

He took her phone from her as she drove, and began scrolling through it. He looked it over, and gave a few nods of approval. "If you want it, I will get it." He assured her. "Shouldn't be that difficult. Just need to make sure we get to it first." He placed the phone back into her hoodie pocket.

"Oh, we're making this happen." She smiled. "The concept art has me really excited."

"Then, I will get it." He grinned. Her smile and excitement were intoxicating. "I want to make sure I see that smile on your face."

She showed her identification to a security guard at the airport, and pulled into the parking lot next to the hangar. "I'm going to miss you, Shelby, baby." She rubbed the steering wheel.

"Don't worry. She will be here when we get back." He told her. "And, if she isn't, I will kill everyone here to find out where she is." An evil grin took his face as he got out of the car.

"There are several movies with similar plots" She commented. "None of them end well."

"Well, I am a demon, so I think I might have an edge on those human vigilantes." He scoffed, looking proud of his strength and prowess.

She fanned herself flirtatiously. "I know it's a bunch of movies, but, damn me again, that would be a fight."

He smiled, and gave her a kiss. "You just have to tell me to win."

She winked, and hopped out of the car, locking it up. She saw Zangrunath had their luggage in tow as they walked to the plane. "This feels like the beginning of a new adventure." She commented as she climbed up the steps into the cabin.

He put their luggage away before he sat down next to her, and pulled her close. "If I am beside you, I will go anywhere."

"To Hell and back." She agreed, thinking about those words. She gave him a curious gaze. "Would I be summoned with you, now?"

He paused, and thought that over for a moment. "I think you would." He guessed as best he could. "Even if it didn't, we would just work hard to get back."

She leaned into him. "Regardless, I'll always be with you." Her hand rested on his chest.

He leaned against her lightly, resting his arm around her waist. "And, I, with you." He responded, giving her a loving kiss.

Their kiss lingered for a minute as the pilot walked by and into the cockpit, laughing at the young couple. As things were closed off and the plane took flight, Ellyria pulled Zangrunath out of his seat. "Let's see about that club." She winked.

Zangrunath followed her, and closed the door behind them. "Yes, let's see what the fun is about."

Saturday, July 17, 2027

Ellyria dashed around the house, grabbing gemstones and herbs. She shoved those into her overnight bag. She checked the bathroom mirror. She wanted to be sure that her outfit was perfect. When that was finished, she joined Zangrunath in the kitchen, packing up the dessert for tonight's dinner in a to-go container. She turned to him with a wide smile gracing her features. Excitement started to overtake her. "Are you ready?" She asked curiously.

Zane smirked, holding back a chuckle at her expense. "Of course, I've been waiting on you."

She shook her head at him, and gave him a playful push. "Let me just grab one of these delicious brownies and give it to Larry."

"Alright. I'll get everything loaded up in the car for the night." He offered, giving her a kiss. His human disguise shimmered into place as he pulled away, grabbing her bag, and the food as he strolled out the door.

Grabbing some tinfoil, she wrapped up a brownie, and followed Zane out the door, trusting that he had locking up the house well in hand. She strolled towards Larry's van with purpose. She was glad to be wearing comfy, stylish sneakers instead of heels. Most mornings when she brought items out to him, she was in work clothes and heels, but tonight was just a dinner date. She stopped on the passenger's side of Larry's van, and knocked on the window.

For some reason, he wasn't in the driver's seat like he usually was. Then again, he was either here or following her for at least sixteen hours every day. It was unrealistic to think that he never moved or left the vehicle. She heard some muttering coming from the back. One voice was clearly Larry's, and the other was lower. She guessed that it was another somebody coming from the Vatican to check on the agent's assignment, but it didn't really matter. She was only tolerant and nice to the guy to keep the Lucifer damned organization off their backs. Larry was, at best, ignorant, and that was good for her. The vehicle shook, and a black curtain moved between the back and the front cabin. She waved. "Hey, I brought dessert." She greeted loudly enough to be heard through the closed window.

Larry popped out into the cabin. He noticed a flash of orange flame come from behind him, and winced, hoping that Ellyria was in too much of a hurry to notice. He sat in the passenger's seat, and rolled down the window. "Thanks." He greeted, happily taking the treat. "Full moon tonight."

"Yep. I've got my monthly visit with Tom. We're having a double date with his girlfriend, Michelle." She smiled. "Anyway, try to get some rest. It's going to be a boring night, as usual."

Larry smiled, nodding as he saw her take a step away. "Will do. Thank you, Elly. Have a wonderful night."

"Thanks." She nodded in kind, and headed towards the car. She hopped into the passenger's seat, and buckled up. "Alright. Let's head to dinner."

Zane leaned over, and stole a kiss from her cheek. "Let's go see Tom, and figure out how this date is going to go." He chuckled, morbidly curious about how tonight's events would play out.

"Well, it's either going to go well or Michelle's memory will be erased. If that happens, we'll have to console an upset werewolf." She sighed.

"Then, I am glad we are not bringing copious amounts of chocolate cake." He commented while driving them towards Tom's new apartment. "That would just be torturous on the guy."

She looked over at him. "Was that a backhanded dog joke?"

Zangrunath looked her dead in the eyes, and didn't hesitate. "Yes, it was." He told her seriously, focusing his gaze back on the road.

She gazed back at him for a long moment before a snicker escaped her lips. "Damn demons." She shook her head, and squeezed his thigh. "You're the worst."

He saw the apartment complex come into view, and expertly maneuvered them to the correct building before parking the car. He leaned over, and gave her a kiss. "You love every minute of it." He smirked knowingly, squeezing her hand once as he hopped out of the car.

She got out, and went into the back to grab her bag, watching as Zane grabbed the dessert. She eyed him for a moment. "I love you." She murmured just for him as they walked up to Tom's place. "Let's do this."

He held the dessert in one hand as he held her hand with his free one. "We've got this." He assured her as she knocked on the door.

A moment passed before Tom answered the door with a smile. "Elly, Zane! Hi, welcome. Please come in." He gestured them inside the apartment as a woman stood up from the nearby couch. He let out a small sigh of relief. "Elly, Zane, this is Michelle. Michelle, Elly and Zane." He told everybody.

Michelle walked up, and hugged Ellyria first followed by Zangrunath. "Hello, you two. I have heard so much about you. All good. Sorry. I would apologize for being a hugger, but that's just how I am."

"Nice to finally meet you." Ellyria giggled, accepting a one-armed hug. "Tom is always talking about how awesome you are."

Zane nodded, getting a hug from the woman, and tentatively hugging her back as he moved over to set the dessert on the counter. "He won't stop talking our ears off about you." He chuckled. "Much to our dismay, he can get annoying."

"Oh, be nice." Elly chastised, putting her bag down near the door. "Good to see you, Tom. Glad to hear that your job didn't give you a hard time with taking today off."

Tom blushed, but nodded. "You as well, Elly. They didn't mind too much. I had some time accrued, so I thought it would be nice to have a proper weekend off." He lied for Michelle's benefit.

"They work you too hard there." She grumbled. "Just say the word, and I'll file a suit against them for violating labor laws." She offered, glancing over to Michelle as she took a seat at the table. "I work for a law firm. Obviously." She commented, flipping some hair over her shoulder. "And, they don't have me doing anything."

Tom shook his head. "That would be overkill in way more ways than one." He gave a small shutter. "Pretty sure things will pick up for you soon." He offered, sitting next to Michelle on the couch.

"They are just a bunch of jerks." She sighed, glancing back over at Zane. "Sorry. This job has just not started out how I imagined it."

"I'm with you on jobs that pay the rent." Michelle chimed in. "I hope it gets better for you. You're Tom's friend, which makes you my friend, and you deserve the best."

Zane leaned in, and gave Ellyria a kiss on the cheek. "It will get better. It will just take some time, is all." He assured her, glancing over at Michelle. "So, what do you do for work?" He asked.

Michelle waved a hand. "Retail. It's Hell, but it is what it is."

Zane let out a small chuckle. "Oh, I beg to differ, but I won't try to argue it. People are idiots." He commented, giving both Tom and Elly a glance.

"Alright, so what do you do that is worse than retail?" Michelle giggled in return.

"I trade on the stock market." He explained with a growing smirk. "It is rather high stakes, and keeps me thinking several steps ahead."

"And, he puts up with me." Ellyria added with a giggle.

Tom laughed at that. "I don't know which is worse, putting up with you, or dealing with Wall Street. Either way, he has a full plate."

"It's definitely putting up with me." She laughed, kissing Zane. "I'm a pain in the ass."

Tom smiled, and squeezed Michelle's hand before he looked at the time and stood up. "Well, let's get the dinner started, shall we?" He offered, heading to the kitchen to get the food going.

Michelle stood, and followed him. "Of course, where are our manners? We didn't even make hors d'oeuvres."

Zane stood up, walking over to the kitchen. He gestured for Michelle to sit down. "We've got this. You ladies can relax while the guys slave away." He teased, moving to wash his hands.

Ellyria rolled her eyes at Zane, but also knew that the ritual did some weird things to him sometimes, like making him want to check her food for poison, which was annoying and hilarious. "Don't mind him. He basically waits on me hand and foot. I don't even know how to function without him."

Michelle sat down at the table across from Elly. "I would say that I'm jealous, but I don't know how I would handle that. I like my independence."

"I'm plenty independent. Just treated like a princess." She smirked. "Probably like Tom treats you. He is always fawning over you, and I can see why. You're super sweet."

"A compliment that I don't deserve." The other woman blushed.

Tom smiled over at her. "Not true. You deserve that and more if I have my way." He told her seriously, carefully filleting some fish to be grilled up.

Michelle chuckled. "I just want what every girl wants. Competitive cuddling and chocolate."

"Hear, hear!" Ellyria chimed in enthusiastically.

Zane shook his head, and chuckled as he cleaned the vegetables, carefully eyeing Tom as he made the food. He leaned in towards the man, and whispered. "Do you have any plan on how to tell her or are you just playing it by ear at this point?" He asked the man seriously, noticing a lack of magic and the supernatural being brought up.

"I have no idea how to do this. Just kinda winging it." Tom mumbled worriedly as he sprinkled some lemon juice into the pan.

Zane paused as he heard that, giving Ellyria a look that could only be described as 'you have got to be kidding me'. He shook his head. He started slicing into the veggies as decisive chopping sounds filled the space, and sighed. "We will take care of it." He muttered, trying to rapidly think of a way to start this conversation.

Ellyria noticed the look on Zangrunath's face. Nothing quite like seeing an angry demon on the weekend to liven it up. She flipped some hair over her shoulder again, guessing what was going on by looks alone. "So, what do you do for fun? Movies, games, books?"

Michelle hummed for a moment. "I don't get as much free time as I'd like, so I tend towards television and movies. Ways to unwind after a long day at work."

"What do you like to watch?" She asked seriously, hoping for a positive response. The last thing she needed to hear was horror movies.

"I'm a sucker for soap operas, and romcoms, but I will watch just about anything as long as it's good." She enthused. "I don't care for bad television. It's not worth my time."

Elly nodded. Almost as bad as horror, but she could spin this. "I always hate those parts of soap operas where a character reveals a deep part of themselves, and the significant other dumps them. Like, what about them really changed?"

Michelle hummed slightly at that. "I kind of get that. It depends on what it is." She surmised. "Like, a serial killer is a whole lot of nope, but, if it's more along the lines of like a secret identity or a power, that would be fine, I think I could live with that if all that stuff existed." She giggled.

Elly smirked. Now, this was where she wanted it to go. "If all of that was real, it would have to be really good at hiding in plain sight." She glanced over at Tom and Zane.

"Exactly, who knows who you would have living next to you then." Zane chuckled. "You could live next door to a dragon and never know it."

"I'm pretty sure that I would notice if there was a dragon next door." Michelle laughed, glancing over her shoulder into the kitchen.

Tom smiled. "I think you would be surprised." He chuckled. "If magic were to exist, I don't see why creatures like that couldn't just change their appearance to blend in." He offered, beginning to plate up the food as he glanced at Ellyria and Zangrunath.

"And, there are plenty of creatures that wouldn't need much to blend in. Witches and werewolves for instance." Elly suggested.

Tom brought over the food, and set the plates down at the small dining table. "The only real issue some of those would have would be during full moons." He commented, looking at everyone before starting to dig in. "Enjoy."

"Oh, thank you, dear." Michelle commented, grabbing her utensils. "I'm kind of glad werewolves don't exist. That sounds terrifying."

Tom started to eat more slowly as he heard her words. "Why would you be terrified of them? They didn't really choose to be that way."

"But, they uncontrollably become wild and attack people." She reasoned.

"Given enough time, I think they could control it." He countered defensively, releasing a nervous laugh. "Besides, wouldn't they have magic to help calm them?"

"If they had magic, maybe it could work." She commented, taking several more bites. She glanced at Ellyria and Zane. "Are you not hungry?"

"Oh, sorry. Just interested in your opinions." Elly responded, starting to dig in.

Zane looked at his food, and began to nibble on it. "I kind of had a big lunch, so I'm not super hungry. I will try to, at least, get some of it down." He lied smoothly. "As for the whole magic thing, I think it would be fun. So many possibilities." He hummed, knowing all too well what it could do.

Ellyria nodded. "Imagine if you could go halfway across the continent in a blink."

Michelle let out a small sigh as she finished her meal. "Traffic would be so much easier to deal with."

Tom chuckled, eyeing Ellyria for a second. "I didn't know you could do that."

"I can't." Ellyria responded automatically. "Yet."

137

Zane released a sigh as he glanced between the pair, and saw the confused look on Michelle's face. "As subtle as a porcupine acupuncturist, guys." He grumbled, shaking his head.

"What?" Michelle gaped. Her mouth wide open in shock.

Tom winced as he realized the mistake. He gazed at Michelle, and took her hand. "There is more to me, and us, than I led you to believe." He told her seriously, gesturing to Zane and Elly.

"Um, okay?" She gulped. "How so?" Her hand shook in his.

He squeezed her hand reassuringly. He took a deep breath, and checked the clock before turning back to look into her eyes. "You know how I was talking about werewolves earlier? A lot of what I said comes from experience."

She nodded. "So, you don't eat people?"

He shook his head. "No. I work really hard to make sure that there's no chance of me hurting people. I work my schedule around the moon, so it doesn't happen."

"I- isn't tonight a full moon?" She asked nervously.

"It is." He nodded, taking a breath as he rubbed her hand with his thumb. "I wanted you to see me for who I am and to prove to you that I have it completely under control."

"And, they know about this?" She murmured as she started to catch up on what was happening. One of her fingers vaguely pointing towards Elly and Zane who she wasn't looking at.

"We're the werewolf busters." Ellyria teased. "He can't get past us."

"They helped me get better control." Tom smiled. "Now, it's a lot easier to relax on full moons as my other self. It's been a year, and it still feels weird."

Michelle did a double take between Tom and his friends. "Do you become an actual wolf?"

"Yes and no. I have heard stories of other people like me being able to do that, but I don't have that type of control yet. For now, it's more like the movies, but much less angry." He explained, looking at Elly and Zane for help as he gathered the empty dinner plates, bringing them into the kitchen.

"He can talk. It just sounds different." Ellyria explained. "And, there's a little bit of a physical transformation."

"He is also taller." Zane added, sitting back in the chair, and relaxing.

Michelle stared at Tom. "Uh, thanks for trusting me."

Tom plugged up the sink, letting the water run for a moment, and setting the dishes inside to soak. He added a good bit of dish soap before turning off the water and walking back to the kitchen table. He stole a kiss from Michelle. "I love you." He told her. "Why wouldn't I trust you?"

"Because I'm normal and might go running and screaming at any moment?" She countered.

He nodded again. "I know. You could." He sighed. "You are worth the risk." Feeling the change starting to take place, he took several steps back.

Ellyria looked around. "Where'd you put the sigil in your new place?"

He chuckled, and pointed beneath them, gesturing to the area rug. "Thankfully, it can be hidden relatively well."

"Ugh. I told you not to do that." She complained, crossing her arms, and leaning into Zane. "Normies can find it way too easily."

He shook his head, and gestured for her to look more closely. "No, it's the rug." He explained, grimacing as he started to change. "I talked to a guy-" a grunt escaped his lips as his limbs elongated, and the hair on his extremities grew at an alarmingly fast rate until it could be described as a coat of patchy fur in places. He took a breath, looking far more composed after the worst of the transformation before finishing his sentence, "and had the sigil stitched into the rug."

Michelle watched Tom's body contort in fascinated horror. She took several large steps back into the wall, making her wonder when she'd even stood up. The only thing keeping her from darting out the door now was the fact that the other couple were much closer to Tom and completely relaxed around the werewolf. "That looks painful."

Tom stood up straight, stretching his body as he adjusted to this new form. He looked into her eyes, with his soft brown ones. Except, now, a deep purple hue ringed around them. "It is, but it gets better over time. What do you think?' He asked.

"Uh, I'm still processing." She responded honestly.

"Take all the time you need. I just want you to know that I promise not to bite." He joked, trying to liven up the quiet room.

"Yeah, he's normally pretty chill. It's me or Zane you have to worry about." Ellyria commented. "I'm going to cleanse my stones on your balcony. Do you want me to smudge your apartment?"

Tom thought it over for a moment. "If you don't mind." He smiled at Elly before he made his way to the fridge to grab a couple beers. "Kind of hard to do things looking like this." He commented. He walked up to Michelle tentatively, offering her one of her favorite local brews of a pineapple passionfruit German ale.

Michelle never felt more grateful to receive alcohol in her life. She drank the beer down to the label before wiping her mouth. "You're doing who, with the what?"

Ellyria rifled through her overnight bag. "I'm clearing bad energy from my magic stones with the moon, and I'm going to go do a ritual to make sure ghosts and other unwanted things can't get in or get the Hell out, if need be."

"To put it in as simple terms as possible. She is going to make sure the magical security system is functioning properly." Tom oversimplified.

Zane shrugged, and leaned back in his seat. "I suppose that is a proper explanation. Though, not what I would have gone with."

"How would you explain it?" Michelle sighed, trying to calm down, and failing.

"She is going to have a magical bubble bath to calm the magic down and, then, pour salt to keep out the ghosts." He told Michelle with a shrug, debating having a drink of his own.

Michelle groaned. "I'm sorry I asked. This is just confusing. Weird is out the window."

"I hate to say it, but weird is pretty normal around me." He eyed her curiously, unsure of her thought process or reactions still. "It gets easier over time."

She looked at him and away again, trying to rectify the man and beast together in her mind. "I hope so." She whispered, drinking more.

Tom nodded, and took a step back from her. He wanted to give her some space to process things however she needed. He sighed, going to sit down on the couch. He turned on the television for background noise, but wasn't watching. "Anyone interested in dessert?" He asked, trying to lighten the mood.

Ellyria called out from the balcony. "Yes! I had to smell those brownies for way too long today."

Tom nodded, and went into the kitchen. He washed his hands, flicking a finger, and extending a claw to carefully cut the treats. He placed them on some paper plates, handing one to Michelle. He popped outside briefly, and left the second on the small balcony table for Elly.

Michelle sat back down, and started to nibble on the brownie. "Thank you. This is good."

"You're welcome." Zane glanced between the couple, reading the room for all but a second before standing up. "It wasn't that hard. Just a recipe I found online." He shrugged, moving outside to give them some space.

Ellyria turned to Zane when he came outside. She'd just finished putting out her gemstones. She glanced at the door. "Well, I don't hear running and screaming." She whispered.

"She is surprisingly calm. It is possible that our calm rubbed off on her." He shrugged. "Who knows? Maybe, she is into it." He commented, glancing inside as the couple silently sat in the room without looking at each other.

"I was." She giggled, stepping over, and raising onto her tiptoes to kiss him. "Eventually."

He smirked "You love every second of it." He wrapped an arm around her. "And, I'm glad you did. It made everything easier for both of us."

She leaned into his form. "And, now, you're stuck with a crazy witch that doesn't think before she acts."

He smirked, and kissed the top of her head. "I wouldn't have it any other way." He whispered to her.

"Thank you, Zane." She murmured, grabbing the plate that Tom left, and digging in. "We'll give them another couple minutes." She suggested.

Zane nodded. "Yeah, hopefully, they will be able to talk this out and be alright in the end." He commented, looking in to see the two still sitting on opposite ends of the couch.

"Maybe, she'll lighten up by the end of the night. She was much more fun earlier." She smiled.

He chuckled, and nodded. "Which is why I am going to just stay like this all night." He gestured to his human disguise. "I'm pretty sure she would be gone if she found out about the other stuff."

Ellyria hummed in appreciation of the tasty dessert. "I don't blame you. Sorry you can't be yourself."

He shrugged. "Don't worry about it. I will make up for it at home."

She shook her head at him. "I'm hearing, 'I'm not only going to be demonic, but I'm going to turn my arms into foam dart guns and shoot you'."

"Something like that." He teased, kissing her cheek.

She smiled. "Alright. I'm going to smudge this place."

He smiled, and nodded. "Alright. Go all magicky, and get this place up to snuff."

She giggled, and grabbed a bundle of sage. She opened the door back into the living room. Stopping for a moment, she raised a finger to the end of the herbs, and lit them on fire, letting the smoke rise for a moment before blowing it out. She started to chant, walking around the place, and waving the smoke all around the outer edges of the room. "Don't mind me." She commented.

"You're fine." Tom watched her walk around the room. His nose flared, and he closed his eyes. He paused for a long moment before sneezing loudly. "Sorry." He apologized, moving to blow his nose with a tissue. "Haven't gotten used to smelling that while like this."

"Just be grateful it's not wolfsbane." She grumbled, heading down the small hallway to the bathroom and bedroom.

"Oh, yeah. That's what I need- a severe asthma attack." He deadpanned, shaking his head, and taking a long draught of his beer.

"Does wolfsbane hurt you?" Michelle asked.

Tom shrugged. "It's kind of like an allergy." He replied, trying to think of the right words. "I can touch it and be fine. If I eat it or smell it, I will have trouble breathing for a while. Eating it will make me sick. Found that out the hard way."

"I'm sorry." She murmured. "I'm glad you're okay."

He smiled. "Thank you." He whispered. "It took some time, but, just like any allergy, you get used to it after a while."

She took a deep breath. "Thanks for trusting me. Wish you would've done it differently, though."

"Sorry." He winced. "I was thinking it over for a long time, and every way just didn't seem to work. No matter how I spun the idea around in my head, you left me at the end. I figured that having other people around would make it less weird and more believable." He surmised.

She sighed. "Other people helped, but seeing you change like that after just being told magic is real is more than a little jarring."

"Again, sorry." He told her, moving a hand closer to her. "I'm not exactly the smartest cookie in the lightbulb drawer."

"I don't know how many idioms you just combined into a weird malaphor." She giggled.

"Neither do I, but I'm glad that you finally smiled." His lips quirking up into a wolfy grin.

"It's easy to smile when you're being a dumbass." She teased.

He chuckled. "Well, that's not hard. That's my M. O." His hand finally stole hers, and he gently rubbed the back of it with his thumb. "If you have any questions, I will answer them. I am an open book."

She shook her head. "I'm still kind of in shock, so you might have to wait."

"That's fine. Take all the time you need." He assured her. "I'm just glad you're staying around."

"I'm not running and screaming, but only because breaking in a new boyfriend is exhausting." She chuckled, scooting closer.

He smiled. "Thank you. I know it's a lot to take in, but I promise to help you in whatever way you need." He promised. "On the plus side, in the winter, I am incredibly warm and soft."

"Do you change on command or just on full moons?" She asked.

"Mostly full moons, but I can change if need be. It just takes a lot of focus." He told her.

She bit her lip. "Is it something you can bite and give to other people?"

He chuckled. "No, that is totally a movie thing. It's passed down. It's a family thing. So, nothing to worry about there."

"Okay." She sighed in relief, looking exhausted.

He wrapped an arm around her. "Yeah, it's not nearly as bad as you think. You can lay down if you want. By the time you wake up, I will be back to normal, and we can talk about it more in the morning." He offered.

She nodded, seeing the other woman walk back into the room, looking equally tired. "Yeah, I think it's about that time."

He nodded. "Go get some rest. Sleep well." He smiled, standing up, and helping her to her feet. "I will clean up around here."

She held his hand for longer than necessary, and slowly moved in for a kiss. "Goodnight."

He squeezed her hand softly, and leaned in to kiss her, making sure to be gentle. "Goodnight. I will see you in the morning. Love you." He whispered.

She smiled, yawning, and heading into the bedroom to get some sleep. "I love you." She murmured as she closed the door behind her.

Tom watched Michelle head into the bedroom before he turned to look at Elly and Zane. "Thanks for coming over, guys. It helped a lot." He released a sigh of relief. "I don't think I could have done it without you."

Ellyria nodded a couple times, covering her mouth as she yawned. "Welcome." She mumbled, grabbing her overnight bag, and carrying it to the bathroom. "I think it's about that time for me, too."

"Get some rest. I still have stuff to clean up." He told her simply, going into the kitchen to continue cleaning up. "Sleep well."

Elly got changed, and wandered back out to the living room, laying down on one of the couches. "Zane?" She murmured, wanting him close as always.

Zane glanced at Tom, and sat down on the couch. He gently rested Elly's head on his lap. "Yes?" He whispered.

She smiled softly, closing her eyes. "I love you. Play nice with Tom."

He leaned down, and gave her a kiss on the temple. "I will. I won't do anything too drastic." He chuckled, gently stroking her hair as he waited for her to fall asleep. "Love you. Sleep well."

145

Hearing his reassuring words, she slowly relaxed. It was a little bright and noisy in the living room, but, within a few minutes, she was sound asleep, using him as her pillow. Light snores escaped her, filling the room with the rhythmic sound.

ARTICLE VII

Zangrunath idly rested in bed as Ellyria slept in his arms. He thought about the last couple months with Elly working at the law firm. He knew that she was happy to have a demon on her side, making things go smoothly. It wasn't as perfect as she envisioned it, but he knew that it could only improve. He smiled down at her, and gave her a kiss.

Ellyria awoke, and grumbled, "don't make me go."

"Sorry, but you have to." He told her seriously. "Come on. I will get breakfast started." He offered, getting out of bed, and heading towards the kitchen.

She growled. "But, Parker treats me like a glorified intern. It's like-" she sighed, "what's the point?" She got out of bed, and started to get dressed.

"Yes, he is a jerk, but he will get what is coming to him." He assured her before leaving the room to get the food going. "Worst case scenario, just scare him a bit. He will either stop or I will kill him. Really no in between."

"Three years at worst." She groaned to pep herself up more than anything. She came around the corner into the kitchen. "At least, I'm actually helping the fun clients," she paused before adding, "when they give me clients."

"You will get there." He encouraged her, looking up from the stove. "I am, after all, still bound to help you."

She pulled on her heels, and sat down at the bar stool at the kitchen island. "I know. You're stuck with me."

"Do you hear me complaining?" He smirked as he slid a plate of bacon and eggs in front of her.

She started to eat. "Nope."

"Good. I know that you aren't either." He leaned on the counter to watch her.

She took several bites before speaking. "Given that I made the deal, you can bet that's right."

He leaned in, and gave her a kiss on the cheek. "I love you."

She smiled, knowing she didn't have to say it back. "And, I you." She finished her meal, and cleaned up. "Now, off to the second layer of Hell."

He laughed, and shook his head. "Not by a long shot. You goof."

"Sure feels like it right now." She groaned.

"This is nothing compared to Hell." He reminded her. He gave her a nudge.

"At least, in Hell, you'd be at my side and not making sarcastic comments into my ear while invisible." She sighed, grabbing her things, and a muffin for Larry outside. "Let's get going."

"This is true." He disappeared with a dark chuckle. "Lead the way my lady."

She walked out the door, tossed her things into the car, and walked over to Larry's van, knocking on his window. "Hey, man." She greeted, plastering on a big, fake smile.

"Mornin'." Larry returned the smile, looking a bit distant. "On your way to work?" He chuckled, already knowing the answer.

"Ugh. Yeah." She handed him the muffin through the window. "I believe you said lemon poppyseed was your preferred poison."

He took the pastry with a grin. "Yes, thank you. It's been a while since I last had this."

"Well, I live to please." She waved. "Off to go be treated like crap by the patriarchy."

"Give 'em Hell." He teased as she walked away, eyeing her like a hawk as she got in her car to head off for the day.

Ellyria sauntered away, heels clicking all the way back to Shelby. "Still clueless." She giggled as she hopped into the car.

"Ignorance is bliss." Zane replied. "Just leave him be. It is better this way."

"It's surprisingly difficult pretending to be just magical enough for him to need to watch me but not magical enough for him to report any strange occurrences." She commented as they pulled out of the driveway.

"Thankfully, you have enough wards and runes around the house to make him think all is normal," he told her. "That helps more than you know."

She nodded. "I get it. It's just silly that he can be thrown off so easily by occasionally hovering a grocery bag into the house when my hands are full."

He chuckled. "The look on his face is priceless."

"He was literally sent to check in on my potential misuse of magic. I don't know why he gets surprised when I use it." She shook her head.

"Probably because he doesn't see it often." He surmised. "The Vatican isn't so much about *using* magic as keeping it in check."

"Oh, I know. Lesson learned." She sighed. "Hopefully, Larry will still be the guy when we move. He's easy enough to deal with."

"If not, you could always sway him with your charms." He smirked into her head.

She rolled her eyes. "You said charms. I heard breasts."

"And?" He asked, sounding confused, which she couldn't see thanks to the invisibility. "If it works, it works."

She grumbled. "I don't like showing my chest off to get what I want."

"I know." He responded. "Just know that I have no issues with you using whatever means necessary to get what you want, so long as no one touches the merchandise."

She barked a laugh at that, and pulled into the firm's parking lot. When she got to her reserved space, she growled. Somebody had taken her spot. Again. "I'm going to cut these interns."

"Would you like me to have their car towed?" Zane asked mentally.

She shook her head, switching over to the mental chat as well. "No, I'm not that spiteful. They probably can't afford to get it out if I do that." She wrote down the license plate number, and parked in a different spot. "I'm going to find out whose car it is and have a chat."

"I can't wait to hear that conversation." He chuckled.

"It will sound like thinly veiled threats and a contract to sign afterwards." She responded, imagining the scene in her mind's eye. She grabbed her purse, and made her way inside.

"I would expect nothing less from greatness." He replied. There was a smile almost visible in his voice despite his current invisibility. As she walked inside, he grew quiet so she could work more efficiently.

Ellyria stopped at the receptionist's desk, and gave her the plate information. "Julie, do I need to see you or security to find out whose car this is?"

She looked at the paper, and nodded. "I can take care of that. That guy has been doing that way too often." She sighed, opening a document, and starting to look for the car's owner.

"Thanks, Jul. How was your weekend? Do anything fun?" She asked conversationally.

She shrugged as she typed on the computer. "Not much. I just stayed home, and caught up on my murder stories." She chuckled. "How about you? Anything interesting in your life?"

"About the same as you." She smiled. "Except, I don't bring work home by watching murder stories."

"I just work at the desk." Julie chuckled as she handed her the paper with the man's name. "There you go Elly. Enjoy."

"Oh, I'm going to enjoy this one." She smirked, looking at the name, and rubbing her temple. "Dammit, Jeremy."

"Don't give him too much trouble. He's new." Julie suggested.

She shook her head. "I'm just going to scare him a bit. I paid my dues as an intern. He can do the same."

"Agreed, but he's kinda cute" She smirked.

Ellyria giggled. "Oh, I see. I'll go easy on him." She winked before strolling over to her miniscule office.

Julie nodded, giving Elly a little wave as she walked away. "Thank you."

"So, what are you going to do to him?" Zane asked curiously, excitement in his voice.

"I'm going to ask for coffee, have him sit down, and tell him off. If it happens again, I'll tow the car." She grumbled.

He let out a small sigh. "I would have just towed it, but you are in charge."

"I'm doing Julie a solid. The receptionist is always a good friend to have." She reminded him.

He thought it over, and gave her a mental nod.

She sat down, and booted up her outdated desktop. It was taking forever to load. "Oh, joy." She complained.

"I know. Ours are much faster," he chuckled.

"I'm going to throw this thing." She sighed as she typed in her password. "They could, at least, give me a computer from this decade."

"Yeah, twenty seventeen wasn't that great for computers." He sighed, trying to lighten it with a half-joke.

"This operating system is ancient." Ellyria complained as she opened the company instant message system, and sent a message to Jeremy. "Well, coffee inbound."

"I will sit back and watch the show." He mentally smirked.

She nodded, checking her emails. "I'll try to make it good."

"Thank you." He replied. "It's almost like watching television. You are my entertainment."

She rolled her eyes, firing off a couple responses before Jeremy eventually walked in with her coffee. She looked up from her work before smiling. "Thanks for bringing that in, Jeremy." She gestured to the seat across from her. "Please, sit." She ordered firmly.

"Um, okay." He nodded, sitting across from Ellyria, and looking at her oddly. "Is everything alright?"

"For the most part, yes. I do need you to do something important for me, though." She waited for him to respond.

"What is that?" He asked, nerves clear in his tone. He shifted uncomfortably in his seat.

She gave him a no-nonsense gaze. "Go out to the parking lot and look at where you parked this morning."

"Uh, what?" He grumbled, standing up slowly.

"You heard me." She told him seriously. "Go look. Then, come back."

Jeremy seemed somewhere between shaken and confused. He slowly walked out of the room, leaving for several long minutes before he walked back into the room sheepishly. "I- um, I'm sorry." He murmured.

She sighed, looking over at him. "It happens. Clearly, you were in a hurry, but, frankly," her voice got lower and darker. "You're not earning any brownie points or favors from me at the moment."

"It won't happen again." He assured her with a nod. "I will go move my car now."

"No." She waved a hand dismissively. "I'm busy, and won't move Shelby for something so silly. It's yours for the day, but, if it happens again, I'm towing it."

"Yes, Miss Grant." He replied, hanging his head in defeat. "It won't happen again. Will that be all?" He asked.

"No, actually," Ellyria smirked. "Julie likes three creams and one sugar in her coffee."

He raised an eyebrow, but nodded. "Okay, I will go get her that now."

"Thanks." She smiled, waving him off, and going back to work. "Now, to pretend they've given me anything to do with my law degree."

Zane mentally smiled. "You've got this. Just a few more hours, and you can come home."

"I'm always home when you're around." She replied in a corny voice.

He sighed as he noticed Steve McDonough walking up to her office. "Incoming."

She nodded, looking up to see Steve at her office door. "Hello, sir."

"Good morning, Ellyria." He smiled as he let himself in. "How are you doing today?" He asked, shutting the door behind him.

"I'm doing well." She responded quietly, smiling despite herself. "Please, tell me you have something? A business deal? Hell, I'd take a prenup at this point."

"I do have something for you, something that I know you will be able to handle." He told her before placing a folder on her desk. "I have a case that needs a certain discretion. The client is a caster like us. He is wanted for a crime he didn't commit." He explained.

She looked at the documents. "A defense case." She responded. "Not my specialty, but, if they're like us, I'll take care of it."

"That is where it gets interesting." He added. His smile grew. "The guy who supposedly did it, has a demon."

"Do we know which one?" She asked.

"No clue." He shrugged. "My guess is that it is a deal, but, if it is a ritual, you are the best person we've got."

She smirked. Finally, something *interesting*. "I would be the expert after March."

"Yes, you are." He chuckled at her as he walked back out the door. "This is yours. Give 'em Hell."

She stood up, and moved around the table to take her new client's hand. "Good to meet you." She greeted. Ellyria gestured to a chair. "Please, make yourself comfortable."

"Thank you." He responded, sitting down in the offered seat. "I'm Michael. Mike to my friends."

She gently waved a hand, and closed the door behind him. "And, I'm Ellyria Grant." She responded.

Mike let out a sigh of relief as she shut the door with magic. "I am glad that you won't think I'm crazy, then. I hate normal people, so boring."

She looked over her shoulder to the blank space. "Zane?" She asked.

Zane appeared next to her, and smiled at the man. "Yes, Ellyria?" He asked.

She smirked. "Thanks. Just needed to prove a point for that one." She turned back to Mike. "You can tell me anything, and I will believe it."

Mike nodded, eyeing Zane as he disappeared again. He looked back at Ellyria before he sighed with relief. "Thank you. That makes me feel better."

She used some magic to flip open his file, starting to glance through it. "So, what's going on?" She hummed.

"About a month ago, I was coming back from a ley line. Just needed to meditate ya know?" He explained before continuing. "On my way back home, I was driving across a bridge when I see this car come speeding across the way. I thought that I was going to get hit, and reacted naturally. Instead of swerving, I put up a wall of force, but the other car veered off before it hit and careened into a bus." He stopped short of finishing his story, trying to shake the memory from his head. "The bus went up in flames. A couple people were injured, and an elderly woman died. I saw a demon come out before sprinting away." He told her, shaking a bit. "Mine was the only other car on the road, and the police thought that I caused the accident. I didn't do anything wrong."

She nodded. "Well, the good news is that it looks like there's some good witnesses to use to corroborate that. The bad news is that, if it is a demon, we're going to need to get to them before it does." She paused for a minute. "If it ran away, it sounds like he was some low-level scum. Zane would've turned to mist before leaving."

"I am hoping that it works out that way. I really don't want to be blamed for the damage that was done. I can still hear the screaming." He groaned, holding his head, and trying to block out the memories.

She reached across the table, and took his hand. "It's okay. After this is all over, we can erase that memory, if you want."

He looked at her. "Maybe. I don't like the idea of messing with people's heads. Even if it is a bad one."

"It's always up to you." She told him. "Now, it looks like you have a good case. I want you to go home, ward the ever-living Hell out of your house, and keep a low profile. I'll take care of the rest."

He nodded. "House is already warded, so I will just keep laying low until you say otherwise."

She shook her head, taking out a piece of paper and drawing a couple simple, linear runes. "With these?"

"No." He told her, taking the paper from her, and drawing far more intricate runes with large sweeping curves and swirls. "These."

She looked them over. "You need to add these." She drew another rune, which was based in the thick, scratching strokes of the demonic language. "With these, if you amp the power up over a few days, even Zangrunath wouldn't be able to get in. Maybe." She gave a cheeky grin. "Regardless, low level demons would be useless against it."

He looked the sigil over, and nodded. "Thank you." He stood up. "I will go home and add those immediately."

She tossed him a charged piece of malachite. "You can borrow that one. I know warding can take a lot out of us."

He caught the gemstone, and smiled, taking a few steps back. He pulled out a piece of opalite. "Thanks. I will give it back the next time I see you."

"You're welcome." She waved. "Have a good day."

"You, too." He replied, tracing sigils into the air before vanishing into a wisp of smoke.

"Nice exit strategy. Not ley walking, though." She turned around to look at the empty space she best guessed Zangrunath would be in. "If there's actually a demon involved, I'm worried about the witnesses."

"Yes, that would mean he either did something to get the demon's ire or it didn't kill its mark. Then, it would be trying to clean up its mess." He appeared, giving a decisive nod as he best explained the demon's reasoning.

She sighed. "I really don't like either of those options."

"Well, lower demons don't really have much control. They just keep throwing themselves at the job until they get it done." He explained.

"So, we also need to figure out who or what is behind this. Otherwise, it will just keep happening." She surmised.

"Yeah." Zane sighed. "If the head is cut off, the demon just ceases to exist on this plane."

She nodded. "Well, then. I'll go make sure the witnesses are as safe as I can make them while we wait for this court date, and you go find out who this demon is and eliminate its master. We'll get some fun for you yet."

He smirked, and gave her a kiss. "Thank you. I have missed going and extracting information the fun way."

"If you go down below, say, 'hi,' to the boss man for me." She chuckled.

He shook his head lightly at her. "I won't do that unless I have to. For now, I will do this the old fashion way. Torture."

Ellyria kissed him, shivering a little bit at the thought of what he was looking forward to. "Enjoy." She told him casually, as if she was telling him to have a fun night out with the boys at the bar.

She grabbed her keys and purse before she marched across the office to see McDonough for a moment. "I'm going to go speak with our witnesses." She told him, quietly adding, "I'm worried about their wellbeing."

Steve nodded. "That is why I let you take it rather than doing it myself." He told her honestly. "You have a better relationship with Zane. He listens to you."

Ellyria nodded. "You need to transfer that thing," she told him seriously.

"I'm working on it." He sighed. "You make sure they are safe." He waved her off.

"You get this court date moved up, and they will be." She quipped.

He nodded. "I will see what I can do."

Ellyria walked out to her car, and plugged in the first address on her GPS, following the instructions before she made it to a gated retirement community. She sighed, but explained the situation to the irate security guard before he finally let her through. The house was a little run down but still nice. She parked, and cast a heavy non-detection spell on herself as she warded the house against demons. Before she knocked on the front door, she went to go talk to Larry, who was still following her in his surveillance van as usual. She knocked, and got into the van with him, letting the spell fade so that he could see her. She sighed. "You're going to see weird shit today."

Larry jumped, and looked startled as the passenger door opened of its own accord. In the back of the van, a body moved and shifted before quieting down again. He glared into the dark space. "Weird how?" He asked as the witch sat down in the Vatican's van.

"Look, I know you are at least familiar with what I am and what I do, but I know you don't always know what I'm *doing*." She covered her face, and groaned for a moment. When she took her hands away, she glanced around the vehicle. A lot had changed about the religious sect's vehicles since she had last stolen documents from one. There was a lot less identifying information in the van that indicated the owner of the vehicle. Her eyes settling on Larry's hip to notice that he didn't have one of the nasty holy magic imbued guns at his side. Ignoring it with a little shrug, she started talking as she'd intended to do in the first place. "I wouldn't normally do this at stranger's houses, but I just got a client that has a demon after him."

A look of startled surprise washed over Larry's face. "Oh, well. I mean, I can't really stop you. You are helping someone. I just need to report anything out of the ordinary." He sneered, looking Ellyria over seriously before offering, "maybe I can let this one slide."

She sighed. "Don't get in trouble for me. I just wanted you to know. I'm, unfortunately, used to the Vatican being around in my life. Thanks to my Mom, I had a bunch of agents at my house when I was younger. I thought they were DEA for several months." She lied smoothly. "I just don't want to live like that again. At least, it's just you." She commented, glancing curiously into the back where she'd heard somebody moving a moment before. "Most of the time."

He did a double take, looking from her into the back. He couldn't see the other occupants of the vehicle, so he waved it off. "Thanks. We aren't bad guys. We are just trying to keep the balance. That's all. Some might see us that way, but people shouldn't be able to do some of the things you do. It's just- wrong. You know?"

"I try not to do anything world altering." She nodded, letting out a sigh. It was true enough. She had used mind blowing magic, but it hadn't changed the world, mostly just her own. "I know there's some of us who don't give a damn about that." She gazed at the house. "Protecting is worth all the energy it takes, though."

"That, we can agree on." He smirked, gesturing for her to step out. "You go do what you need to do. I will be sure to tell them what they need to hear."

She nodded, heading back towards the house. She knocked on the door, and an elderly woman in a pink wig with big, oversized glasses that dominated her face opened it about two minutes later. "Hello, Missus Hayworth." She offered her hand. "I'm Miss Grant, a lawyer representing the gentleman about the incident on the bridge about a week ago."

Missus Hayworth thought about Ellyria's explanation for a moment. "Oh, yes, Mike was his name. Good lad. He was a bit shaken up. Is everything alright?" She asked seriously.

Ellyria smiled at the woman's concern. "He's well for the time being, but it's my job to make him the best case possible. So, I was wondering if I could borrow some of your time to take a statement? I want to make sure that I understand everything that happened."

"Of course." Missus Hayworth replied, letting Ellyria into her house. "Can I get you something to drink?" She offered politely.

"Just water, please." Ellyria responded, sitting at the dining room table. She took out a tape recorder as well as a legal pad and pen. Her eyes darted around the room to check for any signs of current or former demonic presence. "You have a beautiful home."

"Thank you. I work hard to keep it that way." She chuckled, coming back with the water. "So, what would you like to hear?"

Ellyria smiled. "Would you mind if I record this?"

"Go ahead. I don't mind." The older woman smiled.

Ellyria started the tape recorder. "Today is Monday August second at," she checked her watch, "ten fifty-eight a.m. Location is at Missus Darlene Hayworth's residence. My name is Ellyria

Grant. Missus Hayworth, could you please state your name for the record?"

"Darlene Hayworth." She almost parroted.

"Thank you, ma'am. As you know, this is regarding the accident at the Western Avenue bridge. Could you please describe what you witnessed in your own words?"

"Yes. I was walking our dog Lucy at Riverside Park near the bridge when it happened. I honestly don't think I would have noticed if Lucy hadn't barked. I turned, and saw that driver swerve into the bus. Then, the bus caught fire." She paused for a moment, trying to think of the right words. "Then, an animal ran away from the fire. Maybe it was a dog or raccoon? I am not sure, but it was bigger than normal and ran like it was injured or sick. As for Mike, it looked like he narrowly avoided being hit himself. He didn't hurt anybody. It was all whoever was in that other vehicle." She explained.

Ellyria nodded. "Thank you, Missus Hayworth. I'll save my questions for the courtroom. I know you've already written a statement for the police report, but, if there's anything you'd like to add before the time comes, please let me know." Ellyria fished out one of her business cards, and handed it to the other woman.

Darlene thought for a moment. "I don't know if it will help, but I think the driver had a tattoo on his arm. It was big, and looked like the Roman number for one." She gestured to her arm to indicate the size.

"Let the record show that Missus Hayworth gestured from just below her shoulder down to her elbow." Ellyria told the recording.

She nodded, and thought for a moment. "That is all I can remember."

"Thank you, Missus Hayworth. Recording end time eleven fourteen a.m." She clicked the stop button on the machine.

"No problem, Miss Grant. I am glad I was able to help." Darlene smiled.

Ellyria packed up her things, and reached across the table to shake hands before showing herself out. "Thank you so much for your time, ma'am. I look forward to seeing you again."

"No problem. It was nice having the company. Have a wonderful day, Miss." Darlene stood up, showing Ellyria to the door.

Ellyria walked out to Shelby, and took the tape out of her recording machine, replacing it with a new one before putting a label on the old one and placing it inside of her lead lined briefcase for good measure. "With magic involved, it's my best bet." She muttered, resting her head on the back of the seat for a second before starting her car. She had more witnesses to see. "I hope you're having more fun than me, Zangrunath." She told him mentally.

Zangrunath was at the scene of the crime when Ellyria spoke to him. "So far, just more questions." He replied as he quickly surveyed the area, and began to put together where the demon came from and ran to. There was just one problem. The paths didn't add up. He shook his head; something wasn't right. The car crashed the way it did, but there should have been no way for the bus to catch fire. He closed his eyes, and began to sniff around for demons. He froze. There wasn't one demon; he smelled two here. "We have a problem."

"I only accept bad news on the third Thursday of each month between the hours of one and two after I've been served ice cream." She replied sarcastically.

"Well, that is a problem for a different day because there wasn't one demon here. There were two." He informed her.

"Great!" She growled, punching the gas.

"I know. I am just as confused as you." He sighed, and started to follow the trail of the closest scent. "I will see what I can find out."

She smiled. "If you catch anybody, feel free to destroy them with prejudice."

"With pleasure." He smirked mentally.

Ellyria spent the afternoon with home visits to as many witnesses as she could. Over and over, it seemed to be the same story. Mike didn't cause the problem. The demon did. So, why was Mike arrested? That piece of the puzzle, she really wasn't understanding. She arrived at the apartment complex of the final witness around three thirty, and, as she was getting out of the car, the sound of gunshots rang out around the area. She ducked back into the car, and screamed for Zane.

Zane quickly appeared next to her in a puff of brimstone, covering her body with his own. "What is going on?" He snarled the question, searching for the source of the gunshots.

"I was going to see another witness. Then, there were gunshots out of nowhere." She explained quickly as her body fought adrenaline and panic.

"Stay down." He told her as he blinked away, and began to furiously search for the source of danger. He wound through the building before finding a door that was wide open. Cautiously, he approached the entrance, looking inside to find a man laying against the back wall of the apartment. His body was torn to pieces with bullet wounds. He released a growl before starting to search for the shooter. Not finding any enemies nearby, he checked the nameplate on the door, and sighed. "Elly, what was the witness's name?" He asked morbidly.

"Elijah Montgomery." She responded.

Zane sighed deeply. "Well, he's dead," he responded. "Shot the Hell up."

"Demons?" She asked seriously.

"Demons don't use automatic weapons." He told her bluntly, seeing the number of shells on the ground.

"This just got complicated." She grabbed her phone, and hit Steve's contact info. It rang three agonizing times before he answered.

"Hey, Elly. What's up?" Steve asked.

"I'm lying on the floor of my car after hearing one of our witnesses be murdered maybe fifty feet away from me." She told him. "I need a better court date."

Steve audibly deflated over the phone. "I will work faster." The line disconnected almost immediately.

Ellyria sat up in her car, looking all around the complex for anything suspicious. She didn't see anything, so she tried concentrating on magic. She was getting a ping nearby, turning her head to see a flash of a figure before it disappeared. She mentally groaned. "Danger's gone."

Zane growled, and appeared next to her. "What is this case?" He asked her, sounding angry.

"Someone trying to frame a magical person to get them into prison, I guess?" She shrugged. "Regardless, I'm done for the day. Gunshots are where I draw the line."

"We are heading home." He nodded in agreement, gazing back at the apartment, and shaking his head.

She held his hand for a second before letting go. "I love you." Starting up the car, she took off towards their place, revving the engine a bit.

He squeezed her hand lightly. "I love you, too."

They sat in companionable silence for the drive. When they got home, Ellyria locked the door, and immediately started walking to the back door instead. "I'm getting in the hot tub. I need to relax."

Zangrunath nodded. "You do that. I am going to keep an eye out around the house." He responded warily. Ever vigilant, he gazed out the front window.

"Should I strengthen the wards?" She asked seriously, pausing halfway out the back door as she was kicking her shoes off.

He looked for a moment, shaking his head. The only thing he saw out front was Larry and his van. "No. Between a witch, a demon, and the Vatican outside, we should be fine."

"With you around, I wasn't actually worried." She smiled.

He eyed her, and smirked. "I know. I just need to be careful now more than ever before, is all. I can't be as reckless as I was in the past."

She shuddered, finding it hard to imagine Zangrunath being afraid of anything. "What happens now? If-"

"Everything is amplified." He told her seriously. "The good *and* the bad. If I get hurt, it will be excruciating for you."

"Thank you for worrying about me." She walked back inside briefly, and kissed him, walking out back again to get into the hot tub.

"I will always worry about you." He replied, following her out into the backyard, and stealing a kiss. "We are one. We need to watch each other's back."

She nodded, touching the crystal around his neck, and charging it with magic. "We do."

"Thank you." He smiled, stealing another kiss. "You make me far stronger than I have any right to be."

"The same could be said about you." She flirted. "I summoned the Devil because of your help."

He shook his head. "You did that by yourself. I was just there."

She tossed her suit jacket over a lawn chair, giving him a deadpan stare. "I felt how tired you were afterwards. Don't lie to me."

"I literally can't." His voice rumbling deep in his chest as he growled at her flirtatiously. "It was you alone who summoned him. I couldn't muster that kind of power if I tried."

"I used yours, though." She told him. "I felt it."

"You drew some of my power, yes." He sighed, stepping into her space. His face looming over hers as if he were about to steal her lips for a fiery kiss. His fingers trailing down her side softly. "In the end, you were still the one who did it."

She sighed, dropping the argument in favor of enjoying his attention. She giggled at him. It was so easy for her to get him to flip that switch between raging in anger and love or adoration. She started unbuttoning her blouse. "Prepare for a back massage. Today has been Hellish."

He pressed the electronic panel a couple of times for her to get the jets going. "Just be sure to start out slow on the settings."

Ellyria gave him a playful swat as he stalked off, shaking her head at him. It had been five months since the soul binding. The change wasn't so bad anymore, and she only had moments of difficulty, now. She did follow his suggestion though, and soon found herself fast asleep in the hot tub.

Zangrunath finished making her dinner, stepping outside. He smirked as he saw Ellyria sleeping soundly in the tub, lifting her out to bring her into the bedroom. He wrapped her up in a towel to dry her off. Placing her on the bed, he let her rest a moment as he packaged up the meal that he made for her. It could be her lunch for tomorrow. Then, he went back to join her in the bedroom. He laid down next to her, holding her close to him to help keep her safe. He wanted to make sure she was protected. She was his after all.

Tuesday, August 3, 2027

Ellyria's phone rang, waking her up at two thirty in the morning. She saw the caller, and groaned. "Hey, Steve." She greeted in a gravelly voice.

"Another one of the witnesses was killed." Steve told her bluntly, sounding as tired and annoyed as she was now.

"Is there magical witness protection?" She asked seriously.

"Not to my knowledge." He sighed. "Besides, we couldn't do it to people who don't use magic. That would anger the Vatican."

She growled under her breath. "Like warding their houses when I go to visit them?"

"No, that shouldn't piss them off as long as the people in question don't know that magic exists." He told her quickly.

She sighed in relief. "What do you need from me, boss?" Ellyria asked with closed eyes and strong sarcasm. "Just called to give me the fantastic news?"

"Don't bother coming in today. Focus on figuring out what is going on. You will be compensated for the time. This can't keep happening." He told her, yawning as he spoke.

"Consider it done." She told him seriously. "Whoever is coming after Mike just made this personal."

"Good." He responded almost happily as he hung up the phone.

Ellyria sat up. Now, she was wide awake. "Alright. I'm up. Who's dying?"

"Just give me a name and I will mount their head above the mantle." Zane responded with an evil grin.

"I don't know, but we're going to find out. What do you need?" She asked seriously.

"If we can get a demon, we can get a name." He explained with a decisive nod.

She brushed her hair out of her face, thinking. "To Missus Hayworth's house."

"Get dressed and lead the way." He told her. His leg bouncing in anticipation, already prepared for battle.

She hopped out of bed, and got into street clothes. "We can't get into her community at night, so we're flying."

"So be it." He nodded. "Just point me in the right direction."

She jumped into his arms. "Head towards the office. It's not far from there."

He smiled down at her, and stepped outside. His thumb lightly rubbing reassuring circles on her shoulder. He shrouded the two of them in mist, spread his wings, and took off towards the office.

Ellyria kissed his cheek. "Thank you."

"You're welcome." Zane smiled, and gave her a kiss on the temple.

"Who would've known when we met that I'd feel this bloodthirsty." She growled, silently wondering when she became a magical bounty hunter, or whatever this was considered, rather than a lawyer.

"I wouldn't have believed it." He chuckled. "It would have made this far more interesting if you were like that when you were younger."

She shivered. "I would be a literal psychopath now."

"Then, I would have fallen for you in a different way." He smirked.

Ellyria leaned into him. "You're insane."

"Of course, you don't go to Hell and come out a better person." He chuckled as they flew through the night sky.

"I'm going to Hell, and I feel pretty good about it." She giggled.

"I give it a century or two before you snap." He surmised. "Either way, I will be there to see the blood."

She shook her head. "I think my dark side and yours are just a tad different."

"Complimentary dark sides." He chuckled.

"You can be murderous, and I'll be calculating and manipulative." She offered.

"That is fine by me." He nodded, holding her a little closer.

"Yours." She whispered.

"Mine." He replied, giving her a little squeeze.

She pointed down to the buildings they needed. "It's down in there somewhere."

He nodded, and flew closer to the ground. "Just tell me where to land." He responded, glancing from house to house with his superior night vision.

Ellyria squinted, trying to find the right house in the darkness, eventually finding it by sensing her own magic guarding the house.

She was about to point it out when a flash of light lit up the wards. "Not good." She mumbled.

Zane swooped to the ground, and set her down a good distance away from the house. "Stay here. I will go find out what the problem is." He told her as he disappeared, making a beeline for the house.

Ellyria bit her lip before running towards the house. She needed to be there to help, but she was so focused on what was ahead of her that she didn't notice what was looming nearby in the shadows.

A set of demonic eyes trained on Ellyria, and, as she ran to help Zane, the low-ranking demon began to growl, sprinting after her. It wanted to get a snack. It quickly caught up to her and, in a swift strike, razor sharp nails cut her leg. When she toppled to the ground, it began to circle her like a shark.

Ellyria tumbled to the ground in a heap. She screamed at the pain, and her entire body jerked with a convulsion. She hadn't been injured since the soul binding. The worst instances were the few times she'd stubbed her toe or bumped her head. This felt akin to being stabbed twenty times. She righted herself, looking around in a panic. When she saw the glowing eyes of her attacker, her hand moved to cover the injury, and she threw out a hasty wall of force to keep the unknown demon away.

As the wall of force wrapped around Ellyria, a huge wall of fire erupted around the demon. Zangrunath appeared between them, seething in anger. He glanced at Ellyria. "Are you alright?" He asked with a bloodthirsty growl.

"I'm fine!" She growled. "Do what you need to do."

"My pleasure." He growled at the demon that was trying to escape the circle of fire. He chuckled darkly as it tried and failed to run away. Lesser demons were pathetically weak. It was laughable. He walked through the flames unaffected, and ripped the legs off the demon. He smirked as the whelp in front of him recoiled in pain. The squelching sound music to his ears. It began to claw desperately at the ground, trying to get away. Black, ichory blood spilling all over the circle. Zangrunath picked up the demon by its hair, and held it up to look into its eyes. "Tell me who your master is." He demanded, grabbing part of the demon's exposed bone, and twisting it slowly.

The demon released an ear piercing howl, and tried to slash at Zangrunath to no avail. The superior demon kept it at arm's length. By the sheer force of Zane's strength and will, it couldn't get any good licks in despite its best efforts.

Zane growled, and ripped out the bone that was in his hand, tossing it to the side. "Tell me or I keep doing this until you are a breathing torso." He threatened. His nails digging deeply into the other demon's flesh. Pin pricks of black blood started to ooze from the wounds.

The demon screeched and wailed as Zangrunath tore it apart bit by bit. It raised a hand to its throat. There, several garish white scars marked the red skin. The markings forming into a rough, but visible, rune that functioned as a way of silencing overly talkative demons. It was either a punishment from Hell itself or the demon's master didn't care for its opinions whatsoever. Regardless, it showed clearly that the whelp was unable to speak.

"Fuck!" Zane yelled, ripping off the demon's arm, and tossing it to the side. "This was a waste of time."

As Zane turned to walk back to Ellyria, the demon that was bleeding out released a call that echoed through the night. Zane turned to glare at the demon with wide eyes before three more demons leapt through the fire, attacking Zane all at once. In perfect sync, they jumped and clawed at him in an attempt at rending flesh from bone as they landed on him.

Zangrunath let out a scream of pain. When he had a moment to recover, however, he grabbed one of the three demons by its tail. His grip was vice-like as he swung the weakling around like a ragdoll, using its body as a weapon against the other two. He crushed two of the heads together. The second demon falling to the ground in a daze momentarily. With a wrenching motion, Zane removed the tail and spine from the one he was swinging around in one fell swoop. He took the gory and sinewy bone, wrapping it around the third demon, using it to strangle the last demon that had attacked him. He held the demon as he watched the life fade from its eyes, and crushed the head of the second. He looked at the one who had unleashed the call, and found that it was dead as well. He snarled, and turned back around to help Ellyria. He knew she would be in pain.

Ellyria let the wall of force fall, and grabbed onto Zangrunath, tears in her eyes. She had felt every blow the same as him. She didn't even attempt to get up. It hurt far too much to try. When he knelt, she leaned into his shoulder, and sobbed. "Ouch."

"I know." He told her as his body began to slowly regenerate. "I'm sorry. I wasn't expecting anything like that." He growled as he picked her up. "What sort of sick bastard makes a horde pact?" He wailed into the night.

Ellyria concentrated through both of their searing pain for a moment before the injury on her leg healed with magic. She held tightly onto him as she grunted at the sensation of the forced expeditious healing. She did her best at ignoring the associated itching that went along with it. "What is a horde pact?"

Zangrunath shook his head, and looked down at her with concern in his eyes. "In layman's terms, it is as close to summoning me as one can get, but, instead of one, you get six. They can go farther, attack individual targets, and work as a single unit if need be. And, everything they see, their master sees. It is like a hive mind."

"How can we find their master?" She asked, wiping away her tears.

"It works differently from our deal. The person would need a large amount of magic to be able to sustain it, so they would probably be at a ley line right now." He explained, wiping a stray tear from her face.

Ellyria looked at him, and took a calming breath. "Hang on." She closed her eyes, reaching out magically, and feeling the leys. The magic coming to her beck and call. She opened her eyes. It looked like her irises were wreathed in lightning, and, instead of brown, there were black orbs staring back. It was like a miniaturized, controlled version of the demonic transformation she experienced after being marked fallen. "I think that I found them."

"Show me." The phrase partially an order but also a statement of tantamount trust.

She thought for a moment, remembering the passages of her grimoire. She understood the concepts of what she wanted to do, but she had never actually tried before. Part of her had been waiting to test it out in a more controlled setting when she had spare time in case something went wrong, but, at this point, desperate times called for desperate measures. She was exhausted, in pain, and just wanted the threat of a group of demons attacking to be in the past. She pulled magic around them. Her eyes firmly closed as she focused on latching onto the ley line. Keeping concentration and focus, she visualized what she wanted and needed. A gut churning sensation washed over her, and, had her eyes been open, she would've seen night turn briefly into day . before they appeared at the center of the active ley she'd found. Her eyes opened, and her head spun. "Woah," she groaned, feeling off kilter from using the new magic.

Zane felt dizzy as well, recovering quickly, and taking a knee to set Ellyria down. He looked around the area, and saw a van sitting not too far away. Zane took a few steps forward before he paused. The van looked familiar. "What the Hell?" He released a grumble of confusion.

She bent over, and put her head between her legs. "What?" She asked tiredly. The recovery from what she'd just done holding most of her attention now.

"Isn't that Larry's van?" He asked, making sure he wasn't seeing things.

She glanced up. "I see the shape, but your night vision is better than mine."

Zane nodded. He'd forgotten about that detail, mentally sending her the visual. As he did so, he watched the pocket door slide open. A second later, two demons darted from the van, charging at them as snarls and howls released from their throats in lieu of words.

Ellyria heard the door of the van open, and the vehicle's engine start. She reached deep into herself, and added weight to the barely visible vehicle. She heard the chassis buckle, and a scream of frustration. She tried to stand, but the magic she'd used the day before and just now had been too much. She fell.

Zangrunath growled, and turned his arms into blades as he charged the two demons. He deftly dodged the attacks, and, in short order, sliced them into minced meat. He glared at the van, storming towards it, and changed his arms back. He wrenched open the door, ripping it from the vehicle with a metallic screeching. Reaching in, he dragged the driver from the vehicle and threw them towards the center of the field, closer to where Ellyria was nearly passed out. He had time, now, to look at the driver. It was Larry, and he looked terrified to see a demon far larger and more intimidating than what he had managed to summon.

"Zane." Ellyria muttered through exhaustion. She wanted to sleep, but knew it was way too dangerous. She tapped the ley to try to regain her strength in a more expeditious manner.

Zane strode forward, and picked up Larry by the collar of his shirt. "So much for playing the fool." He thundered. Where Ellyria had unconsciously borrowed his power before, he was doing the same, now. The clearing they were in rumbled, and the surveillance van tipped onto its side, crashing into the trees beside it, thrown like a child's toy by the wave of powerful magic.

Larry looked between Zangrunath and Ellyria. His eyes wide. He tried to wiggle out of the demon's grip, but was too exhausted from the pain of losing his demons, being thrown a hundred feet, and the magic from all the executions he'd orchestrated. "Fuck you both!" He spat into Zangrunath's face. "You are what's wrong with this world. A half angel that does literally nothing good for a people who are suffering. I'm glad that you went to that church. I hope that the Vatican hunts you for the rest of your life. You deserve to live in fear just like everybody that you terrify with that unnatural power of yours!"

"You framed the innocent. You killed people for speaking the truth. The Vatican observes, keeps the order. What sort end justifies the means?" Zangrunath accused, shaking Larry, and hearing a satisfying pop.

"He was just going to use his power to mess with more people." Larry bellowed and coughed as he struggled with the pain of being made a demon's puppet. When would his literally damned summons make it back? He needed some backup here. "And, those people were just as bad. They wanted to protect that monster. They could have helped that bus, but they stood there and watched as people died!" He coughed again, and blood came out, splattering on his face. He grew pale, processing that this was the end. His head turned towards Ellyria. His eyes dull and cold. "No witch I observed ever helped anybody other than themselves. Rot in Hell, bitch."

"I trusted you. Murderer!" Ellyria screamed the accusation, pointing at him. Magic formed as she lost her temper, and a pointed spire of earth shot from the ground near her hand, extending and careening towards him in an instant. The clearing was silent for but a moment before a loud squelching echoed throughout as the makeshift, natural spear pierced Larry through the heart. She started to hyperventilate, realizing what she'd done, and the magical stalagmite crumbled to the ground, reforming with the earth. Blood sprayed everywhere, covering both Zane and Ellyria.

Quick on his feet, Zane sidestepped Ellyria's attack, holding the Vatican agent firmly in place. He glared into Larry's eyes, watching the light fade, and knowing exactly where his blackened soul would be headed. He dropped the shish kabobbed body before he walked over to Ellyria, holding her close. "It's okay. He's dead."

She held him tightly, and sobbed. "That doesn't get easier."

He nodded, and gently rubbed her back. "I know. That is why I try to distance myself from everyone."

Ellyria held him tighter. "No. You don't. Not from me."

"Everyone but you." He corrected. "You are the only one who matters to me."

"Mine." She murmured, nuzzling into his shoulder.

"And, you are mine." He responded. His wings wrapped around her momentarily. He enshrouded them in mist, and picked her up, taking flight towards their house. "Let's go home."

She fumbled with her phone as they flew, sending a text message to Steve. 'Threat neutralized. I'll be in tomorrow.'

"I'm off today." She mumbled tiredly, pocketing her phone.

"Get some rest." He told her quietly. "You used a lot of magic, and we both were injured." He stroked her hair lightly. "I will make sure we get home safely."

She nodded, and closed her eyes. "I love you." She whispered as she drifted off.

"And, I you." He murmured, giving her a kiss on the cheek. Zane made it home in record time, and set her down in the bed. He grabbed a washcloth in the bathroom, and dampened it, wringing it out well. He wiped the blood from her face, getting any spots he could find, and helped her out of her gore covered clothing. Finally, he tucked her in, and laid down next to her. He gave her another kiss, and fell asleep at her side. It had been a long day, and he needed rest too.

Ellyria awoke before Zangrunath. Light filtered through the windows, and she saw her demon sleeping beside her. Resting peacefully. She smiled, running her fingers down the side of his face all the way to his hip. Her fingers ran back up, and she saw his eyes open. "Good morning. I didn't know you could sleep." She smiled softly as she met his black gaze.

He smirked at her, and stole her hand to kiss. His lips meeting the inside of her wrist. "I don't need to. Doesn't mean I can't do it if I want to." He responded, running a hand down her side like she did to him.

She shivered at his touch. "I just want to be close to you, right now."

He nodded, and put his wing over her. His tail wrapped around her waist, holding her close to him. "That is fine."

"Let's make this my first and only defense case." She murmured as she rested on his chest.

"Agreed." He sighed with relief. "That sucked."

"It did." She wiggled her leg. "I never want to get hurt again."

He made a face, and kissed her. "I'm sorry that I let that happen to you. I should have been there to protect you." His tone sincere and apologetic.

She shook her head. "I should've paid better attention. It's my fault."

"I ran ahead without making sure that there was nothing that could hurt you. The fault is mine." A hand ran up and down her back. "I have superior senses to you, millennia of experience in tactics, and could have easily created a duplicate for protection. I failed you."

"We can argue this all day." She shook her head. "I'd rather not. I'd rather be grateful that it wasn't worse."

He nodded, and sighed, squeezing her a bit as he did so. "Let's just relax." He told her, brushing her hair from her face.

She laid there for a minute before her stomach growled, ruining the moment. "Stupid human body." She complained.

Zangrunath sighed, and sat up. "I will make you food," he offered as he picked her up, bringing her with him, "but I still want you close to me."

She sat on the counter where he put her down. "No eggs, please. Just not feeling it."

"Toast and bacon, then. Maybe some jam on the toast." He suggested as he started moving around the kitchen to make her breakfast.

"Thank you." She smiled at him, watching him intently as he worked.

He smirked, and turned to look at her. "You are very welcome.

She chuckled at the look in his eyes, deciding that changing the subject was best before breakfast was delayed. "I want so badly to actually use my specialty at work." She sighed. "Instead, I get to play a magical detective."

He nodded as he put the strips of bacon in the pan. "At least, you are doing something. It's better than sitting behind a desk all day pretending to work and hating everything."

"I kind of do hate everything to be honest." She frowned.

"There are moments, yes." He looked over at her for a moment, reaching over to the loaf of bread, and popping two pieces in the toaster. "You are going to get the opportunity to do it soon enough. Once this case is over, I know that you will get something."

"I would take anything at this point. I just want to sink my teeth into a contract and tear it to shreds, figuratively speaking." She blushed.

He laughed at her description. "Depending on the contract, you might get to do that literally." He spread strawberry jam on the toast, and plated up everything for her.

She licked her lips. "This smells great."

"Well, eat and see if it tastes just as good." He smiled, placing the plate in her hands.

She took the plate, and started to eat. "You always take such good care of me."

"I try my best." He watched her for a moment, leaning up against the counter.

She pulled the piece of toast from her lips, and looked at him with some emotion as she chewed. "I dread the day you have to take care of me as an old lady. So not sexy future demoness."

"You will always look the same in my eyes." He told her honestly, going to the sink to clean up the small mess he made.

She took another bite. "I don't want to imagine it. I don't know why I brought it up. I hate the idea of it."

He shook his head at her. "You will be a sexy demoness. Hell makes sure you are at your absolute peak performance. Stop worrying about all of that. You are powerful, and that is what I see."

She chuckled at him, hopping off the counter. She took her plate into the living room. She hit the power button on the computer. "I'm going to play some games. Maybe something with tower defense."

He smiled, and followed her into the living room. He turned on his computer. "You do that, I'm going to figuratively destroy the world by playing strategy games."

She grinned at him. "Enjoy."

ARTICLE VIII

The room was empty besides Zane who was always there. "It's a Monday sort of Tuesday." Ellyria groaned at her desk as she looked over her emails.

"At least, it is a four-day week." He offered. "It will be shorter than normal."

She sighed, looking at her messages, and growing very still. "Excuse me a moment. We may have finally struck paydirt." She quickly stood up, and fought to walk, not run, to Steve's office. "Is it true? Are we brokering a merger with the W's?"

Steve glanced up at her, and smiled. "We are working on something, yes. Nothing has been finalized yet, but, so far, things are looking good."

Ellyria turned her head as Parker came up behind her and touched her shoulder. It made her shudder with revulsion. "Good morning, you two. We're having a meeting with the law team starting in ten minutes. Be ready to talk deals."

"Thank you, Parker. I am aware." Steve responded with a sigh, standing up, and grabbing a few items from his desk.

"I'll be there with bells on." Ellyria replied with a wide smile, going to her office to grab everything she needed. "By Lucifer's blackened throne, yes." She muttered.

"Congratulations." Zane mentally smirked. "I know you will get this deal solidified."

She made her way into the conference room with the confidence of somebody who owned the place. "You bet I am."

Ellyria sat beside McDonough, and clicked her favorite red pen to be ready. Her trusty legal pad in front of her as Parker loaded up a presentation on the projector. She read the contract that was posted on the screen, starting to frown deeply the further along she got.

"This is awful." Zane mentally sneered. "This is them basically buying out the company."

"The company with the highest net revenue becomes the chief controlling entity." She muttered back to him. "Of course, they make more money. There's two of them."

"Then, fix it." Zane replied. "You did study for this, right?" He asked rhetorically.

Ellyria snapped out of the conversation to find Parker looking at her intently. "Miss Grant, good of you to join us. Now, as I was saying, I'm quite pleased with this deal. Would you care to share your- expertise?" He jeered the final word.

Ellyria put her pen down, and leveled him with a murderous gaze. "I think that, if you'd like White and Whitaker to be your boss, you should definitely sign that atrocity."

"What?" He quipped.

"Article four subsection 'B'. Controlling stake goes to the company with the highest net revenue." She deadpanned. "That's my biggest concern. The second being that this requires us to relocate to Worcester."

He shook his head, and shrugged. "Okay, moving isn't a problem. We can easily get everything transferred over within a year."

"This document gives us sixty days and, may I remind you, voids my contract, sir." She reminded him seriously. He probably thought that it was a bonus to get her out of this place.

McDonough spoke up before Parker could chime in, and smiled at Ellyria. He knew that she, of all people, would get this shored up. "Then, what would you recommend Miss Grant?"

"I would recommend that the section about controlling parties be changed to 'most resolved cases within the past five calendar years, and, if you believe relocating can be done in a year, I suggest changing it to two years to leave room for error. Since I remember the lease on this building was recently signed for another year, I would shoot to be relocated by the end of that term to avoid paying month to month." She replied confidently and firmly.

McDonough spoke again. "Why is there a move involved?" He asked Parker. "Why can't we have the same company, but with two separate branches? Wouldn't that help increase the number of clients we can take in? You know, accessibility."

"I completely agree." Ellyria nodded, gazing at the dumbfounded Parker. She thought for a moment, and turned back to look at the contract, directing Julie to scroll down for her. The final article had her seething. She turned to speak directly to McDonough and Hannon. "The future company in Worcester is to be dubbed Parker, White, and Whitaker. This writes both of you out of partnership."

McDonough glared at Parker angrily. "What did you do?"

Parker stretched his collar as the sweat was rolling down his face. He couldn't meet Steve's eyes. "It was a lot of money."

"You already signed this, didn't you?" Ellyria demanded.

"What type of idiot turns down a one hundred thousand dollar raise!?" He quipped.

Ellyria stood up. "Show me McDonough and Hannon's partnership contracts."

"I don't know how that will help." Parker shrugged, snapping, and pointing at Julie to get the documents for her. "The deal has already been made."

"Show. Me. Their. Contracts." She growled, leaning forward on the conference room table like she was preparing to jump over it just to strangle him.

Julie ran into the room, looking down and away to avoid having the anger of the room directed at her. She handed Parker the file folders.

"Fine." He replied, tossing the folders across the table. They landed just short, sliding the rest of the way before bumping into her hand. "Good luck." Parker sneered as he walked out of the room.

Ellyria looked to McDonough and Hannon. "I'm going to need overtime." She grumbled before storming towards her office. "And, get me Parker's *current* contract." She called out.

"Granted. Give me five minutes." Steve growled as he left the office, going to fish out his former partner's contract from their file storage room.

"There has to be verbiage in here that voids the new one." She whispered to Zane as she slammed her office door, and started to dig into McDonough's documents.

Zane gave her a mental nod. "Of course, there has to be." He told her seriously. "No contract would ever be that one sided."

"If this deal goes through, my employment contract is void. I wrote my contingencies with the completion of the penthouse in mind, and, Lucifer damn them to Hell, it isn't done yet."

"You will get that penthouse." He promised her. "If need be, we can pay double."

"Sorry, but I need to focus." She told him as she started to read and make highlights. She sent an instant message, and coffee appeared a few minutes later along with Parker's contract. She sighed. This was going to take a while.

Wednesday, September 8, 2027

The office was dark. The only illumination coming from Ellyria's computer screen and a small desk lamp. She smiled, and

giggled. She was so far gone that she'd hit slap happy. "I found it."
She jumped up out of her seat, nearly toppling the office chair
over. "I found it!"

Zane spoke for the first time in hours. "What did you find?"
He asked curiously.

"Parker's contract. The old one states that he needs approval
from all partners to sell, trade, or otherwise dissolve the firm.
There's some old verbiage that has changed since the old partners
retired, but the intent is there. And," she started to laugh
maniacally, "he just voided his own partnership by going over their
heads."

Zane appeared next to her, and smirked. "That is hilarious."

"McDonough, Hannon, and Grant has quite the ring to it." She
suggested.

"Yes, it does." He chuckled, giving her a kiss. "Good job. I
knew you could do it."

She picked up all the documents, and looked at the time. "Oh,
Hell. I've got to be back here in six hours."

He glanced from the clock over to her. "Will you be okay to
drive?" He asked seriously.

"No." She responded immediately as she packed up. "I need
you to drive."

He nodded, and turned into his human self. "Let's get you
home."

"I want a shower." She complained as they walked out to the
car.

Zane walked behind her, stopping when he noticed that
something was amiss. He placed a hand on Ellyria's shoulder. "I
don't think we are driving home." He growled, eyeing the damaged
car.

Ellyria took in the damage, and her chest tightened as she tried
desperately not to cry. A whimper escaped her lips. "Parker is
going to pay." She muttered darkly in lieu of giving in to her
heartbreaking feelings.

"If you want me to cut his brake lines, I will." Zangrunath offered.

She shook her head. "No, he's about to see his world burn." Exhaustion hit her, and, secrecy be damned, they were getting home. She tapped the leys, and carefully started to knit together the tires and repair the damage to the classic vehicle. "Nobody messes with this car." She growled possessively.

"I love it when you get angry." Zane smirked, opening the door for her.

"I'm going to write him out of law on the east coast." She threatened as she started to get more irritated. Tired, hungry, and frustrated was not a good combination for her at all. She huffed, crossing her arms as she flopped into her seat.

He got into the car, and placed a hand on her thigh. "Calm down. You are too tired."

Ellyria groggily looked out the windshield. "I never liked that touchy misogynist, and I'm going to make him pay."

He started Shelby, and she roared to life, sounding angry. "I think she agrees with you."

"I want to see him watch his world fall apart in front of him." She sighed.

"I know you will." He smirked, giving her a kiss. "Close your eyes, and I will get us home quickly."

She closed her eyes, and sighed. "Sorry. I've been exhausted and hangry for hours."

"I will make sure you get a big breakfast in the morning." He promised.

Ellyria yawned. "Let me sleep in more than normal, please. I'll get in right at nine instead of early."

"Will do." He nodded, knowing she couldn't see it. He got them home in record time, and, by the time they were there, Ellyria was out cold. He lifted her up, and put her to bed, holding her while she slept.

Zangrunath's wake up call was the only reason Ellyria stirred. She yawned, and groggily looked at him. "I'm up." She groaned, sitting up. She knew she didn't have all the time she usually did. "I'm going to go take that shower.

He smiled, and pulled away. "Go enjoy it. I will have breakfast ready when you get out." He promised, hopping out of bed, and making his way to the kitchen.

She got cleaned up, and put on one of her nicest outfits before strolling out into the living room with her heels in hand. "I am as ready as I'm going to get today." She announced.

"You look dressed to kill." He commented as he placed a nice big breakfast in front of her. "Enjoy. If you want more, I made extra, just in case."

"Take me now." She deadpanned as she eyed the food with a different kind of lust altogether. She dug into her meal, and didn't stop to even look at him until her plate was clean. Ellyria glanced at the clock. "Ack! We've gotta go."

Zane nodded, and disappeared before talking into her head. "Lead the way. I will follow you anywhere."

"Parker's going to be pissed that my car is intact." She surmised.

"He will never figure it out." He chuckled.

She shook her head, still feeling beyond frustrated with the man who would become her former employer very soon. "If he ever does, it'll be because I killed him."

"If that happens, I will bring the popcorn." Zane replied. "You are going to ruin that man's whole career."

"Oh, yes, I am." She sneered. She grew quiet as she drove to work, smiling to herself. When she pulled into her parking spot, she noticed that the sign had been tagged sometime overnight. "Oh, it keeps getting better."

He chuckled. "Well, it was his funeral for starting a fight with a nephilim."

"I made a deal with the actual Devil. I am coming out on top of this thing." She replied mentally as she strode out of the car with her head held high. She pulled her briefcase to her with magic and locked Shelby. "Let's go destroy a career."

"I can barely wait to see this." Zane's grin was palpable in her head as she strode confidently into the office on a mission.

She walked into the office, reached over Julie's desk as she sat on the counter, and dialed the number to speak to the office. "This is Miss Ellyria Grant. I'm calling a partner's meeting in five minutes. Thank you." She turned to Julie. "Have Jeremy brew a fresh pot of coffee. We're going to need it, and please have security ready." She slid off the counter, and walked into the conference room with a wink at Steve.

Julie nodded, and began to get everything ready. As Ellyria walked in, McDonough looked at her curiously. "Please tell me you found something?" He asked, sounding hopeful.

"Bow down to me in glory." She whispered, giving a little curtsey.

He released a huge sigh of relief, and sat down in a chair. "Thank you! I didn't get any sleep last night after that incident." He smiled widely. "I will actually get some rest tonight."

She sat down, and crossed her legs. "You're going to be paying me a lot of overtime. I left at three a.m., and Parker tried to mess with my car."

He sighed deeply, but nodded. "It's fine, if I know you like I think I do, you just saved this company."

"Oh, and so much more." She grinned, watching Daniel Hannon and Joseph Parker file in.

Parker looked at her, and smirked. "Good morning, Miss Grant. Did you have a nice drive into work this morning?" He asked.

"Yes, I did, sir." She smiled with false sweetness. "I might have been a bit *tired*, but it was better than driving *smashed* after a night out."

Parker raised an eyebrow at that, and shook his head. "So, what is this meeting about?" He asked impatiently. "I need to head to Worcester soon." He glanced at his watch.

She leaned over across the table, and looked deeply into his eyes. "Why is that? You're no longer a partner here. The new contract is void."

He paused, and looked at her critically. "What are you talking about? I have my name on this company." He retorted.

"You do now, but, when you were made partner, you signed a contract that makes your partnership null and void if you do anything without the consent of the other partners. It seems the old bosses didn't trust you." She smirked.

Parker's eyes went wide. He looked at her in shock. "No, no, no. That contract was over when these two took their places. That doesn't work in this situation."

She looked down at the documents. "I don't see an end date on here."

He walked over, and took the paper from her hand, looking it over quickly. "There has to be an end date." He started to look visibly frustrated.

"So, we're done here, right?" She asked.

"You bitch." He spat, pulling a fist back before it was caught by McDonough.

"I wouldn't do that if I were you." Steve told him seriously. "That is, unless you want to be fed that arm." He warned Parker, knowing that it wouldn't be him doing the feeding.

Parker was seething in rage now. "No! I own this company. I own you." He shouted as he began to walk towards the door. "I am going to bankrupt all of you and wipe my ass with your savings accounts!" He idly threatened as he slammed the door to the conference room, shattering the window in the door with the force.

Steve sighed, and looked at Elly. "Thank you Ellyria. You saved the company." He offered his hand to shake.

"I just did my job." She responded.

"And, you did a good job at that." He smiled at her before a car alarm went off outside.

"I'm going to go kill him, now." She growled, marching out the door, and running in her heels into the parking lot. "Zane." She told him mentally. "Can I borrow some strength for a second?"

"Take as much as you need." Zane replied, lending her his power as requested.

Ellyria ran up to Parker as he was bashing into Shelby with a baseball bat, and decked him as hard as possible in the face, knocking him over the side of the car with the force.

Parker fell onto the ground, and slid on the asphalt. He stood up on wobbly legs, and spit out a bloody tooth. He growled, standing up, and charging at her. "You ruined me!"

Ellyria didn't know what to do, so she ducked, feeling Parker's momentum throw him over her. He fell back onto the ground. She stood up straight, and stomped with all her might onto his chest. "You ruined yourself, and you will not mess with that car, dirtbag."

He groaned in pain as he felt and heard cracking in his chest. He rolled to the side, and gasped for air.

She turned around, starting to walk away as she heard the security guard calling out from across the parking lot. She didn't see him reach for her until she was already on the ground.

"I'll kill you!" Parker wheezed as he tried to pull her towards him, and his hands went for her throat.

Ellyria's eyes went dark black, and her skin started to change before his eyes. "I will destroy you." She responded, kicking him in the groin with her heels.

Parker instantly went pale as a ghost, falling over in pain. He fell to the side and tried to crawl away. He glanced back at the beginnings of Ellyria's demonic looking transformation, and shuddered. His body in agony, he tried to get away faster, but stopped, cowering in fear when he saw her looming over him.

Ellyria stood up, and kicked his side, making him roll over again. "If you ever touch me or my car again, I will make your life a Hell so miserable that you will beg me just to end it."

He whimpered, and nodded. "I won't do it again." He shivered as he looked up at her. "I'm sorry!" He sobbed, curling up as he prepared to be beaten more.

Ellyria glanced over at the approaching group of onlookers, and looked to McDonough. Her eyes were still the darkest of obsidian. "I'm going to go write a restraining order." She told him, pretending to cry, and covering up her face so others didn't see. "Let me know if you need anything."

Steve looked a little shocked, but nodded. "If I do, you will be the first to know."

She quickly ducked into her office, using random bits of the errant magic she'd picked up, trying to make the changes clear up. "Dammit." She murmured as the adrenaline and Zangrunath's power started to fade from her.

"Calm down." Zane soothed.

"Trying." She sighed. "I just assaulted a guy."

"No, you didn't." He told her. "It was self-defense. You did nothing wrong."

She rubbed her temples. "I technically broke laws."

"If it ever comes to that, there are people who will back you up." His voice low and calming. "Besides, he is not going to press charges."

"I'm okay." She took a breath, muttering the phrase over and over.

Zane sent her calming thoughts, and quietly spoke into her head. "You are fine. He attacked you, destroyed your property, and tried to sell out a company he had no right to sell." He reminded her. "He has more pressing matters to worry about like embezzlement and fraud."

"I'm sorry." She pulled up a restraining order form on her computer. "He's not coming near me again."

"He would have to get through me first." He growled possessively into her head. "Mine."

She felt the mental caress of the word. "Just don't forget whose you are." Ellyria replied, yawning widely.

Zane sent her a mental smile, and let her continue her work. "Just let me know when you are ready. I will take you home."

"He smashed Shelby again." She sighed.

"I know." He sighed. "You will probably need to have it towed back to the house so you can fix it."

She waved a hand. "Would you mind calling? I just want to get this one thing done right now."

"Of course." He smiled, appearing next to her in his human form. He looked sharp and attractive in a business suit. He picked up her office phone, and started to make the arrangements she asked for.

Ellyria grew quiet. She focused on getting the task at hand done, and, once it was completed, she brought the printed document to Julie at the front. "I need this to be approved at the courts." She sighed. "Can we have Jeremy messenger it over, please?"

Julie nodded, and took the pages from her. "Yes, I will have him get it there as soon as possible."

"Thank you." Ellyria responded tiredly, making her way to McDonough's office. She yawned again. "Do you need anything? I'm exhausted. Only got a couple hours of sleep."

He shook his head. "No, go home and get some rest." He told her before he added. "In fact, take the rest of the week off. You helped us keep this place, and got assaulted because of it. You deserve it."

"Paid leave, I hope." She winked.

"Yes. Now, go rest." He waved her off. "I will take care of everything here."

"Thank you." She smiled. "See you soon. Let me know if there's anything you need."

"Will do." Steve told her, going back to his work at the computer.

As Ellyria walked out of the building, she could see Shelby being loaded onto a tow truck, and Zane walking over to her. "You ready to go?" He asked her, already knowing the answer when he saw the exhaustion in her eyes.

"Yeah." She replied with a small voice as she took his hand.

"Alright." He led her away from the building, making sure that any prying eyes were long gone. Once they were well hidden, Zangrunath turned into his normal self, and picked Ellyria up. He shrouded them in mist, and flew them towards the house.

She leaned into him, starting to cry. "Not my car."

"I know." He soothed, rubbing her shoulder. "We had to make it look believable. She will be home in an hour at most, and I will have her in the garage. You can fix her whenever you are ready."

Ellyria sniffled. "It's not what it is, but what it means. I made a promise."

"I know." Zane replied. "I know what it means to you, and I won't let you break that promise."

She nodded. "Thank you."

"No problem." He smiled, giving her a kiss on the cheek. He landed in the backyard, and brought her inside. He placed her on the bed. "Sleep well."

"I'm gonna mess up my sleep schedule." She complained.

"Then, stay awake until a normal time." He offered, knowing she was too tired to try at this point.

Ellyria sat up, and the room spun. "Dammit."

"I figured as much." He chuckled, tucking her in. "Just sleep. We have four days to fix it, after all."

"Fine." She growled crankily at him.

He gave her a kiss. "Sleep well. Love you."

She curled up, cuddling into a pillow. "Night, love."

ARTICLE IX

S tanding in her backyard, Ellyria was bundled up for the cold weather. She didn't think she needed the power of the leys to keep her Dad around for the night. She set up the ritual, and, in no time at all, her father's specter was in front of her. "Hey, Dad." She smiled. "Thanks for showing up a few months ago."

"No problem, sweetie." Samuel smiled. "It was the least I could do. You needed help."

"Yeah." She sighed. "It was a painfully bad day."

He made a face. "I'm sorry."

She rubbed her head unconsciously at the thought. "So much has happened this past year. I don't even know where to start."

"Well, how is school coming?" He asked seriously.

"I actually passed the bar in May with a 280." She smiled. "Then, I started working at a law firm at the end of June."

"I'm glad." He looked a little teary eyed. "Just wish I could have seen all that."

She shook her head, trying not to cry sympathetically. "I didn't walk. It would've been too bittersweet."

"I still would have liked to see it. I miss a lot like this." He gestured to himself.

"You get to see Mom, though, sometimes." She smiled at the thought.

He chuckled, and shook his head. "No, actually. I don't. She is busy being herself."

"I'm sorry." She frowned. "That sucks."

He smiled. "It's fine. She is busy, and I know that, when I do see her, it will be well worth the wait."

Ellyria looked steadily at her father. "I did world altering magic this year too." She changed the subject. "Stuff that Mom's probably angry about."

"Like what?" He asked curiously. "Can you bring people back from the dead?"

"Honestly, I don't think that would be so difficult, but I think I might actually get smote for trying." She paused. "I summoned the Devil himself."

Her father froze, blinking several times. "What?" There was no way that he'd heard that correctly.

"He's also a fallen angel. I needed to know what was happening to me, so," she shrugged, "I asked the only source I knew of for sure."

He sighed. "Well, at least, you got out of it scot-free. Right?" He asked nervously.

"We changed my deal while he was here." She waved flippantly, but her expression became smug. "It's kind of too much information, but Zangrunath will always be around to take care of me."

He nodded. "At least, you are happy."

"I am." She told him, looking down at the ground. "I'm so close to getting what I want that I can taste it."

"Did you enjoy getting there for the most part?" His tone becoming serious.

"It was a lot of hard work, but I enjoy what I do. And, I'm incredibly good at it." She answered as honestly as possible. After a long pause, she finally decided that it was time to say what she'd been waiting to ask. "I asked Zangrunath to stay inside for tonight. I wanted-" She sighed, looking up at the sky, and holding back tears. "I'm so screwed up, Daddy."

He looked at her broken expression, wishing there was some way that he could help his baby girl. "No, you're not, sweetie." He started calmly. "You are unique. I know you might think that you are something beyond reason, but, I can assure you, you are not the first."

"I've killed people," she explained, "brutally, and for things that could have been much worse. And, what's worse is-" She took a breath, wiping away a tear from her eye. "I can never have kids anymore. If anything, that's my biggest mistake. I didn't realize what I was doing. What I was giving up."

Her father grew quiet for a moment as he processed her words. He nodded sadly. "I killed people, so I understand that. I do." He paused, trying to think of what to say in response to her other news. "I- you might not be able to have kids, but you can still be a Mom." A sad smile took his lips. "I know that, if you do, you will be great at it."

"They won't be magic, though. I kind of inadvertently ended our family line." She waved a hand, and their family grimoire appeared in her hands. "Nobody will use this again after me."

He frowned. "Somebody will use it. As much as I dislike the idea, I would rather have someone use it than have the knowledge in there be lost to time."

"I gave away the pages of demon code to save myself." She told him.

"Who did you give it to?" He asked, letting out a deep sigh, and rubbing his temples.

"Good ol' Lucifer himself." She gulped with a bitter chuckle. "That was terrifying."

He groaned when she said that before looking into her eyes with a forced smile. "I guess that's better than it falling into the Vatican's hands. That would have caused a war, had that happened."

She wiped her face, and shook her head. "I won't start the next holy war."

"It wouldn't be a war so much as an extermination. You gave it to the right being." He smiled at her. "I know that he will definitely make sure that it's kept out of the wrong hands."

She reached out to try to touch him, and her hand went through his. "Dammit." She sighed, glaring at her hand. After a minute, she looked up to him. "I'm sorry. It can't be too much longer. I have an important meeting tomorrow."

He nodded in understanding. "It's fine." He lied. "I know you are a busy person, now. Just try to stay out of trouble. Alright?"

"I always do." She smiled. "I might be a partner at the firm when I talk to you next year."

"I look forward to finding out." He smiled.

"I love you, Dad." She whispered to him.

"I love you, too, sweetie." His smile was bright for her as he fought away the sadness of knowing that they would be apart for another year. "Take care."

Ellyria watched her father fade away, and stood up to head inside where Zane was at his computer desk playing games. "Thanks." She whispered to him, coming up behind him, and hugging him around his shoulders.

Zane smiled, and turned his head to give her a kiss. "It's fine. I know you like to have private talks with him. It is no big deal." He replied, sending hordes of minions at an enemy he was fighting against.

She sniffled. "This year made me miss him a lot." She stood up, and started to walk down the hallway to get ready for bed.

He quickly finished up his game, and followed her to the bedroom. "At least, you can still talk to him. There are people who don't get that option." He told her in a reassuring manner as he sat down on the bed, watching her go about her ablutions.

"I know." She whispered while cleaning her face in the bathroom mirror to avoid having him hearing the emotions there.

"You know you can always talk to me about anything. Right?" He asked.

She nodded. "I do, but you hate it when I cry. I don't like seeing you in pain like that."

"I would much rather be in pain than have you feel like you need to hide or suppress things." He told her seriously. "I can take it. I am pretty durable." He chuckled.

She finished what she was doing in the bathroom, turned around, and climbed into his arms. "It's just me rehashing the same shit on a different day."

He held her close, and gave her a gentle kiss. "You like to make up things in your head. Just take a calming breath next time you think something is going to go wrong and watch as it doesn't. Okay?"

"I will try." She told him as she laid down next to him. "Now, get over here, and cuddle me."

He smiled, and laid down, pulling her close to him like she asked. He gave her a squeeze. "Better?"

"Much." She smiled. "Goodnight, Zangrunath."

"I love you, Ellyria." He replied, giving her a kiss. "Sleep well." He stroked her hair as she laid in his arms.

Monday, November 1, 2027

Ellyria pulled into her parking spot at the firm, and hopped out of Shelby. She had a big smile on her face as she walked immediately into the conference room. "Hello, McDonough. Hannon. How are you this morning?" She asked.

"Doing well." Steve McDonough greeted with a smile. "How about yourself? Have a good weekend?" He asked conversationally before the meeting got started.

"Oh, you know. Got to see some distant relatives." She smirked.

A knowing smile pulled at his lips, and he nodded. "Good to hear."

"I hate to skip the formalities and get straight to the brass tacks, but I have a client coming in an hour. You wanted to see me?" She began.

Steve nodded again, and looked at Daniel Hannon. "Yes, we wanted you to look over this new contract we are working on and get your thoughts on it." He slid the folder to her with a serious expression.

She opened the file folder, and started to read it over. After about a minute, she looked up. "You really want me to be your partner? "

Daniel smiled. "Well, yeah. After you helped us keep the place, it's the least we can do. You know what you are doing, and we are both glad to have you be our partner."

She beamed at them. "I will, of course, have to read this over, and how do you feel about a branch in New York? I have my eye on a penthouse that I can bid on next year."

The two looked at each other, and nodded. They looked back at her. "That is fine by us." Steve responded.

"Thank you!" She grinned.

"You're welcome, but, before any new branch gets made, we still have work to do. So, go make sure our clients are taken care of." He chuckled, waving her out the door.

"Of course." She grinned, standing up, and heading to her new office. She closed the door, and locked it behind her for a moment. "Zane." She whispered.

"Congratulations." He mentally enthused. "I knew you would get it."

"Get out here, and hug me." She demanded.

He chuckled, and appeared next to her, lifting her, and spinning her into an embrace. "There, a big hug for the big new position you got."

She stole a kiss from him. "Thank you."

"You are very welcome," he stole one more kiss, knowing she had work to do, and clients to see.

She unlocked her door. "It's all starting to fall into place."

"Just a little while longer, and the deal will be done. Then, it will just be the two of us." He smiled before disappearing.

"You, me, and a New York penthouse." She smirked, getting to work for the day.

"I look forward to that day." He agreed before going quiet so she could work in peace.

ARTICLE X

Ellyria paced back and forth like a lioness in the living room as she stood behind Zangrunath's computer screen. "I can't believe that they're starting the bidding at midnight." She groaned. "They're killing me softly."

Zane shook his head, and pulled her to his side. "Calm down, and relax." He told her, giving her a kiss. "You want this, and I will get it for you. I am not worried about the price. We have the money."

She looked at the current account balances on the documents strewn across the table. "I know. I'm just anxious. This is new to me."

"I can tell." He chuckled. "You haven't stayed still in the last thirty minutes. Your legs are going to give out before the bidding ends."

"It's only two minutes to midnight. I'm fine." She grumbled.

"Then, prove it to me by sitting down and being calm." He responded, patting his lap for her to sit in.

She sighed, and took a seat as she was told. "There. Happy?" She asked, checking the clock anxiously.

"Only slightly." He wrapped his tail around her waist, focusing on the screen. "You are still a nervous wreck." He glanced down at her.

"I just know what I want." She sighed, bouncing her leg impatiently.

"I know, and you will get it." He promised, kissing her cheek, and placed a hand on her leg to calm her. "Trust me."

Saturday, July 1, 2028

She watched as the site ticked over to a new screen, refreshing quickly, and Zangrunath's fingers got to work on the keyboard. She shut her eyes. "Oh, I can't watch."

"Relax." He soothed as he put in a small starting bid. "All these other people have no idea what they are dealing with." He chuckled as he saw several other bids come in. He shot the price up a bit. A few more bids came in, raising the bid to fifteen million. He laughed as he doubled the price in one go, making several other bidders leave in short order. "Play hard, live harder."

"I know we have it." She gulped. "And, I know it's probably going higher, but that's a lot of money."

"Nothing that I can't get back." He shrugged as fewer buyers were starting to bid as the price continued to go up. "Just close your eyes and focus on the image of us relaxing on the balcony."

She sighed. "We're going to have to buy all new everything."

He shook his head. "No, we don't. Just because we have the penthouse doesn't mean everything needs to get more expensive. We can still bring a good bit with us." He placed another bid, raising the price to over thirty-five million.

"Are we selling this place, then? I've kind of grown attached to it." She frowned.

"Only if you want to." He responded. "We could always just rent the place out."

Ellyria thought about that. "We would make a killing."

"Extra money, yes." Zane chuckled. Several bidders left, leaving only one other person. He raised the bid again. "If you wanted a killing, I would suggest video games."

She chuckled, and nudged him. "Oh, very funny. Time to throw in the towel mister millionaire. You ain't winning this."

He cracked his knuckles, and sent the price up to forty million. "There. Either they stop or I put it to fifty."

"I really don't want to imagine spending that much." She whined in distress.

"Just think of it in pennies." He joked as he waited for a moment with nothing changing. "It is silly when you think of it that way."

She giggled. "Like the greedy cartoon duck with the top hat and monocle."

"Give me some time, and I could make that real." He smirked, as the other person left, leaving them the last remaining bidder. A few moments passed, and the screen changed, informing them that they were the winner. "Now, the place is ours."

She pulled him in for a tight hug. "Oh, sweet, merciful Lucifer, yes!" She exclaimed.

He gave her a kiss. "Feel better, now?" He asked, already knowing the answer.

Relief washed through her. "Yeah. Thank you. My devilishly handsome hero."

"You are very welcome. Now, go get yourself a celebratory drink while I take care of the paperwork." He chuckled, starting to chat with the seller.

She stood up, and moved to the kitchen where she grabbed a cola and whiskey, filling an oversized glass with double the whiskey over the soda. "Your favorite drink for me to have."

He smirked as he saw the beverage. "Well, that will do the trick." He commented as he began to complete the necessary paperwork, focusing for a few minutes until that was finished. He sat back a bit, and turned to her. "We will have the keys by the end of the week."

"Really?!" She bounced a bit in excitement.

He nodded, and smiled. "Yeah, the last inspections were finalized just a couple weeks ago."

She lifted her glass. "I'll drink to that. Woo-hoo!"

He smiled, and walked up to her. As will I." He stole a sip from her glass.

"I haven't actually gotten drunk in forever." She smiled. "Good thing we've got a four-day weekend ahead of us."

He gave her a kiss. "Then, let me help you with that." He moved to the kitchen, grabbing a bottle of whiskey so she could get properly drunk. He walked up to her, and raised the bottle up. "Cheers! To the penthouse."

"To the penthouse!" She took a large swig of alcohol before sauntering over to the television. "Let's watch campy horror movies and make a drinking game out of it."

He took a large swig from the bottle, and smiled. "Alright, and anything that they get right about Hell is a double."

"Ha! I love it." She chuckled. "After I'm good and not sober, we can have some fun."

"That was the plan." He smirked as he sat down next to her. "I want to see how much you can remember in the morning."

Sunday, July 2, 2028

Ellyria groaned on the bed, gripping her forehead. "Oh, Hell."

Zane chuckled quietly. "Been there, didn't even get a t-shirt. Do you remember anything?"

"I remember seeing like nine of you, but it was probably double vision and a duplicate." She grumbled.

He laughed at that assessment, and stood up to go make breakfast for her. "I will be back in a minute with some water for you."

She covered her face with a pillow. "Ibuprofen, too, please."

"Coming right up." He called back. He got the water and drugs, and returned to give them to her. "Here you go." He kissed her softly. "You just relax, and I will be back in a bit with food."

"You are a gentleman and a scholar." She weakly smiled before taking the pills with the water.

He left her in the room for a bit as he made breakfast for her. A secret smirk graced his features. He was excited about today. He had gotten the keys to the penthouse yesterday while she was in a drunken stupor, and he was going to surprise her with a visit. He just wanted to have some fun with it first. He just needed to get her out of bed for his plan to begin. He came back into the room about thirty minutes later with a nice big breakfast for her. He sat down next to her, and placed the tray in her lap. "Here. This should help soak up the rest of the alcohol."

"You always know exactly when to spoil me with a full English breakfast." She smiled.

"Years of practice." He smiled.

She dug in. Her headache was still there but gradually improving. By the time she'd silently finished eating, she put down her utensils. "I don't remember actually eating yesterday."

He chuckled at that. "You demanded that you didn't want to lose your, 'fun mood', so that is accurate. If you need more, just ask."

"Oh, no. I'm stuffed, but I will probably be just as hungry for lunch." She warned.

"Duly noted." He smiled. He looked her over for a moment before he decided to enact his plan. "That reminds me, we will need to go chat with the seller of the penthouse in a while. Something came up."

"Oh, no." She pouted. "What happened?"

He feigned a sigh. "Don't worry. We still own it. There was just an issue with the building. Something about things going too quickly and corners being cut in the building process." He lied smoothly.

"Dammit. I knew it was too good to be true. When will it actually be done?" She growled.

"It's looking like early next year." He replied, making a face.

She whined. "Next year?! What happened to the keys in a week? That's a huge mistake!"

"Don't worry. I am taking care of it." He told her calmingly, giving her a tight hug.

She hugged him back. "Okay. We've got a meeting in New York, then." She pulled away, heading towards the closet.

"Yeah." He replied, smirking as she walked away. She'd taken the bait hook, line, and sinker. "It should be pretty eventful, so brace yourself for anything." He took a moment to let his human form shift into place.

"So, I'm hearing, dress like a lawyer?" She asked.

He shook his head even though she couldn't see it. "No, be relaxed. I will take care of everything. Your demon is on it."

"Alright." She shrugged, coming around the corner wearing jeans and a t-shirt. "I'm ready."

"Good." He wrapped an arm around her. "Let's go get this sorted." He smiled as he led her to the door.

"Yeah, let's get the pain over with." She sighed. "Who even works on Sunday? Other than land developers that just screwed up a forty-million-dollar deal."

"Don't worry." He reassured her. "I gave them an earful."

She deflated. "Sorry. I'm sure you handled it very well."

"It's okay." He gave her a kiss. "You are just annoyed, is all. You have every right to be."

She hopped into Shelby, and closed her eyes. "If you don't mind, I think I'm going to try to sleep off the rest of this hangover on the way there."

"That is fine. I will wake you when we get there." He told her.

"Thanks." She yawned, settling in, and relaxing to the hum of the engine.

"No problem." He smirked as she slowly drifted off to sleep. He knew she would be mad at him when she found out that he'd lied. However, once she was inside the penthouse, she would forgive him near instantly. He quietly chuckled to himself. This was the first time he had lied to her. He had a feeling he could do it after the soul binding, but there was no reason to do so up until now. Why he wanted to do it in the first place, he didn't know, but he did know he wanted to give her a nice surprise. This would do the trick, so he made sure to get her there quickly and safely. He was looking forward to giving her this surprise.

Zane drove for about three and a half hours, enjoying the speed and hum of the engine. When he pulled into the underground garage, he turned to Ellyria to gently wake her up. "Hey, we are here."

She sat up, gazing blearily all about. "Hey."

He smirked, and gave her a minute to properly wake up. "Come on. We have business to attend to." He hopped out of the car, going to get the door for her.

She looked around. "Where are we, anyway?"

"At the meeting point." He lied with a smile. "We need to go up and meet them."

"Alright." She shrugged as they found a room with a bay of elevators. "This is nice." She commented. "At least, it looks like they know what they're doing."

"Yeah, it's not bad." He replied as he led her to the last elevator, and used a key to open it. He stepped aside to let her in first. "Come on. We are almost late."

Ellyria looked at the key in his hand. "They messengered over a key just for a meeting. Someone's feeling guilty."

"Yeah. They were really apologetic over the phone." He chuckled as the elevator rose. "They insisted that we do this today."

She shrugged. "With how much money you wired them, they damn well better be sorry."

He smiled, knowing she was going to be in shock when the doors opened. "Yeah, it was a pretty penny."

"I know. A disgusting number of pennies." She rolled her eyes, looking at the lack of numbers on the elevator door panel. "What level are we even going to?!"

"I think it is pretty high up there." He replied, looking up, and trying to play the fool for just a moment longer as they neared their destination.

"Now, they're just trying to make us feel bad." Ellyria rolled her eyes.

As they hit the top of the elevator shaft, Zane turned to look at her. "I don't know. I think the view may make up for it all." He commented as the doors opened to their new penthouse.

Ellyria gasped, looking at what she was seeing, and doing a double take. "Oh, my god." She whispered. "Wait a second. I thought that you couldn't lie to me you jerk!" She spun around, and gave him a good smack on the chest as fiery anger burned in her eyes.

He brushed off the swat she gave him. It was nothing to him. If she really wanted to hurt him, she could. A smile stole his lips, and he chuckled. "I realized that I could lie to you not too long after the soul binding, but had no reason to do it. That was, until they delivered the keys yesterday and you were too drunk to remember it. So, I decided to have a bit of fun. Sorry."

She looked at him with tears pooling in her eyes. "Okay." She jumped into his arms. "I like these sorts of lies."

He smiled, and held her. "Don't worry. I will keep them to a minimum." He wiped away some of her tears, going in for a kiss.

She held onto him tightly. "Well, show me around, you sneaky little demon."

He smiled, and carried her around the house, showing her the different spaces. There was more than double the amount of room here than at the house, so they had plenty of space to grow. He showed her the much larger kitchen, which he knew was going to get well used before he brought her outside to the balcony. "The view is beautiful." He commented, smiling as the wind blew her hair.

She kissed him before gazing around the city. "This is everything I dreamed it would be and more."

"Good. I'm glad you like it." He brought her back inside. "We will have to get a few things, but, thankfully, it won't take too long.

I can do most of that stuff while you are at work as long as you don't mind me leaving you be for a few days."

"That's fine. Things have been boring lately." She sighed. "You can take time to do whatever we need." She leaned into him.

"You will probably want to ward the place first." He suggested.

"Of course, I will. I don't want the Vatican to sense anything that comes out of here." She replied.

"Then, it looks like we have a busy week ahead of us." He gave her a hug.

She groaned a little in frustration. "I have a busy three days, starting now. I still have to work Wednesday through Friday." She summoned her wand, and started to draw runes along the walls.

He watched her for a moment as she started to work. "I can't wait to move in. It has been too many years in the making."

She grinned at his excitement, growing quiet for a while as she went about her task. As she was finishing the last rune, she told him, "I'm going to start channeling now."

"Go for it." He replied, leaving her to it. He wanted to figure out where everything would go. "I am going to see where the computers are going."

She smiled, "you do that." She rubbed her hands together, and summoned her magics, touching the first and last runes, and channeling as much of her energy as she could into the wards.

Zane came back a little while later with a few sheets of paper in hand. A quick glance over the pages was all it took to notice diagrams of the locations of their furniture and other items. "Okay, I have a good idea of where everything is going. I just need to put a sigil here, and I can jump back and forth to make the moving go smoothly."

"I should be able to ley walk safely between places, too." She told him as she continued to focus on the magic. "Though, that takes more energy than warding."

"You just focus on doing your work. As long as I have the sigil, it is like walking through a door for me." He told her. "It takes almost no energy."

"I'm so jealous. Do what you need to do. I'll keep this up."

He smiled, and kissed her. "I will." He walked into the master bedroom, and began to draw the demonic glyph that would allow him to travel the vast distance in mere moments.

Ellyria concentrated until she found her power waning about two hours later. She reached deeply, and used as much ley energy as she could get before eventually calling it for the night as she panted, leaning against the wall. "Might've overdone it." She murmured to herself.

Zane walked up to her, and shook his head. "Of course, you did." He sighed, pulling her into his arms. "You got excited to have the place, so you wanted it done sooner rather than later."

"It's not even done yet." She sighed, leaning into him. "They still need more."

"We can worry about it tomorrow." He told her as he walked her into the elevator, pressing the button for the garage. "Let's get you to the house so that you can get some rest."

"I don't want to leave." She complained.

"I know." He replied, holding her a little tighter. "But, you will complain more if you sleep like garbage." He explained, knowing her too well.

She closed her eyes, feeling the elevator come to a stop. "Fine. There's always tomorrow."

"Of course." He smiled. "Tomorrow, I will be able to go back and forth. It will make getting here faster." He got her into her seat, and walked around to his.

She looked over at him. "I'm fond of the private elevator. I don't have to deal with people after a long day."

"It is nice." He nodded in agreement, and rested a hand on her leg.

Her mind was whirling as she realized that she finally had the penthouse she'd wanted for so long. "I've got to start talking with Steve and Daniel about the New York office." She leaned into him, and complained. "I have done nothing but sleep today."

"There is nothing wrong with that." He assured her. "You had a long day and weekend."

"I'm sure that I had fun." She giggled. "Even if I don't remember it."

He gave her a soft smile. "Well, we will try to redo it at a different date. Then, you can fully remember it."

"I look forward to it." She yawned. "I'm exhausted."

"You used too much magic. Of course, you are." He told her quietly. "Get some sleep. I will get you home safely."

She nodded. "Goodnight, Zane." She whispered as her head rested on his shoulder.

He smiled as she rested against him. "Sleep well."

ARTICLE XI

Monday, December 24, 2029

Winter vacation started for Ellyria after the end of a long workday. After a romantic dinner for two, things were getting heated. Caught up in the moment with Zane, she was ready to enjoy her first vacation in far too long. As Zane was leading her towards the bedroom, she opened her eyes to look up at him, and froze. Something she saw out of the corner of her eye caught her attention. "Zane! Behind you!" She shrieked.

Zane turned to see where she was looking. He looked at the intruder and froze in place. "M- my king?"

Lucifer lounged idly on the couch of the living room, looking far more human than the last time they saw him. He assessed the situation, and smirked at the two of them. "Oh, don't mind me. Continue as you were. I can wait until you are finished."

Ellyria looked at Zane, unsure of what to say or do and starting to turn bright red with embarrassment.

Zangrunath looked at Lucifer and, then, towards Ellyria who was thoroughly embarrassed. He felt rage build within him, but knew there was nothing he could do about it given who was on the couch. He stepped in front of Ellyria to help cover her up. "We were just-" His lips couldn't finish the lie.

"Oh, really?" Lucifer asked with a grin. "Because that looked like the beginning of the fun." He chuckled at his general.

Ellyria hastily covered up. "You choose now of all times to lie?" She asked Zangrunath before turning to the Dark Prince. "It was the beginning of my first vacation in a very long time." She sighed in frustration.

"I figured as much." He shrugged, looking at Ellyria. "You don't have to cover up. Be comfortable around me. I am, after all, the Devil. I work with Lust herself. There is nothing I haven't seen before." He chuckled, trying to lighten the mood.

Ellyria sighed. "I think I'm good like this."

"Do you feel more comfortable?" He asked with a knowing smile.

"I would feel better returning to where I was about two minutes before you appeared, but I'm currently about as comfortable as I'm going to get at the moment." She blurted.

He shrugged again. "As long as you are relaxed." He turned to look at Zangrunath. "What about you? Comfy?"

"Pissed." Zane told him honestly.

"Why is being comfortable important? This is clearly not a social visit." Ellyria interrupted.

Lucifer gazed at her, and nodded. "You are a smart one." He sat upright. "I want you to be comfortable because I find that all job opportunities should be as relaxed and laid back as possible." He smirked at the pair, completely in control of the situation at hand.

Ellyria shook her head, and tiredly took a seat on the couch, looking at Zangrunath. "Job opportunities." She murmured with a whirling mind.

"Well, this is more of a promotion for Zangrunath, assuming you can do it." He replied, glancing at his demon with palpable amusement.

"A promotion?" Zane asked in confusion.

"To put it simply, one of your superiors thought it would be *funny* to try besting ol' Lucy, and decided to go rogue." He chuckled for a moment before his face became stern. An aura of danger starting to grow around him. "So, I want the two of you to go destroy him so thoroughly that even all of God's angels couldn't put him back together again."

Ellyria went pale at the look on the face of the Devil himself. He was far too close for comfort; she gulped as fear washed over her, turning to Zane. "What do you want to do?"

Zane stared at the King of Hell, and sighed deeply. "I don't think we have much of a choice in the matter."

"You always have a choice." She told him seriously. "I guess I shouldn't beat around the bush. What do you want out of this? We're doing it."

"I get a promotion, but what I want is to spend time with you." He replied, gesturing to the room. "You are what I want." He told her honestly.

"Do I need to write a contract for that or are you going to handle it?" Ellyria asked Lucifer, knowing that her contract with the Devil already covered her own lifetime.

He waved a hand. "That will be easy enough."

Ellyria nodded, taking a breath, and tapping the leys. Her eyes turned black, and her skin started to become a more demonic red. "Where was his last known location?"

He raised an eyebrow at the changes he saw in the other fallen angel. "Brazil." His response quick and factual.

She searched the leys, sensing for any oddities. "Well, he's not there anymore." She commented before feeling a blip of magic even farther off. Her eyes opened. "I think that was Argentina." She blinked several times as the odd demonic changes slowly reverted. She saw the baffled look on the Devil's face. She sighed, trying not to roll her eyes. "There's not much information that we can find on fallen angels. I can't control the back and forth the same as you and others since I'm only half. Instead, for me, it comes out when I use strong magic."

"Clearly." Lucifer chuckled. "I just don't understand why you don't use it all the time. You would be quite formidable if you did."

Ellyria glanced at Zangrunath. "If I wanted to end the world, I could. It wouldn't be difficult. I'd much rather watch the light fade from people's eyes when they realize that they didn't read the fine print."

He hummed. "I think I can understand that." The Dark Prince nodded. "I prefer the world the way it is, so thank you for not doing that. Still, don't be afraid to stretch your wings a bit." He chuckled.

Ellyria shivered as the memories of her one experience attempting to fly with her spectral wings washed through her mind. "Been there. Done that. I don't think I like to fly that way. I'll settle for ley walking."

"Well, it was worth the shot. Thank you for doing this for me. I would do it myself, but, much like yourself, the earth doesn't like it when I have fun." He barked a laugh, and quickly calmed himself. His eyes pierced into them. "Feel free to go back to your fun. Just be sure to get that done for me soon. Ta-ta for now." With those final words and a wave goodbye, he vanished into the air, nowhere to be found.

"I suffer from severe word vomit around that being." She sighed.

Zangrunath nodded, and sighed. "He has that effect on mortals. They want to express their deepest desires in front of him."

"Does it ever go away? In Hell, maybe?" She asked.

He shrugged. "I tried to lie to him there, but, between that ability and the code, he is exceptionally good at seeing through deceit. I think it is his divinity."

She nodded, thinking about his words. She consistently forgot about the demon code, which was a problem. She needed to think about that first and foremost when dealing with demons and the Devil. It was a bad habit that she needed to break sooner rather than later. "That would make sense. Huh." She paused even more thoughtfully. "I never really considered which abilities were from my father and from my mother. I can obviously combine them, so I'm not sure which is part of my divinity or not."

He waved a hand, looking and sounding a little annoyed. "Well, whatever it is, have fun with it."

"Are you okay?" She asked.

"You are lucky." He told her seriously. "You have the powers of both humans and angels. I just have the borrowed powers that come with being a demon. I will never get that in my entire eternity. That is what you and the Prince of Darkness have in common." He gestured to where Lucifer had been sitting.

"Why couldn't you?" She asked out of nowhere. "We share a soul."

He shook his head. "That would break the code. Only a person born of divinity can wield those powers. I wasn't born with them."

She conjured a ball of magic that glowed in her hand, and carefully placed it in his. "I didn't mean the divine powers."

"That is just magic." He told her as she placed the ball in his hands. "It's like holding a candle to an inferno."

She sighed, looking down, and feeling like she was somehow taking something that he wanted away from him. She wanted to give that to him. She shuffled off to their bedroom, feeling less-than. He'd never rebuffed anything she'd suggested quite so hard before. "I think I'm going to sleep before we go to Argentina."

He nodded, and looked around the room. "Yeah, I will get this flight arranged, and clean this place up while you sleep." He sighed as he began to clean the room up after the visit. "Sleep well."

"Thanks." She whispered, heading into the bedroom, and hearing the door click quietly behind her. She slid down the wood there. "I just want you to be happy with your footing. Whatever it takes." She mumbled before crawling into bed. "Count on the Devil himself to turn a vacation into work and cause our first fight."

As Ellyria went to bed, Zane cleaned up before he sat at the computer. Why did Lucifer have to show up? He had planned a fun vacation for Ellyria, and, in less than an hour, the Prince of Darkness had ruined it.

He thought about the disagreement; he didn't mean to be mad at her. It was mere jealousy. Envy. It was difficult not to be jealous of something you couldn't have, and he didn't want to think about what would happen if he ever did get his hands on the kind of destructive power Ellyria had. Some things shouldn't happen, and this was one of those things. He shook the thought from his head, and started to book the flight.

Hopefully, tearing the rogue general into a fine mince would help him clear his head.

Tuesday, December 25, 2029

Zane awoke Ellyria early in the morning. She looked outside, and it was still dark enough to see the city lights. She leaned in for a kiss, but he didn't move the rest of the way in to join her. She sighed. "I'm assuming you probably packed our bags?"

"Yeah." He nodded. "We will need to get going here soon in order to hopefully keep up with this one." He told her simply.

She got up, and changed clothes. "I'll be ready in five."

He nodded, heading to the kitchen. He quickly made her a sandwich to eat on the way to the airport. He handed it to her as she came out of the bedroom, and led her to the door. "Alright, let's get going."

She took the food, and followed. "This feels like those first days of college." She commented, looking at him. She frowned when he didn't look back.

"How so?" He asked, moving by muscle memory at this point.

She looked at him, and shook her head. "No reason." She replied, but, internally, she remembered dancing around him and their feelings. She thought that the fly by night breakfasts and his cool attitude were a thing of the past. Clearly not.

Zane led them to Shelby; he got in, and started her up. He waited for Ellyria to get in and get herself situated before he began to drive them to the airport. Luckily, the streets were relatively clear at this time of night, and he was able to rev the engine a bit, weaving between the other, much slower, vehicles.

Ellyria finished her simple meal, and looked at him. She felt her heart sink, but her gut clenched tightly in anger as well. "Look at me, Zangrunath." She demanded.

He turned his head to look at her and, then, back to the road quickly to make sure they were safe, "what?" He asked, sounding impassive.

"What's wrong with you? I know there's a lot going on, but you haven't looked at me. You didn't kiss me good morning, and you didn't open the door for me." She snarled like a demon. "This is stupid. Dammit all to Hell. I don't care about anything else. I love you, and I'm not going to let this screw up what we have."

Zangrunath continued to drive, letting out a sigh. "I love you, too. I do." He began, glancing over at her.

"But," she interrupted, "you were about to say but."

"But," he added with a growl, putting more emphasis on the word. "I am jealous of you. Alright?" He sighed deeply as he drove, shaking his head like he was trying to forget about the last few hours entirely. "I just want to get this over with so that we can go home and be together. Okay?" He asked.

Ellyria took his hand. "I'm sorry." She whispered in a watery voice. "If it's any consolation, I don't want power or standing or any of it. I just want you. You can have it. All of it and me."

"Don't be sorry. I know you don't want any of it. You would have preferred to have a normal life over all of this." He responded, knowing that to be true. "I want you, but I can't have that power you have. If I were to have it," he trailed off. His mind raced before he shook his head again. "It would be better if I didn't." He finished, leaving the details out. It was best if he left

215

that as vague as possible. He didn't want to scare her with the darkest parts of him that Hell had brought to the forefront.

She squeezed his hand, curious but too emotional and exhausted to pursue the lead. "I would make every single mistake and choice again if it meant that I could be with you." She stroked the back of his hand with her fingers. "Use me as a tool if you need to. If I'm at your side, I don't care."

He pulled her hand to his lips, and gave it a kiss. "I would never use you like that. Given the ritual and your deal, it should be the other way around." He chuckled mirthlessly, looking into her eyes. "I would go through Hell several times over if it meant that I get to end up beside you." He finally smiled at her.

"Mine." She whispered to him.

He squeezed her hand. "Mine."

They arrived at the hangar, and she stole a kiss from him. "I love you, Zangrunath." She whispered to him before they hopped out of Shelby. "Let's go get you a promotion to lead general or whatever." She hummed. "What would that make you?"

"Well, I won't be one of the seven main generals, but I would be right under one. So, it would be like a human lieutenant." He explained as they got onto the plane.

"But, the guy we're after is one of those generals. Isn't he?" She asked, genuinely curious. Who were they going after? Was it a good or a bad thing that the Devil was vague? She shivered as the realization struck. He didn't strike her as the type to accidentally omit something; he was purposely vague.

"If he were, we would have much bigger concerns. We would need more help than just the two of us if that were the case." He surmised.

She thought about his words. "I thought that your boss said someone above you needed handling. I'm confused."

"Yes, but he never said which one." He sighed "There is a hierarchy of who runs what. There is Lucifer at the top, and he has seven demons under him who oversee everything. They rival him in power, and he also didn't say who decided to tick him off. Fuck." He groaned, suddenly having the same realization that she had moments before.

"That's what I thought." She nodded. "We'll figure it out. You're strong. I'm strong. Together, we could end the world. We can beat one demon."

"I admire your enthusiasm. We probably will, but it is probably going to hurt." He nodded, and gave her a soft smile before he sighed deeply, taking his seat on the plane.

She gave him a peck on the cheek. "It's not so much enthusiasm as understanding that we're kinda screwed one way or the other. I expect pain."

"There will be," he frowned, "but I will try to keep it to a minimum."

"As long as I have it made up to me after this is done, I'll be fine." She leaned into him, taking his hand. "I will help any way I can to make this go well for you."

He leaned his head on her. "Thank you. The sooner we get this done, the sooner I can make it up to you. So much for my gift to you." He sighed.

"I know. It was a nice vacation idea." She pouted.

He shook his head. "No, I actually got you something. I was going to give it to you later today since you like this day for gifts so much." He told her with a serious expression that turned into a soft smile. "I just never had the chance to give it to you."

"I thought today was just another stupid Pagan holiday that the Christians converted when they took over." She chuckled as she used his words.

"Oh, it is," he chuckled, "but I still wanted to get you something."

"You're so sweet." She smiled, kissing him. "I got you something, too."

He put an arm around her, and rubbed her shoulder. "Then, when we are done with this, we can exchange them."

"I look forward to it." She closed her eyes, and leaned her head on his shoulder. "I'm going to get some more rest. Seems like the crazy will kick into gear as soon as we land."

He nodded. "You do that. We will be going until he is put down when we get there, so do your best to be at one hundred percent."

She nodded. "Nothing quite like demon slaying on Christmas."

"Paint the halls with blood and gore." He sang.

"Grandma got sacrificed in a blood pact." She sang back tiredly.

He chuckled, and gave her a kiss on the forehead. "Sleep well. Love you."

"Darling." She murmured before falling asleep.

Zane gently held Ellyria's hand as she rested. His mind focusing on the task ahead for a while, but turning back to the woman beside him. He was surprised by her. They had disagreed before, but, today, she had deescalated him from a fit of jealous rage. This was a new feeling to him. He had never had somebody that could do something such as that before, proving, yet again, that his witch was special. He knew that he would protect her with everything that he had in him now and forever.

Several hours later, Ellyria ate a bland meal of airplane snacks. It wasn't great, but it was something. She would need to have fuel in her system for whatever would happen tonight. The pilot's bell rang to inform them that it was five in the afternoon local time. She looked at Zane. "Demon hunting after dark." She commented.

Zane nodded. "I would much rather be doing this during the day, but we will work with what we have." He looked out over the city of Buenos Aires, trying to see any sign of the demon as they descended, and murmured, "where are you?"

"Do you want me to check again? It's been a few hours." She asked.

"Yes, please. I don't want him sneaking up on us." He responded.

She nodded, and tapped the leys. "He's heading north by northwest." She told him. "Feels like there's something big that way. Probably a ley convergence like Stonehenge."

"He is probably trying to get stronger, then." He growled. "We need to cut him off before he gets there."

"We can do that. I can still ley walk. Honestly, I don't know why we didn't come that way in the first place, but you were already chartering the plane." She shrugged. Her eyes were still black, and her skin started to change colors. "I'm just going to take the big guy's advice and keep it going for now."

"Good." He nodded as the plane landed. "I chose this because you needed the rest. We were not going to go into this halfcocked and tired."

Ellyria nodded. "It's fine. We've got the money anyway." She unbuckled her seatbelt, and sat up. "Let's do this."

Zangrunath smiled, and turned into his demonic self. A growl escaped his lips. "Let's." He opened the door to the plane, and picked Ellyria up, shrouding them in mist. He started flying in the direction she had indicated a few moments ago.

Ellyria continued to concentrate, pointing for him like a dowsing rod. "At least, I'm helpful on this adventure." She grumbled.

"You are always helpful." He smiled. "As long as you are by my side, you are helping."

She kissed his cheek, suddenly pointing directly west. "Okay, that was weird. He, like, jumped."

He quickly veered in the direction she pointed. "I don't know how he did that. He might have used a sigil to go between points."

"You're the expert." She shrugged. "You like to keep all the demonic secrets close to your chest even though I'll probably be like you one day."

"I don't do it on purpose. It is out of habit. Mortals aren't supposed to know how we operate. You are the exception because we are bound. When this is done, I promise I will explain it to you." He explained, rubbing her back soothingly.

"Thank you." She smiled, leaning into him. "It would be nice to know what I'm in for besides reading about the whole making demons thing." She shivered.

He nodded. "I won't be able to help with that. The process is designed to weed out the weak and make sure the strong thrive. Hell thrives on strength."

She nodded. "I get it. It's just a lot of blood."

"You will be fine. You are strong. I know you will become a powerful demon." He smiled.

"I will." She replied more confidently. "Either way, I'll be yours forever." She pointed suddenly due north. "Okay. He's gotta be screwing with us."

He growled, changing directions. "He better not. This needs to be over and done quickly."

Ellyria sighed. "I can expedite by ley walking if you want."

Zangrunath thought it over, and sighed. "Let's do it. I don't really want to, but I want this over with. I just have a bad feeling."

Ellyria nodded, understanding how he was feeling completely. "I would prefer to be on the ground for this, then."

He nodded, and flew towards the ground, setting her down gently as he landed. "Let's get this done."

Ellyria looked at the setting sun. "Yeah. Let's finish this before it's too dark for me to see the fight." She took his hand, concentrating hard before a flash of light and a jerking motion brought them into the center of a clearing. She looked around for a second. Her gut sank. Her eyes met Zane's before she pushed him out of the circle they'd jumped into with a wave of magic. "Get out!" She screamed. "It's a trap!"

Zangrunath flew backwards out of the circle, seeing a magical barrier quickly enclose Ellyria inside. He nearly toppled backwards before he caught himself and landed square. His eyes darted around the clearing, checking for any danger before he ran up to the wall of force and began to pound against it. "Elly!" He yelled.

Ellyria ran up to the wall, and found it to be solid. Her eyes panicked. "Zangrunath." She murmured to him. "It's in my book. This circle. It's a magic siphon." She dropped to her knees as she felt magic start to slowly leave her. Her eyes flickered between black and her normal brown.

"Fuck!" He shouted. His eyes darted around for the demon they were after. "Where are you? You cowardly excuse for a demon!"

There was a long moment of silence before a flash of light appeared next to Zangrunath. "I am right here." The ex-general grinned as he drove his fist into Zangrunath's face, throwing him several feet away from the circle. He licked the demonic black blood from his hand, and chuckled. "I was expecting something stronger, but," he paused, gazing at Ellyria. He licked his lips. "You are the reason for him being here, aren't you?"

Ellyria stepped back. She was disgusted by this unknown demon, deciding that engaging with him wasn't worth the little time or energy that she had. Instead, she found herself running to the center of the circle. She looked all about before wrenching as much energy from the earth as possible. The leys came to her aid, and she felt a surge of power. She stomped, and the wall around her flashed with bright light. She did it again before she realized that this one was already weaker. She glanced off to where Zangrunath landed. She bit her lip. "I love you." She whispered, pouring as much of her magic as possible into him as fast as she could.

Zangrunath felt his wound close instantly, and his gaze focused on Ellyria. "No." His eyes wide as he momentarily lost sense of his usual calculating nature, dipping into his wrathful side. He shot towards the demon. Now that he'd seen their enemy, he shouted to get the demon's attention. "Sathanas, let her go!" His arms turned into blades, and he unleashed a flourish towards the general.

Sathanas took the attacks with practiced ease. They were nothing but flesh wounds against his power. He began to chuckle as he felt the wounds close faster than Zangrunath could make them. A Cheshire smile dominated his lips as he gained the upper hand. Sathanas raised a foot, and kicked Zangrunath square in the chest, creating distance between them. He heard bones cracking in the other demon's chest as he turned towards Ellyria. "No." He told the pair. "I want the power to overthrow Lucifer. She has it. I'm taking it, annihilation ritual or not." He started to laugh maniacally.

Ellyria fell to the ground in pain as Zangrunath's ribs cracked. "Ah!" She screamed. By some miracle, she was still conscious enough to send him the magic he needed to heal the wounds and then some. She could feel the magic of the leys starting to weaken. She had taken a lot. She saw the other demon, and reached out a hand, concentrating hard between sending Zangrunath power and using it. Blood came from her ears as she tried to tear him to shreds with her power; a small wisp of matter sloughing off starting at his horn.

Sathanas noticed Ellyria, and growled. He made a quick series of hand motions, sending spikes from the ground into her legs in a manner eerily similar to how she'd killed Larry years previous. "You can stop that. Just let me take the power already. It will be easier on the both of us if you just give in." he smirked.

Zangrunath felt the pain that shot through his legs, and released a roar. His wings became wreathed in flames. He blazed towards the target of his wrath. "You are going to die!" He yelled, grabbing Sathanas by the arm, and ripping it off in one quick fluid motion. Now that the other demon was somewhat disarmed, he took the opportunity to stab him several times.

Ellyria screamed in agony. Her focus on everything external faded. She cut the spikes from her with two swift hand motions, and healed herself, gasping in pain. Her breaths came heavily; her movements growing sluggish. She curled up, and let out a sob before giving Zangrunath everything she normally held back from using. Her magic was running out, and, these things, she couldn't let the other demon have. Her energy manipulation and matter creation. The connection to the leys. She felt her heart skip a beat as it was all torn from her. She choked, and sputtered.

Sathanas sneered at Ellyria, and felt that she was all but spent. He could feel power coursing through him. A smirk pulled at his lips before his gaze met Zangrunath's. "And, so it is done." He laughed as he waved a hand, sending several spikes shooting up and through Ellyria's chest and torso.

Zangrunath released a strangled noise of loss and heartbreak, not unlike a whimper, though it could hardly be described as that. He watched helplessly as he felt the moment Ellyria died. He died countless times before, but, this time, was a million times more painful than anything he had ever experienced. He fell to his knees, and wailed in grief, feeling the other half to his soul leave this plane. He held his head in his hands for all but a moment, and, in that moment, something snapped inside of him. He glared at Sathanas, standing up, and starting to slowly stalk towards him. "You are dead." His voice rumbled in a low timbre as he instinctively used Ellyria's powers to create armor of pure holy light around himself.

Sathanas froze as he noticed golden tears falling from Zangrunath's eyes. They flowed upwards, and formed what looked like a shattered halo above his head. He shook his head slowly as he began to back away. "N- no. No demon should be able to wield the powers of divinity. That breaks the code." He stammered.

"Fuck the code." Zangrunath growled, creating a greatsword of light in his hand. "I am going to eviscerate you and spread your atoms across space time. To Hell with the repercussions!" He yelled to the Heavens as he instantly appeared next to Sathanas, and swung the sword with practiced precision. The strike knocked

Sathanas back into the barrier, shattering it as he flew through the force field.

Sathanas tried to cast a spell, but found that nothing happened. His eyes went wide as he saw Zane appear next to him again, striking him into the ground. Thanks to the massive amount of power being used and their durable demonic bodies, a massive crater started to form where the battle raged on with Sathanas at the bottom of the growing pit. He wearily attempted to stand up. The magic he'd taken from Ellyria already waning from him thanks to the injuries he'd sustained. He got to a knee before Zangrunath jumped onto his back, and a cracking noise rang out through the clearing. "Please, no." He begged, trying vainly to get away.

Reacting quickly, Zangrunath's hand moved at an impossibly fast rate. Above them, what looked like miniature black holes appeared. Small stars formed around them. Zane drove the sword through the base of Sathanas's spine, and wrenched his head back by the hair. He turned the body to look him in the eyes. A symphony of sickening squelching sounds rang out in the moments before Zane ended his existence. "I have been around for over three thousand years, and, in that time, I have done countless rituals. None of which ended like this." He paused as tears welled up into his eyes again. "Then, you decided to overthrow Lucifer himself, break the code, steal Ellyria's power," his voice broke. "The woman I love! You killed her right in front of my eyes." He began yelling only to grow deadly quiet to the point that he was leaning forward to snarl the words directly into Sathanas's ear. The earth below them started to rumble as he raged. "I sentence you to death. No amount of magic, holy or otherwise, is bringing you back!"

Zangrunath quickly and violently tore Sathanas into small pieces. He completed the task with practiced ease, as if he were ritualistically dismembering the demon for the millionth time in his life. With each chunk of rent flesh, he hurled the pieces of Sathanas into the inky black voids that hovered above them. When there was nothing left of the demon to destroy, he stood up. His back arched as he cried to the Heavens at the loss of his Ellyria.

Ellyria's eyes opened quickly. She breathed easily. Looking around, she found the room unfamiliar but comfortable. Art decorated the walls, and the room was made up in an elegant Victorian style. She sat up slowly, and jumped when she saw the familiar form of Lucifer. "Ah, shit." She groaned.

Lucifer sat at a desk good distance away from her. He leaned back in his chair, turning to gaze at her. His usual unruffled expression was missing. Instead, he looked annoyed and dismayed almost beyond recognition. He barely looked at Ellyria, and his hand moved to cover his face. "Calm down. I already have enough to deal with after this. I don't need anything from you right now. He waved a hand at her flippantly as he muffled a groan.

"I'm just realizing that, even though I died before my deal was done, I still went to Hell." She commented. "I think. Honestly, I expected tormented souls, fire, and brimstone. This ain't bad."

"The souls wouldn't shut up." He sighed, sitting up slightly to look at her. "As for this," he gestured to the room, and shrugged, "it is what I desired. So, I made it be. Then, there is your deal-" The King of Hell trailed off. Even he didn't want to bring up the failure of epic proportions.

"Oh." She covered her face, and groaned loudly. "I worded that amendment explicitly for a reason, but didn't take unnatural death into account. Crud."

"Yes, quite." He nodded. His eyes gazed at her and through her, seemingly piercing through her soul. "Not to mention the annihilation ritual that had yet to be completed. Both of which I messed up by sending you on a suicide mission without knowing what he'd done."

She nodded, feeling her magic missing. It was with Zane. Zane who wasn't here with her. She grew still. "Dammit." She growled, feeling weak.

Lucifer sighed, and stood up. "Because of my mistake of epic proportions, congratulations! You get to go back." He announced, walking up to her with an unreadable expression in his eyes.

She stood up in turn, staring back into his dark, and mildly terrifying, eyes. She gulped. "I'm not staying?"

"No, not yet." He replied, gazing down his nose at her as if inspecting something that he intended to purchase or destroy. "You still have a ritual to finish, and I need to deal with the aftermath of what your other half just did." He shook his head. "My brother is never going to let me live this down."

"W- what did Zangrunath do?" She stuttered, panicking, and completely ignoring his last sentence. "Is he okay?"

"Oh, he is perfectly fine." He told her with a dark chuckle. It was obvious that his annoyance was once again growing quickly. "He just used your powers to temporarily become one of the four horsemen of the apocalypse in order to make Sathanas no longer exist." He stared blankly at the wall behind her for a moment, processing his own words. "He did get the job done, though." He added, trying to look at this disaster with the thinnest of silver linings.

Ellyria closed her eyes tightly, and let out a sound of frustration. "I usually stop before I get to that point."

"Thank you for that." He told her with a nod. "Though Zangrunath could control what he was doing, I doubt he could've stopped himself. Demons don't normally fall in love, so they tend to go overboard when they see the person they are bound to die in front of them." He sighed, looking her over with that assessing gaze again. "Go up there and take your powers back, please. I need to go have a chat with the council."

Ellyria opened her lips to respond, to ask more questions. She always had more questions. Instead, she awoke in a great deal of pain. She felt blood trailing down her skin. She blinked several times, gazing up at Zangrunath, coughing. "Zane." She whispered weakly as her heart beat steadily.

Zangrunath jumped as he heard Ellyria's voice and felt her body begin to move again. He pulled away, seeing her wounds start to heal. He looked at her face when he heard his name. Pulling her against his chest, he held her, crying as he did so. "Elly."

"Not so tight. Everything hurts." She mumbled, groaning. "Boss man sent me back."

He chuckled at her words, and loosened his grip. He didn't want to hurt her more than she already was. "I thought I lost you forever." He sniffled.

She shook her head. "Should've checked Hell before you got that far."

He gave her a kiss. "I wasn't sure I could find you." He replied, starting to wipe away his tears. "I never failed to protect someone, so I thought," he trailed off.

She noticed the physical changes about him that her magic created. Somehow, they made him more beautiful to her. "Shh." She wiped away a golden tear. "We. Are. One." She leaned into him, wanting to sympathetically cry just at the look of him even though she knew it would just make matters worse to start crying herself. "Can I get my magic back?"

He nodded, and gently placed a hand on her chest, channeling her magic back into her. "That power; I shouldn't have used it. It wasn't mine to use. I'm sorry."

"I wanted you to use it." She told him, breathing a little easier, now. "I just normally stop before I get that far."

"I know. That is why you should have these. Seeing you," he didn't finish that sentence, but he continued with the rest of his thoughts. "Made me snap." He told her honestly. "I didn't care what happened as long as he died."

She finally started to cry in pain and emotional anguish. "Can we sleep, please? I'm exhausted."

He felt a few tears fall, and nodded, knowing exactly how she felt. "Yeah, let's go to the plane and sleep." He told her, starting to fly towards the airport, leaving the devastation he caused behind them.

"No." She shook her head. "I ley walked us to Chile. Just find a hotel. I don't care."

"Okay." He replied, giving her a kiss. "That is fine by me." At her order, thanks to demonic magic, he instantly learned the location of the nearest city, flying her towards where his instinct directed him. He kept looking down at her, making sure that she was okay. He watched as Ellyria's eyes closed, and she eventually drifted to sleep in his arms, snoring lightly. Zangrunath smiled down at her. He stroked her hair comfortingly as he flew. He arrived at a hotel in short order, waving a hand to disguise them with demon magic, and rented them a room. He brought Ellyria to the room, and closed the door behind them. The full force of both his and her exhaustion hit him. He laid down in bed, holding her in his arms as he promptly passed out.

ARTICLE XII

Ellyria took all but a second to realize she didn't recognize the room she was in. Where was she? She groaned in pain. She did feel the form of her demon beside her, and she turned to look at him. "Zane?"

Zane stirred awake when he heard Elly's voice. "Yes?" He asked.

"Where are we?" She asked. Her stomach growled ravenously.

"A hotel in Chile." He told her as he let go of her. "You asked me to fly somewhere close instead of heading back to the plane."

She got out of bed, and ran to the bathroom, returning a minute later wearing freshly repaired clothing. "The poor pilot needed a break, too."

He let out a sigh. "We pay him enough so that he doesn't mind working a holiday. He wouldn't mind."

She slid into his arms, holding him close. "Regardless, I didn't want to fly."

"I don't blame you." He responded, holding her in kind. He groaned. "I am still sore after that."

She nodded, and tried not to cry at how much it hurt to breathe deeply. "We are sore. Let's just get room service and relax until we're better. I don't think I can do much more magic than I already used to fix my shirt today, but I think I have a plan to get home."

Zangrunath nodded. "I am fine with that. I don't really want to go anywhere right now." He rolled over, grabbing his cell phone. "I will let the pilot know that he can head back whenever."

"Sounds good." She lounged on the bed. "I want to visit as many countries as we can on the way back home."

"I will never say no to that." He smirked knowingly, and dialed the pilot before ordering room service for her.

Ellyria waited for Zane to be off the phone before she spoke again. "Now you know firsthand that I can end the world. Would've been kind of cool to see the fireworks."

Zane rested next to her, and looked into her eyes. "I never doubted that for a second. Though, you might be able to see the aftermath." He chuckled.

"Well, it's either scorched earth or a crater." She commented.

"Yes." He deadpanned. "Wasn't really thinking. Just kind of did."

"I don't need to see it, then. I'll just look it up next time one of the online satellite maps refreshes." She giggled.

"Or check the news." He laughed before his countenance changed. He sighed, and wrapped an arm around her. "I don't want to lose you again."

She cuddled into his chest. "You can't." She responded. "My contract amendment screwed the Devil over."

He looked into her eyes. A chuckle bubbled up in his chest before spilling into a fit of laughter. "Of course, you would beat the Devil at his own game." He suddenly gripped his side from laughing so hard. "Ouch."

"I know. I feel it, too." She gripped her side as well, and groaned. She paused before adding, "you've got me like this for the rest of my natural life. I used the good words." She smirked.

He leaned in to give her a much-needed kiss. "I wouldn't change it for a second."

A knock came from the door. "Room service!" A voice called to them.

Zane sighed, and stood up. He walked to the door, and answered it, quickly getting the food from the man. He shut the door behind him. He came back to bed a moment later, and sat down next to her, offering a tray of food. "Here you go. Sorry it's not my cooking."

She took the plate, and started to shovel the meal into her mouth. "Too hungry to care."

He smirked, watching her eat for a moment as he relaxed. "That's okay."

A few minutes later, Ellyria finished her meal, and laid down on the bed beside Zangrunath. "I love you." She whispered.

He smirked, and turned into his demonic form. He wrapped his tail around her waist, pulling her close to him. "I love you."

Thursday, January 3, 2030

Ellyria and Zangrunath held hands, walking the streets of Mexico City. They idly chatted until they happened across a bar that seemed strangely out of place. Zangrunath stopped, assessing the building with confusion and wonder. "That doesn't seem right." He commented.

She glanced over at the building, and did a double take. She reached out a hand, feeling the energies there. "Huh." She hummed. "It feels magical."

"Yeah, but that wasn't what drew me to it." He responded, looking at her instead of the building. "It was the name."

"Dilrith." She whispered. "That's not Spanish."

"No, it is closer to the Spanglish version of demonic." He told her seriously. "It means demon slayer."

She looked up at Zane. "Hard pass, then? Though, I admit that I'm curious."

He chuckled. "Oh, no. We are checking this out." He smiled, and led the way to the entrance. "I doubt that they have any idea of what the name means."

"Doubtful." She deadpanned. "I would bet on it."

"You're on, and the usual wager?" He asked with a smile.

She thought for a minute. "Double it."

He chuckled, and nodded, holding out his hand as they entered the bar. "Deal."

She shook on it. "Agreed."

As the two entered the building, they saw license plates from across the globe decorating the walls. There were a few patrons idly chatting. A country song came to an end, and rock music picked up afterwards. At the back corner of the room, a large man stood stoically in all black clothing, eyes gazing around the bar for any signs of trouble.

Over at the bar, a middle-aged gentleman making drinks wore a surprisingly well tailored outfit despite their surroundings. The slacks were designer, and the button up might not have been, but the silk tie instantly negated the thought that anything he wore was cheap. "Hello." The man greeted the couple who entered with a thick European accent without looking up from his workstation. He had medium brown hair that could have either been blonder or darker when he was younger, but patches of white there now made it difficult to tell. It was just barely long enough to pull into a small tail at the base of his neck and slicked back. His goatee made him look even more distinguished. He finished wiping a spot on the counter, and looked up, revealing icy blue eyes.

Zane looked at the man for all but a second. "Fuck." He swore, knowing instantly who was tending the bar.

"What?" Ellyria instantly tensed at Zangrunath's reaction.

He gazed at the man for a moment longer, and the bartender gave him a curious look in return. He turned his attention to Ellyria for a moment to address her question, but he never turned his body away from the man behind the bar, keeping him in his sights in the corner of his eye. "Have you ever heard a ghost story and thought to yourself that there is no way that could ever happen?" He asked, seeing the bartender come around the counter to approach them. "Well, there is a ghost standing in front of us."

Ellyria looked the man up and down. He didn't seem like a witch, but she sensed some sort of magic. She thought quickly before asking Zane quietly enough for only him to hear. "Is that ghost you're mentioning us or him?"

"Honestly, both." He told her as the man stopped right in front of them.

"Is everything alright?" He asked with evident concern in his voice. "Do you need anything? A drink? Maybe, some food?" He asked with eerie calm as he assessed the pair. He seemed to size up each of them in an instant, looking them directly in the eyes in the next moment.

Zane nodded. "Yes, everything is fine. Just wasn't expecting the place to be quite like this. That is all."

Ellyria broke the piercing eye contact of the bartender, and glanced at Zane. "Well, I think I'm in desperate need for alcohol after the last few weeks."

The man smiled, and waved a hand towards the bar. "Well, that I can help with." He moved back behind the bar. "What can I get you?" He asked.

"Whiskey and cola. Mostly whiskey." She told him, taking a seat on a stool, and mentally asking Zane. "What is this guy?"

"I will take a double of what she gets." He ordered with a sigh before sitting. He watched the man start to make the drinks, and replied in the same manner. "He was the Vatican's number one demon exterminator before he up and vanished one day." He explained, continuing to eye the man cautiously. "No one knows why he left. Everyone thought he was dead, but, obviously, he wasn't."

Ellyria nodded, assessing this former Vatican agent. She stiffened. "I think I found why he quit." She murmured into his head. Outwardly, she pointed at the gold band on his left ring finger. "Who's the lucky lady?" Ellyria asked conversationally.

The man smiled, and handed them their drinks. "Her name is Lily." He responded, leaning on the bar as he did so. "She is devilishly beautiful." He smirked at the double meaning of his own words. His mind working through the facts and trying to figure out exactly what this was all about. The weight of the holy weapon on his hip heavy on his mind.

Zangrunath coughed around his drink, and took a moment to calm himself. "Oh, I bet she is." He deadpanned, realizing who the man was referring to.

Ellyria took a drink, and realized it wasn't as cold as she liked. She focused for a second, and subtly froze the glass without moving her fingers, taking another sip. She looked up to find the bartender's eyes boring directly into hers.

"You know, miss." He began simply, a smile starting to grow on his lips. "If you wanted a colder drink, you could have just asked." He chuckled lightly, turning towards Zangrunath. Now that all the moving pieces slid into place, he could relax into the situation more. "Yes, she is, but you already knew that. Didn't you, demon boy?" He teased, leaning against the bar.

Ellyria was dumbstruck. "How did you do that so quickly?"

"You or him?" He asked, pointing to Zane.

"Yes." She responded.

He chuckled. "I could smell him the second he walked into the door." He looked at Zane before regarding Ellyria for a moment. "I could also smell demon coming off of you, but it wasn't until you cooled your drink that I realized I had a witch here with her demon."

Ellyria searched all about. Nobody seemed to be startled by those words. "Okay. I'll bite. Are we all weird here?"

The bartender laughed. "It's a matter of perspective really, but the ones here right now know what's up."

Ellyria sighed. "Well, this trip just got a lot more interesting."

"Yes, it did." Zane gestured to the bartender. "Ellyria, meet Tarso Helge, the demon hunter."

Tarso extended a hand. "Nice to meet you."

Ellyria shook hands with the man. "Retired, I hope. I feel it if you take him out, that hurts."

"Oh." Tarso hummed, raising an eyebrow at her words. He noticed the annihilation ritual seal on her back. The details starting to piece themselves together as they came to light. He looked at the demon. "You two are soul bound. Interesting." He smiled. "What is your name?"

"Zangrunath." He sighed, holding out his hand to shake Tarso's.

She made a face. "You can just tell that?"

He shook his head. "Your scent has a stronger demonic smell than normal. That, and I can see parts of the seal on your shoulders. It is kind of a giveaway."

She looked at her outfit, and realized how much of her back was exposed. "Oh, I'm so used to normal people that I forgot others could see it."

He waved a hand. "It's fine. I just haven't seen a seal that detailed in several years."

"Uh, yeah." She sighed, remembering the mark of the fallen in the center of the seal. She closed her eyes, and concentrated on the shirt knitting itself together to cover her upper back and shoulders.

Zane glared at Tarso. "Could you please stop staring at her back?"

Tarso chuckled, and nodded. "Alright." He took a step back. "Would you care to go downstairs to have a more private conversation? There will be fewer prying eyes." He offered.

"I guess so." Ellyria shrugged. "I admit, I'm curious."

"Then, let's head downstairs." Tarso smiled, waving the bouncer in the corner over to run the counter for him.

Zane glanced at Ellyria before releasing a deep sigh as his body automatically stood up. She'd already made up her mind, and the ritual was taking over soul binding or not. "Fine. Let's go."

"Sorry. We never see magical folks outside of Tom and Steve. I'm kind of invested." She admitted.

"It's alright." He nodded. "We still have a couple weeks before we need to head back home."

Tarso smiled at the pair as he led them down a set of stairs to the private portion of the bar. They walked down a long hallway with several doors that each had strange symbols on them. At the end of the hallway, a set of heavy doors dominated the space. He swung them open, and brought them into an area that looked like the one above. Now, it contained far more exotic patrons. Two demons flanked the doors, standing guard as they walked in. There were creatures of varying shapes and sizes sitting about the bar. Each one eyeing Ellyria who seemed out of place among the group of weirdos and misfits.

Tarso brought them to a private booth, and gestured for them to sit down before he closed the shutters behind him. "So, what brings you two to Mexico?" He asked, sitting down across from them.

"Christmas Day demon slaying became a vacation trip." Ellyria shrugged.

Zane chuckled. "You make it sound like that is a casual thing."

"Yes, why are demons killing demons now?" Tarso asked.

"Because someone asked us to." She responded vaguely.

He gave her a curious look, but nodded. "I won't pry too deep, then." He looked like he was about to ask something else, but his manners overrode the question. "Are you hungry? Can I get you something?"

Zane shook his head. "Don't need to, but she might."

"I could eat." She nodded.

"Alright." Tarso smiled. "What can I get you?"

She didn't need to think. "Well, we are in Mexico. Tacos."

He chuckled. "Alright. I will be back in a moment." He stood up, and left the two of them alone. The shutters to the booth remained open when he walked away.

Ellyria looked out of the private booth. "Okay. I think I saw someone with scales out there."

"That wouldn't surprise me. I saw a few people out there who I wasn't expecting to see." He eyed the odd fellow in the booth on the opposite side of the bar. "Pretty sure there is a dragon in here." He added nonchalantly.

"Excuse me, a what?" Her expression between amazed and baffled.

"A dragon." He repeated with a chuckle. "You know angels and demons exist. Did you really think that dragons don't exist?"

"I- uh," she stuttered. "Ugh. I should've realized when we met Tom."

"It's okay. The general population doesn't need to know. Secrecy was one of the reasons behind the crusades, so most creatures went into hiding." He took a sip of his drink.

After hearing that, Ellyria took a large gulp of her booze, remembering one battlefield from their trip to Europe over her graduation. "Especially the other weapons of war," she quoted his words. "Oh, you jerk."

He smiled. "All is fair in love and war."

"I love you." She whispered to him before mentally adding. "You don't have to say it out loud. I'd hate to ruin your demonic street cred."

He leaned down, and kissed her. "I love you." He replied out loud. "I don't care what they think. You are the only one that matters to me."

She smirked, taking a drink, and staring down a demon that was watching them. "This has been the weirdest vacation of my lifetime. So far."

"I don't plan on them getting any weirder, so this should be the pinnacle." He nodded at Tarso when came back with a plate of tacos in hand.

"Here you go." Tarso smiled, setting the food down in front of her, and sitting across from them again. He pulled the shutters to the booth closed to allow them privacy. "Enjoy."

Ellyria breathed in the delicious scent before digging in. "Yum."

"I am glad you like it. Grazie." He nodded respectfully.

Between bites, Ellyria asked. "So, no offense, but how does one go from what he called you," she pointed to Zane, "to all of this." She gestured to the bar. "Sounds to me like an interesting story."

Tarso chuckled at her words. "Well, it is an interesting one. I started by working as a soldier. After that, I was chosen to join the Pontifical guard when I killed a demon. The Vatican was my employer for over twenty years before I met somebody on a mission that I couldn't find the wherewithal to kill. I fell harder than Lucifer from the pearly gates in love with her." He smiled at the memories. "It wasn't easy getting out by any means, but I did. Now, I live here, making sure that others like myself are kept safe from prying eyes."

Ellyria almost had her drink come out her nose at his mention of Lucifer, but she kept it together. "I would imagine that getting out was much harder than you make it sound. The Vatican is persistent." She groaned.

"They are." He nodded, knowing exactly what she meant. "It helps when you have friends in both high and low places. You don't work for the Vatican without making some friends."

"Say no more. Of all people," she thought about the rather obvious marks on her back that he'd seen. "I know all about that."

Tarso smiled, and nodded. He was going to speak again before a loud commotion came from the main bar, making him quickly stand at attention, ready to receive the signal for an oncoming fight. His eyes narrowed, and the booth doors swung open. Two children with bat wings coming from their back flew in, jumping into his arms. "Daddy!"

A demon woman sauntered in a moment later. She smiled, releasing a sigh. "Sorry, dear. They woke up from a nap, and their wings had come in. They insisted we come see you." She looked at the two people in the booth with him. "Sorry for the intrusion." She apologized.

Ellyria bit her lip, and shook her head. "No, it's perfectly alright." She smiled at the kids, and looked at Zane significantly. "I'll be right back."

Zane saw the look in her eyes, and nodded. His gaze followed her for a moment as he watched her walk to the bathroom. He didn't see any demons follow her. There would be Hell to pay if they even tried. When she was out of sight, he sighed, and looked from the blond haired and black-eyed boy and girl to Lilith's disguised form, which was as statuesque as any model or actress and equally blonde. "I wasn't expecting settling down and motherhood to be so inviting to you."

Lilith gave Zane a serious look, and shook her head. "Be quiet, mister-to-Hell-with-the-repercussions. Don't think that, even though I am here, I haven't heard about that little adventure you had in Chile."

Zane sighed. "It is a long story that isn't suited for children." He nodded towards the twins who were flying above their father who was trying to catch them playfully.

Ellyria returned with slightly puffy eyes mid-conversation, and started listening intently to catch up. Her eyes kept darting over to the children. She took a deep breath, and tried to relax.

Lilith leveled a gaze at Zangrunath, and smiled. "It's alright. I was only teasing. Don't get your tail in a twist."

"I will try not to." He smirked.

Tarso paused what he was doing, and turned to Lilith. "Alright. I think it is time we went home for the day." He smiled at the kids who were overjoyed by the idea of their father coming home early. He gave Zane a nod. "It was a pleasure to meet you, general." He gave the demon a mocking salute.

Zangrunath chuckled, and gave him the finger. "Get out of here. It was nice to meet you, too."

Ellyria shook her head, and laughed. "Oh, boy. Someone teased you while I was away."

He shrugged. "I managed."

Tarso smiled, leading the kids away. "It was nice meeting you, Ellyria. Have a great evening. Don't worry about the food and drink. It's on me." He waved as he left.

"I'm still paying." She grumbled, turning her attention to Zane once the happy family was out of sight. "Sorry I bailed on you there."

"It's fine. I figured that you needed to get some air." He soothed.

She sighed wistfully, looking to where the family just disappeared. "Yeah."

Zane moved a hand to hold Ellyria's. "Are you alright? You are normally far more composed." He worried.

"They have what I want." She shrugged. "Hellish desires and all that."

He sighed, and nodded. Of course, she put it in terms that he could understand. "I'm sorry. If there was a way, I would give that to you." He apologized earnestly.

She leaned into him. "I know."

He squeezed her hand, realizing something important. "I owe you on our bet."

"I'll collect tonight." She looked at a few bar patrons. Every demon in the place gazed at them unabashed. "I think we're going to be busy."

He nodded, and looked at the patrons. "Yeah, they look like they have questions."

"Well, it can't be worse than meeting your boss. Bring it on." She finished the sentence a little louder for their benefit.

Zane sighed at the shutters to the private booth. The only thing private about it was that people couldn't always see the occupants.

He waved for the few people who were watching them to come over.

Three demons crowded the booth, body blocking the exit. One of them had shoulder length black hair. His hazel eyes regarded Zangrunath, completely ignoring Ellyria. "You really got a promotion while in the middle of a ritual?"

"Yes, Zorron. It is possible to multitask." Zane smirked, wrapping an arm over the back of the booth to rest on Ellyria's opposite shoulder. "Enjoy your time here while you can because I will not let you slack when I get back."

Zorron shivered, knowing of Zangrunath's reputation despite the softer side he'd already presented today. "Yes, sir." He squeaked, stalking off. That was all he was really interested in, his comrade becoming the new general.

"Wrath, sir?" A second demon who had a large, pointed nose and aristocratic cheekbones asked. His human disguise was pale with brown, shaggy hair. He licked his lips, eyeing Ellyria before bowing at the waist towards Zane. "Ozmong, sir." He explained. "Can you tell us the tale of what happened in Chile?"

"No." Zane deadpanned. "Sathanas won't be coming back ever. The rest will remain between myself, Ellyria, the council, and the Dark Prince."

Ozmong nodded, regarding Ellyria like she was about to become his next meal. "And, you. You're the one who summoned Wrath?"

Ellyria tried not to raise her eyebrow or show any indication of surprise. She could only hope that she succeeded. A few years of being a lawyer helped if nothing else. She realized that there were seven generals, but she hadn't put the puzzle pieces together until it was shoved into her face. The seven generals were the seven deadly sins, and Zangrunath, her Zane, was one of them. Wrath himself. She recovered relatively quick, given her revelation, and smiled. "Yes, of course, I did. He wouldn't be here to make you look like you're about to wet yourself otherwise. Stop simpering."

She sneered. She glanced over at Zane, suddenly surprised by her own reaction.

Zangrunath smirked, and gave her a silent nod of approval. "Ellyria is the most powerful witch that has ever existed." He commented, pulling her slightly closer against him. "And, she is mine." He added with a rumbling growl, making Ozmong step back in fear, cowering behind the third demon that had approached their table.

"At your service." The last demon bowed. His hair a striking red color, and his eyes emerald green to go with it. "Thyneakas." He greeted with a respectful nod, but no bow or other sycophantic behavior as seen with the previous demon. "I merely wanted to introduce myself to the infamous Wrath and his lady." He stated, seeing another figure walking towards their booth that gave him a shock. He nodded at the man before finishing what he came here for. "May I ask what led you here to your visit today?"

"Curiosity about the place." Zane responded honestly, watching as both Ozmong and Thyneakas backed away from whomever was approaching.

Thyneakas nodded, flipping a gold coin in Ellyria's direction. "Have a drink on me." He offered.

Ellyria caught the coin, looked at it for mere seconds before duplicating it, and flipping the second back at the demon. "I can pay for myself, thanks."

With that, the demons scurried off, shooed away by a singular man who was dressed in an expertly tailored suit. He grinned, nodding as he looked them over. "Oh yes, Tarso does like to keep eyes on his kind." He gazed at Zane when he said that before copying the same procedure for Ellyria. "It is odd, however, to see a nephilim in here, though." He added quietly so only the couple could hear it. His short, wavy hair was black, and a piece of his bangs lazily fell into his face. Intense brown eyes stared back, and a well-built physique hid beneath the vest he was wearing, made even more obvious by how tight the clothing was against his form.

Ellyria sighed. "It's odd to see any of us ever. I've never met one."

"Who are you exactly?" Zane asked the man curiously.

The man chuckled, and bowed. "My name is Azazel." He smirked at the demon. "I have seen many people. But, a fallen? You are the first I have seen here." He took the opportunity to sit down across from them.

Zangrunath noticed the telltale signs of another demon. The haughtiness and smell of brimstone being chief among them. However, there was something off about it. He gazed back at Azazel. "To what do we owe the pleasure, mister nephalem?"

Azazel smiled, and looked at Ellyria. "I simply wanted to come meet my kin. There are not many of us around these days."

Ellyria took a drink, looking between the two. "Well, besides you and Lucifer, I'm the only other one I know of, and I'm not a demon. Yet." She shook her head. "I'm sorry, but did you just say nephilim and nephalem? Could you explain the difference?"

"You won't fully become one." He informed her. "You will gain some features, but you will still look mostly the same. The only exception being when you actually tap into that power that you hide. As for the rest, you are half angel, half human. I am half angel, half demon. Thus, the similar yet different names."

"Good to know." She responded simply.

"It seems you already know most of what to expect." He chuckled, looking at Zane. "You're lucky. You get her like that for eternity."

Zane released a low, possessive growl, and pulled Ellyria closer to him. "Don't look at her like that." He demanded.

"Okay." Azazel shrugged, putting his hands up in the air. "I was only commenting. I didn't mean anything by it." He teased.

"Stop." She growled at the two of them, eyes going dark.

Zane nodded, and went quiet. The order from the ritual kicking in. Azazel just smiled softly as if he knew he'd just learned something or otherwise gained the upper hand. "I am glad to find that I am not the only one around anymore." He stood, nodding at Zane. "Keep her safe." He added, excusing himself from the table.

"I will." Zane promised, gazing into Ellyria's eyes as he said the words.

Ellyria's eyes faded back to normal. "Sorry. Lost it for a second there."

"It's alright. You are allowed to get angry occasionally." He reassured her, understanding completely.

"I swear, since the whole birthday thing three years ago, it happens more and more." She shook her head. "Doubt I'll need much of a ritual by the time I actually go."

"He just confirmed it." Zane smiled. "It's okay. You are still perfect to me."

Ellyria chuckled. "I know. You're incredibly happy, proud, and possessive about it." She kissed him, and shook her head at his antics.

"I am yours and vice versa." He retorted.

She chuckled at him, and winked. "Let's go get a room. You owe me tonight."

He smirked, standing up, and offering a hand. "Doubled, as I recall."

"Yes, indeed." She smirked, taking his hand. "I know you'll make it worth my while."

"Yes, I will." He led her out to the front to go pay for a room for the two of them.

A few minutes later, when they were alone, Ellyria asked. "Would you mind if we stay for a day or two?"

"We can stay as long as you want." He promised with a kiss.

"If it weren't for everything back home, I'd be sorely tempted to stay much longer." She told him honestly.

"Relax, and stop thinking. When we have time, we can always come back." He told her before helping give her their agreed upon prize several times over.

Saturday, January 5, 2030

Ellyria was enjoying a hearty breakfast of huevos rancheros with green sauce in the bar when Tarso, Lilith, and their kids walked in. She glanced over at them, and felt jealousy overtake her. "I'm such a bitch." She whispered to Zane.

Zane tilted his head to the side. His back was to the door, and he hadn't noticed the new additions yet. "Why do you think that?"

"Envy." She mumbled.

He turned to look at the family. He sighed, and gave her hand a squeeze. "I love you," he whispered, "no matter what."

She nodded. "I love you. Maybe, we'll adopt once the ritual is over. It shouldn't be a problem."

"We can do that." He smiled. "We will just have to explain a lot of weirdness to them."

"Yeah." She sighed. "We'd have to explain a lot regardless, but," she paused, looking at the little ones. Tears welled up in her eyes. "I want to be someone's Mom."

He rubbed her hand with his thumb. "You will be, and you will be great at it. You do whatever it takes to obtain your goals. You'll even make a deal with the Devil."

"Been there. Done that. All I got was a stupid seal." She laughed. "Sorry. I know we've been over it. I don't mean to keep rehashing it."

"It's fine." He kissed her cheek. "You just overthink things sometimes."

"I know." She sighed, seeing the kids playing around with their new wings still. The boy was near the bottles at the bar, and she saw him knock one over, quickly reacting by catching it with magic. "Woah, there, buddy. That was almost a really big mess."

The young boy turned, and smiled at her. "Sorry. I wasn't paying attention." He flew over, and gave her a big hug. "Thank you. My name is Adrian. Will you be my friend?" He asked, quickly being distracted by his sister playing with a demon over by the doors. "Lacey!" He called out as he ran off.

Ellyria looked at Zane, and placed a hand on her chest. "Might've just melted a little bit."

"You are still in one piece." He assured her.

She leaned into him. "Maybe we should leave."

"You want to go home, then?" He asked seriously.

"I don't know." She responded weakly. "It's probably better than torturing myself through staying."

"We still have a couple weeks before you need to go back to work." He replied, doing some quick math in his head. "We can either go somewhere else and have fun or we can go home and relax. I have a late present to give you." He offered.

"Yeah. I do, too." She nodded. "I guess it's time to go home."

"Home it is, then." He replied. "Am I calling the plane or are we going Air-Elly?" He chuckled.

She laughed. "I will ley walk. I'm not feeling like flying right now."

He smiled, and helped guide her out of the building. "Well, whenever you are ready." He offered, allowing for her to lead the way from there.

"It feels like there's a ley right behind the building." She shook her head. Why wasn't she surprised?

"Of course, there is." He held her hand as they strolled to the back of the building.

When they got around to the other side, Tarso was waiting. Ellyria jumped in surprise. "How did you do that?"

"I own the bar. I know every way in and out of the place, and I wanted to know why you didn't say goodbye before you left." He leaned against the wall, and chuckled at her surprise.

"Uh." She hedged, seeing Lilith and the kids nearby. Her eyes cut from them to him.

He glanced from the kids to Ellyria. "Oh." He replied. The levity about him from moments before completely gone as he finally caught up on what was going on. "I'm sorry."

"It's fine." She tried to respond flippantly. "I just want what I can't have. If you ever need anything, look me up. The law offices of McDonough, Hannon, and Grant. Cambridge, Massachusetts. We should be opening an office in New York soon, too."

"Well, if I ever need a lawyer, I will do that." He told her honestly, looking the two of them over. He saw her glance at the kids again, and smiled. "You will be a great mother one day. You might not be able to have them, but there are plenty of kids out there who would gladly call you 'Mom'."

Ellyria looked down with a bitter smile before looking back at Tarso with black eyes as she connected with the ley. "Thanks." She told him, holding a hand out for Zane.

Zane took her hand, and smirked at Tarso. "Stay out of trouble."

"Same goes for you." The demon hunter chuckled, but his eyes were on Ellyria as he said it.

"I do stay out of trouble. It tends to come to me." She sighed, ley walking them directly into the penthouse living room. She took a deep breath as lethargy hit. "That might be the longest one yet."

"Are you going to be okay?" He asked her seriously as he held her.

She nodded. "Yeah." Though, as she said it, her head spun. "Just need to lay down for a bit."

He nodded, picked her up, and brought her into the bedroom. He laid her down on the bed. "There you go. I am going to replace the food in the fridge." He made a face. "You rest."

247

"M'kay." She mumbled, passing out.

He smirked as she fell asleep, going to take care of the house. When he finished, he came back to the bedroom, laying down next to her. He wanted to be close to her for a while.

Sunday, January 6, 2030

Ellyria slept until an ungodly hour the next morning, finding Zangrunath comfortably watching her when she awoke. "Hey." She murmured.

"Hey." He smiled, kissing her nose. "Are you feeling better?" He asked.

"Like I'm hung over, to be honest." She told him. "Probably, should've built up to that."

He rubbed her shoulder reassuringly. "It's alright. We are home, now. We don't have to go anywhere unless you want to. Besides, we have Shelby."

She smiled, and stretched. "I'm glad we're back. I think I just want to be lazy today."

"That is fine by me." He nodded, looking at the clock and chuckling. "Would you care for some brunch in bed then?" He asked.

She checked the time, and giggled. "If it can be called brunch at two thirty in the morning."

He shrugged. "It's brunch time somewhere. Want anything in particular?"

"Not Mexican. I had my fill." She responded honestly.

"Alright. Bacon and eggs with pancakes it is." He smiled, getting up to go make her food.

When Ellyria was alone in the room, she looked up to the ceiling and quietly whispered to any entity that would listen. "Please, just let me be a Mom when this deal is over." She closed her eyes, and decided to get some more rest while she waited for her meal.

A long moment of quiet hung in the air before Ellyria heard a sound like a silver bell. The room became silent again, and, a few minutes later, Zangrunath came in with the food. "Here you go."

"Did you just ring a bell?" She asked, sitting up to eat.

He looked at her strangely, and laughed. "No. Why would I do that?"

She gazed back at him, and frowned. "I guess, I'm just so tired that I'm hearing things."

"Hey." He reached out, gently holding her chin so she would look at him. "As long as it's just a noise, it's fine. If it's voices, we have problems."

"If I'm hearing voices, it's probably a new power." She shook her head at the thought, digging into her meal. She really didn't want to imagine any other powers coming her way.

"Kill them all." Zane muttered into her head whimsically.

She winked at him. "I could, but one or both of us are becoming horsemen to do it."

"Both." He nodded. "I want you by my side."

"Do you know which one you were for that fight?" She asked curiously.

"I am not entirely sure, but I think I was War." He guessed for her.

She thought about that. "I'd probably end up being famine since I can tear matter into shreds."

He nodded, looking off into the distance. "You would cause a plague of destruction."

"Probably." She agreed. "Let's not find out for a good long while, though. I think that might actually kill me to try."

"Agreed." He shook his head to get rid of the thought, turning to look at her after a moment. "So, what do you want to do at three in the morning? The sun won't be up until nearly 8."

She smiled, finishing her food. "Let's go relax in the hot tub, assuming we left the heat on while we were out."

"Alright, but, first, let me go make sure it is warm." He smiled.

Ellyria looked around the room, and sighed. "I don't know what that ringing was, but, hopefully, I didn't just make another deal with the Devil." She muttered to the otherwise empty room.

Zangrunath arrived back a few minutes later. "It's good."

"Great." She smiled, getting out of bed.

He walked over to her, and wrapped an arm around her. "It's cold out there. Below freezing. I want to make sure you get there safely."

She chuckled. "I will stay near you, then. My fiery demon."

He nodded, holding her close as he opened the door. He helped her over to the hot tub, which was steaming. "My lady." He offered, waiting for her to get in before he joined her.

Ellyria stripped down, and slipped into the heated water with a little shiver. "Cold, but so, so worth it." She sighed.

Zangrunath followed behind her. He let out a sigh of relief, and sat next to her. "This was a good choice."

Ellyria curled up against his side. "The deal's done this year. Call it intuition or what have you. We're so close. I can feel it." She tried to explain.

He wrapped an arm around her, holding her close. "I am a little curious to see what happens when this is all over. I have never been around after a deal's completion. This will be a first."

"We'll find out together." She smiled. "I'm glad I could make that deal when I did. I don't know what I would've done or how I would react if you disappeared suddenly without a trace."

"Violently and with extreme prejudice." He smirked, knowing her too well after so many years.

"I would make you come back." She promised.

"You would summon Lucifer again in order to do it, too." He guessed.

Ellyria grew quiet for a long time. They were both enjoying the companionable silence. "I don't know what the next milestone is after this." She murmured.

"Everyone has the same feeling around this time." He told her. "Pretty sure that you will know what it is when it happens."

"For right now, I just want you." She smiled. "Maybe, in a few years, I'll figure out the rest."

"That's fine. I am okay with this right now." He smiled, kissing her forehead.

She looked out at the sky. "I think I'll miss this most one day-when I die." She sighed at the thought. "Seems like you don't get good views in Hell."

"It depends on where you go." He responded. "This is nice, but there are some things that beat this by a huge margin."

"Oh?" She asked, turning to look at him properly. "Tell me about it."

"It depends on the time of year, but, if you go at just the right time, you can see the souls come down like snow." He smiled. "It is quite the sight."

She kissed his lips. "Somehow, you make something that should be horrifying sound beautiful."

He ran his hand down her back. "You have to be able to see the beauty in things you wouldn't normally consider."

She held onto him tightly. "Thank you, Zangrunath. I love you." She murmured. "Can we continue where we left off on Christmas Eve after we get our gifts?" She asked.

"Of course, we can." He chuckled. "I love you."

"Thank you." She smiled appreciatively. "My gift is," she laughed. "Well, I dug deep. You're hard to shop for since there's a lot you don't need, and we normally just buy whatever we want all year."

"Thank you." He gave her another kiss. "I would have just settled on time with you. You are a pretty great gift."

"Thank you." She murmured, pulling away slightly. "Let's get this late gift giving show on the road before I turn into a prune."

Zane smiled, lifting her up and out of the hot tub, and bringing her inside. He got them both situated with nice warm towels before carrying her to the couch where they both sat. "Well, I am not entirely sure how this is all done, so why don't you go first?" He smiled.

She smiled, and stood up. "Close your eyes, please, and no peeking." She returned holding an elegantly wrapped package the size of a sweater a few moments later. She placed the box in his hands. "You can open your eyes, now." She told him while sitting beside him.

He opened his eyes, and looked down at the box before looking back at her. He smiled as he unwrapped the box. He opened it up, and saw a set of tidily organized and typed documents detailing a business deal in which Grant Construction had won the bid to demolish a parcel of decrepit buildings. "Damn." He replied in shock before he looked back up at her. "But what do you want me to do with it?"

She chuckled. "I want you to have fun destroying them however you please."

A grin pulled at Zangrunath's features. He laughed hard, leaning in to give her a kiss. "Thank you. No one has ever done that for me before."

She smiled as they gazed into each other's eyes. "I want you to be happy." She held his hand. "And, I know pulverizing things into dust does just that for you."

"Thank you. Now, you close your eyes." He instructed, standing up, and getting her gift. He came back a few moments later, gently placing a crimson red box into her hands. "You can look now."

Ellyria opened her eyes, trying not to laugh at the look of the packaging. "It's wrapped exactly as I imagined." She commented as she started to undo the paper, revealing four metallic rings, each one with demonic runes on them. She looked up. "I don't speak enough demon to know what this is exactly." She looked up at him.

He chuckled. "That would make sense. I wanted to be able to give you some closer, more personal, time with me, starting with your vacation."

She carefully placed the box down, and kissed him. "Thank you. You thoughtful, amazing demon."

"I am glad that you like it." He smirked into the kiss. "Love you."

She looked into his eyes, and sighed with relief. They were home and on vacation. They could relax. "I love you, darling. Now, where were we before the Dark Prince interrupted?"

ARTICLE XIII

Monday, July 1, 2030

The alarm hadn't gone off yet, but Ellyria was awake and stretching. She looked over at Zane, who was typing away on a laptop, and smiled. "Hey. Today's the day."

Zane set the laptop to the side, and leaned down to give her a kiss. "Morning." He smiled in return. "Excited?" He asked her as he went back to working on the laptop.

"I am." She smiled, rolling out of bed, and starting to get dressed. "It's going to happen today. I can feel it."

He watched her for a moment before he closed the laptop. "Well, let's get this started." He got up, going to make her a big breakfast.

Ellyria walked into the kitchen, wearing a red dress that cinched at the knees. Her heels were black, and she looked out the penthouse window, observing the city. "Thank you, Zane. You took my idea from a decade ago and made it a reality. It's better than I imagined."

"You did most of the work." He shrugged. "In all honesty, I didn't do much on this deal short of the money and taking out a few people. Most of my other deals involved bloodshed and carnage. You had the easiest deal by far." He smiled as he cooked.

"Regardless, thank you for helping me make it happen." She moved into the kitchen to make herself a drink. "I know it's early, but I'm going to make a celebratory mimosa."

He chuckled. "That's fine. I don't mind driving you to work." He told her as he plated up the food.

"Thank you." She smiled as she poured the drink into a champagne glass. She moved back over to the window, taking a sip. "Now, this is perfect."

He placed the food on the kitchen island for her. "Enjoy."

She kissed him on the cheek, sitting down, and starting to eat slowly. She hummed. "You always know when to go all out."

"I know you." He smirked. "A decade of being together will do that."

"The best, most crazy, insane decade of my life so far." She chuckled, taking her time to eat. After a little while, she finished her meal, and stood up. "Let's clean this up, and head to the new office."

"I will get this going. It won't take long." He offered, cleaning up the mess.

Ellyria helped with the dishes before she grabbed her things. "Let's go complete a ritual." She smirked, tossing her dark hair over her shoulder.

He smiled, and took her hand. "Let's." He led them to the elevator. "I am curious to see what happens after this is done."

"I'll feel it. Won't I?" She asked. "Seems like a very Hellish thing to do."

"You will." He nodded. "I don't think it will be painful, though. Just a gut feeling." He told her as best he could since he was never around for the aftermath of a deal before.

They walked to Shelby. She took a seat on the passenger's side. "I knew this would happen ten years ago, but I didn't expect to know when my soul was about to be forfeited. And, strangely enough, I'm not worried. I know it will be in Lucifer's able hands."

He sat down, and started the car. "I will also be here to keep you safe. You aren't going to die anytime soon."

"I certainly hope not." She glanced over at him. "I've been doing some research on my Mom."

"Oh? Have you found anything of note?" He asked curiously as he drove them to the new building.

Ellyria nodded. "One of her domains is longevity of life, so I might be around for quite a while."

"Well then, be ready for a long and interesting life." He smiled.

"It could never be boring with you by my side." She responded.

He chuckled, at all the fun ideas he had in mind for their future together while he pulled into a parking spot. "Here we are."

She took his hand, and squeezed it. "I want you by my side today, mister Grant." She laughed about their inside joke from the time her assistant thought they were married.

"Of course, my darling wife." He laughed, giving her a kiss.

She hopped out of the car. "Let's go open the New York office." She smiled, strolling towards the door slowly so he could catch up.

He got out of the car, walked up beside her, and took her hand. "Lead the way. I want to watch you complete this deal."

She nodded, walking into the building. She stopped at the receptionist's desk. "Good morning, Gloria. Could you please call a meeting for nine thirty? I'd like to gather the team to start the day."

"Of course, Missus Grant. I will let them know as soon as possible." The middle-aged woman responded, picking up the phone, and starting to make the calls.

Ellyria waited for Gloria to be off the first call. "Just Miss. Thank you."

Gloria blushed, glancing at Zane. "Sorry. I saw that you were together and assumed."

"It happens all the time. Just be careful about assumptions. They can get people in a lot of trouble." Ellyria replied before walking towards her office. She walked by Yvette's empty desk. "Did my assistant make it in yet?" She asked.

"Yes, she is out getting coffee at the moment." Gloria told her.

"Great. Thanks." Ellyria smirked, closing her office door behind Zane. "Every damn time I bring you, I swear."

Zane nodded. "Sorry that I am devilishly handsome."

She laughed. "I don't actually care what they think. We are one. I feel married to you. It's just the principle of the matter at this point."

"Well, if it ever becomes a problem, we can easily make it real." He offered with a smile. "It wouldn't be too hard to get done."

She raised an eyebrow as she unpacked her briefcase. "That is not something I ever expected to hear from you."

"I don't care whether we are or not. I just want to make sure you are happy." He explained.

She thought about his words as her computer booted up. "There's just one problem."

"What is that?" He asked curiously.

"The one I'd want to marry us is very difficult to summon." She laughed.

He chuckled. "Then, I guess, we will just have to send him a letter."

"Might as well make it official with the only one that matters." She shrugged, responding to an email, and taking a deep breath as she readied herself for the meeting. "Alright. Time to finish this."

Zane smiled, and gave her a kiss. "Alright. I will be right beside you."

Ellyria stood up, and started walking towards the conference room. As her office door shut, two staff members stood from their computer desks, and ran in front of her. She heard noise coming from the room when one of them opened the door. Her assistant, Yvette, called out, "she's coming," in a quiet but urgent voice. Ellyria pulled the door open, and stepped in, looking over at Zangrunath with a smile seconds before he disappeared. Her smile became a frown. "Zane?" She asked both aloud and mentally. There was no response from Zane as she stood by the door.

Ellyria turned to the office staff all gathered around, and realized they were all waiting for her. This is what she'd wanted, but it was wrong. She took a breath, and gritted her teeth. She had to get through this meeting first, and, then, she could figure out what happened. "Good morning!" She greeted with false happiness, trying to get through this while her mind raced with thoughts and ideas about making Lucifer pay for lying to her.

Ellyria pulled out her phone, and texted Steve. 'I need you to give me an emergency phone call in five minutes. I need an excuse to get out. Something just went magically wrong.'

'Sure thing.' McDonough replied.

The five minutes were too long for Ellyria. Grueling and agonizing were feelings that had nothing on how she was feeling right now. She tried not to visibly sigh with relief when Steve's call came in.

"Hey, something's wrong. Get out of there, and explain what just happened." He told her when she answered.

Ellyria covered the receiver uselessly. "I'm sorry. This is McDonough. You can go about your days. Thanks, team." She stood up, and marched to her office on a warpath. "Zane's gone."

"What?" He asked in confusion. "Didn't you add an addendum to your deal?"

"Yes, an ironclad one with the King himself." She responded. "He and I are going to have some words." She snarled.

There was a nervous sigh on the other end of the line. "Please don't go overboard." He replied as calmingly as possible.

Ellyria growled, trying not to let the demonic changes of being a fallen angel overtake her. "Too late." She responded. She could feel the heat Zangrunath was feeling all over her body. She imagined that it was like what hot flashes were like. "I'm getting my soul bound back one way or another."

"Just don't get seen." He sighed. "Good luck." He muttered as the call disconnected.

Ellyria pocketed her phone, and grabbed her things. "I'm sorry. This is an emergency." She told Yvette on her way out the door. "Call me if I'm needed for anything."

"Will do, Miss Grant." The other woman replied, seeing Elly march out with a fiery passion in her eyes.

Ellyria hopped into Shelby, and sped home. She parked, taking the elevator up. When she got to the penthouse, she flipped through her grimoire. She reread her contract three times. "I don't get it. You should be here." She grabbed her chest, feeling the loss. "You should be here."

She gulped, trying hard not to cry. This wasn't right. Zane should be here. The air started to crackle with electricity as she struggled to contain the anger and turmoil inside of her. "Screw subtlety!" She shouted to the Heavens, stomping hard on the ground. For once, she took everything. Her eyes darkened to black, skin became red, and spectral bat wings suddenly dominated her back. Magic pulsed around the warded penthouse, dangerously writhing around her like it would break free at any given moment. She cloaked herself in the palpable magic around her, disappearing from New York, and reappearing inside of the towering pillars of Stonehenge.

Behind nearby stanchions, people screamed and darted away in fear of the devilish woman that appeared out of thin air. She didn't bother even looking at them. Her sole focus was on what she was here for. Zangrunath. He belonged here, and she needed to have him. "Mine!" She screamed in a language she didn't know. *He* never taught her demonic. They thought there would be time for that.

A burst of magic rolled out from her location so powerfully that it caused a tremor and thunder crack. She channeled for as long as she needed. The ground shattering, being remade. Over and over. Gravity lost hold at the hands of the quickly fluctuating magic. Bodies, cars, and anything not battened down lifted into the air before Ellyria disappeared from the scene entirely. Moments later, a sonic boom rang out, setting off car alarms, and dropping all the lifted objects back down onto the ground.

Zangrunath sighed when he realized where he was. He didn't think that he would be back here so soon, but, now, he knew he wouldn't be able to see Ellyria for, at least, a few days. Their contract terminated. The ritual ended. He didn't want to do this, but his job demanded it. Making his way to Lucifer's familiar tower, he nodded as he walked past the demon manning the desk. This was official business. At the bottom of the ancient stairwell, he found the Keeper of Contracts. "Did it all go through properly?" He asked.

The blind demon nodded, and turned to Zangrunath with a toothy grin. The clank of his keys a dissonant melody. "Yes. The ritual completed successfully. Her soul has been collected. Now, we just wait for her to die."

"There will be some time before that happens." Zangrunath growled. He solitarily made his way up the stairs, stepping out of the basement of the tower before he felt a quake ripple through Hell. His eyes darted all around before he looked upward. From here, the spire where the Dark Prince resided loomed above him more than usual. The shaking returned a moment later, and Zane noticed the magic forming at the top of the tower. He spread his wings, and began to fly with haste. Someone or something was attacking Hell itself.

As Zane flew up the dark spire, he found Lucifer already waiting at the area where the magic was forming. Unlike their last meetings, he was not his usual, angelic self. This time, he was fully embracing his power over the underworld. His skin was crimson red and literally dripping blood. The leathery material of his batlike wings was tattered. White hot flame made it near impossible to look directly at the wings. Ten horns raised from his head, and a flaming crown hovered just above them. He gazed at the portal that was forming with mirthless eyes that seemed to damn a person by looks alone.

He glanced over his shoulder as he saw his legions and generals amassing around the tower. "Go back to your stations!" He bellowed, causing shockwaves to emanate from his person at the power of the order. He glared directly at Zangrunath. "Except for you." He growled at an impossibly low timbre. "This is your doing." He jabbed a finger towards the portal.

"What?" Zangrunath asked nervously, trembling at the sight of his King.

"Ellyria is doing this." Lucifer muttered as his gaze focused on the portal, waiting for the arrival of the one who had earned his ire. "No one breaks into my domain unannounced."

After a moment of pressing darkness and cloying heat, Ellyria looked upon a landscape she'd never seen before. Out of the corner of her eye, she saw the figure of the one she'd come to see. She reached out a hand, dragging him to her as space nearby began to disintegrate. "You took him! That wasn't the deal!" She raged in demonic.

Lucifer growled, and instantly flew into her face. He grabbed her by the wings, throwing her into the roof of the tower. She hit hard. Wind knocked out of her, and the ceiling crumbled. "I took no one!" He snarled. "He was going back in a few days!" He landed on top of her, pinning her to the floor of his office. "You couldn't be patient, could you?"

Ellyria pushed him back with magic. A beat of her wings had her standing. Her control was waning. It wouldn't take much for her to lose it. Running amok in Hell became a very real option in her mind. In her periphery, everything she touched or approached disintegrated; Lucifer himself the only exception. "Give him back. He is mine. Not yours."

"Calm down before I make you regret your next sentence." Lucifer demanded. His tone promised pain and misery. "You have violated laws you cannot fathom against Heaven and Hell. I can promise you that this is not the answer. Do you want your precious demon back?" He growled.

Ellyria glared at Lucifer. Finally, her mind caught up, registering the change in his appearance. She recoiled, and she inhaled a breath of air. She started to shake. What had she done?

She shook her head. "If I stop now, I pass out." She finally replied, sounding defeated.

He stared her down. "Go home before I make you." He ordered. "I can't kill you, but I can do other things. You broke into my domain, and that is not to be taken lightly." He pointed a finger at Zangrunath. "He is going to stay here. Before you see him again, you and I are going to have a chat."

Ellyria glared back at Lucifer. Her eyes fiery and defiant, like their first meeting. "Fine." She jeered, instantly disappearing with a booming wave of pressure. Ellyria appeared in the penthouse. As soon as her feet hit the floor, she passed out cold.

Lucifer growled, and turned to Zangrunath. "I hope, for your sake, she is worth it because you won't be seeing her for some time." His form shifted back to his usual angelic form. "I will make her life a living Hell while you are here, and you are going to suffer as well."

Zangrunath made a face. The earlier fear still lingered in him, but, now, annoyance grew in his chest like a cancer. He nodded at the Prince of Darkness. "I expect nothing less." He sighed, wishing that Ellyria had waited instead of losing her head.

Lucifer smirked evilly at Zangrunath. "Of course, it is what I do." He chuckled. His gaze boring through Zangrunath as he uttered the words, "one year of hard labor. Now, I will see to her."

"Of course, my King." Zangrunath bowed. He flew down into the ash and lava pits of Hell, beginning the grueling process that awaited him.

Lucifer smirked. He appeared in the penthouse. A flash of light the only harbinger of his arrival. He saw the woman on the floor, and kicked her side. "Get up." He demanded. "You and I are going to talk."

Ellyria didn't move, but a second, harder kick woke her. She rolled over, coughing with wide eyes. The room spun. She gripped her head in pain as she groaned. "Ouch."

He stared down at her, walking a slow arch around her, and sitting down on the couch. "You are in a lot of trouble."

Ellyria sat up. Her wings were fading in and out of existence. She looked into his eyes in defeat. A sigh escaped her. "I lost control." She clutched her chest as she felt Zangrunath's pain. "It's my fault. Punish me, not him."

"Oh no, you two are one. The punishment goes both ways, and, if you think that is bad, wait for what I have in store for you." He shook his head, and stared back with cold eyes.

Ellyria nodded. "I don't understand what rules I broke."

"For starters, you went to Stonehenge, and, looking like a demon, ripped a portal to Hell in broad daylight. People saw you, and were recording videos with their phones." His chest rumbled with a growl. "That is six things right there. Not to mention declaring war on Hell itself." He added. His face set into a stern grimace.

"Do I get bonus points for channeling famine?" She groaned, slumping back onto the floor again in exhaustion.

"Then, there is that. Mortals shouldn't access the horsemen." He shook his head. "By all rights, you should be dead right now. Made to suffer for all of eternity in the deepest pit of Hell with Zangrunath as your punisher."

She sobbed. "I understand. Just get it over with, then."

"I can't." He reminded her. "Your deal with me made it so. You must die of natural causes. I have to keep you alive."

Ellyria started to cry. "I can't even die correctly."

"Be quiet. You could have done nothing. Everything would have been fine. But, you- instead of thinking," he paused to allow the words to sink in, "something a lawyer should do, you went off the deep end." He spat, a mocking tone eking in.

Ellyria couldn't help but sob. She'd made so many mistakes in the past, but this was the worst. Her lips opened, and she spoke. It was a compulsion to do so. Zangrunath explained Lucifer's divinity to her once before, but she wasn't thinking clearly. She didn't realize what it was causing her to do this. Every deep thought and secret that lingered in her heart and soul came out of her in that moment. "I want him. He is mine. We wanted you to marry us. I want children of my own, but, since we can't have any, I think we'll adopt-"

"For fuck's sake be quiet." Lucifer demanded. "You will get him back, but it will be *after* you've received your punishment. He is going to be working his demonic ass off while you are going to be here in a Hell of your own making. Then, I might let you get married."

Ellyria nodded hollowly, curling into a ball as Zangrunath's pain washed through her. She let out a little yelp as torment rolled through her.

Lucifer stood up, and strode forward, looming over her. "Stand up." He ordered. "If you want him back, this is the price."

Tears silently rolled down her cheeks. She struggled to stand, stumbling until she was vertical. She wobbled in place. She met his eyes. All the changes brought on by her tirade gone. It was just Ellyria. Much the same as a decade prior when she'd accidentally summoned a demon. "Yes, my King."

"Good." He nodded. He traced a sigil into the air, forming a complex pattern that hovered in the air in front of her. It glowed with the searing color of a brand without giving off heat. He stepped to the side, staring her down. "For the next year, you will go about your business as normal, feeling everything Zangrunath feels doubled over." His eyes assessed her reaction carefully.

She looked back dully. "Yes, my King."

He crossed his arms over his chest. "Place your hand on the seal, and bear your punishment."

Ellyria's right hand became a fist at her side. Her left opened, slowly moving to touch the seal. She saw tremors coming from it. She expected tantamount pain at any moment. Seconds before she touched the sigil, she gazed at him, tears still falling. "Zane's going to feel this too, isn't he?"

Lucifer shook his head. "No, only you. That is your punishment. Knowing that his torment is your fault, and bearing it doubled over." His tone that of judge, jury, and executioner.

She nodded, and moved her hand the remaining inches to touch the magical brand, which wrapped around her hand, twisting up her arm where it blackened, burning into her flesh. Her lips formed into an 'O' shape. The pain forced her to gasp before she wailed in agony. Her body convulsed, and she fell limply to the ground with a thud.

Lucifer watched with disinterest for a moment. His cold gaze looking through her. "Enjoy your time alone." He muttered, disappearing in a burst of light.

Ellyria writhed and twitched on the floor. She wished that she could pass out, knowing that the embrace of death or unconsciousness wouldn't come. She chanted the words, "I did this," over and over like a mantra. She crawled to the table where she left her phone.

It took half an hour on the floor as her voice steadily grew hoarse from her screaming, but she managed to text Steve McDonough. 'Home. Not good.' Her fingers refused to function after that. She sent the message, tossing her phone aside. Rolling onto her back, she cried while staring up at the ceiling.

An hour later, Steve frantically knocked on the door of the penthouse. "Ellyria! Is everything alright?" He called.

The door swung open for Steve, and he was greeted by the sounds of agonized screaming. Ellyria writhed on the ground in a pile of her own sick, sweating bullets. "Help." She begged.

He ran over, and picked her up, moving her to the bathroom. He set her down in the tub. A worried gaze studied her. "What happened?" He asked.

Ellyria lifted her branded arm as she kicked and flailed in the tub. Another round of chanting began. "I did this." She sobbed.

Steve eyed her arm, and sat down on the floor. He sighed deeply. "You pissed off the Devil." His words a whispered statement, leaving no room for question. Even he could hear the annoyance in his tone.

"T- t- they're," she stuttered out, "torturing him."

"And you're feeling it, aren't you?" He asked rhetorically.

She nodded, tears running down her cheeks. "I m- messed up."

He nodded. "I bet. Focus on me, if you can, and explain what happened."

"I-" she sighed, "broke every rule there is."

He pinched the bridge of his nose. "How badly?" He asked.

"Search demon in Stonehenge on the internet." She whispered, clutching her chest.

Steve groaned, unlocked his phone, and pulled up a search engine. His mouth popped open in shock as he watched the shaky, mobile video in horror. He saw the demonic visage of his business partner, and did a double take, looking between her and the screen for a moment. His eyes glued to the screen as a portal opened, taking her with it, and the video came to an abrupt stop. He locked his phone, growing quiet for a long time as he processed the information. He knew from Ellyria's insistence that she was powerful, but this- "what the fuck."

"I'm sorry." She breathed.

"How are you not dead?" He asked seriously. "That should have put a mile wide target on your back."

Ellyria pointed. Her arm shook. Her voice hoarse still, but powering through the words. "There's a copy in the first drawer on the right side of my desk."

He got up, and marched over to her desk, finding the copy of her contract. He read it over several times before shaking his head. "He can't kill you, but he can torture you." He groaned as the puzzle pieces started to click into place. He started to understand the problem, now.

She released a sob. "I should've died. I should've just died. It hurts."

He leaned against the wall, and slid down. "Dammit, Elly. Why did you do it?"

"They took him. He wasn't supposed to go." She whispered.

"So, the contract ended, and he went back." He sighed deeply, and looked at her. "You went through all of that, and you still didn't get him back?"

Ellyria held up one shaking finger. "One year."

"One year?" He asked. "What does that mean?"

"I get him back in one year."

His eyes went wide. "You are going to be like this for a year?" He exclaimed.

"Yeah." She mumbled, grunting as she forced herself to stand on wobbly feet. "I'll get used to it."

He stood at a much faster speed, and gently pushed her back down. "Don't force yourself." He told her. "Take your time. I will cover for you. Family issues."

She shook her head. "I got used to the last seal. I can deal. Just give me a week or so."

He looked nervous. "Okay, but, please, don't overdo it. I want you to take as long as you need for this. Don't come in if you can't think straight."

Ellyria's eyes closed. "I'm more concerned about sleep right now."

Steve nodded. "If you need me to get you something to help with that, I know some people that can get you the strong stuff."

"Please." She whispered before adding. "I'm such an idiot."

He nodded, and sighed. "No, you just didn't think." He offered a hand to help her out of the tub. "You go lay down. I will be back as soon as I can." He offered, moving towards the door.

"Thank you." She whispered again as pain lanced through her back. She gritted her teeth together to keep from screaming. It came out as a grunt instead. She looked over at Zangrunath's desk, and frowned as she stumbled her way to her bedroom where she fell into bed and prayed for an end to the suffering. "I'm sorry, Zane."

COMING SOON

Zangrunath and Ellyria will return in Terms and Conditions
Book Three:

Fine Print

Ellyria and Zangrunath are reunited, but things are far from
perfect. Greed continues to drive the witch, and Zane will always
try to give her what she wants. When all of their adoption leads
dry up, Elly falls into a depression.

Their lives take a turn once again when Ellyria's mother arrives to
deliver a gift straight from Heaven, but it comes with a secret that
must be kept at all costs, including from Lucifer and The
Almighty. With all new priorities in mind, the couple change
everything to protect their family. Favors are cashed in, incredibly
powerful magic is used, and they can only hope that it is enough
to protect them from legions of enemies.

More deals are struck, but each one seems to come with another
damning consequence. Ellyria just wanted a normal life, but,
before casting the annihilation ritual, she should have read the fine
print.

ABOUT THE AUTHOR

Terms and Conditions is M. W. McLeod's first trilogy in The Veil setting. They currently reside in Arizona, and enjoy playing Dungeons & Dragons with their friends. After years of writing fanfiction, they branched off from borrowing a spark of others' worlds to casting their own type of spells. They are fascinated with tall ships, and are a self-proclaimed caffeine addict, flavored coffee being the poison of choice.

www.beyondtheveilauthor.com

Twitter: @MWBeyondTheVeil

Join the discussion at:
https://www.facebook.com/groups/mcleodsradreaders

CPSIA information can be obtained
at www.ICGtesting.com
Printed in the USA
LVHW082124110821
695091LV00011B/355